The Makings

of

Violet Frogg

Patsy Trench

Prefab Publications

While this book is a work of fiction one or two real and recognisably famous people appear in it. Their lives and their personalities have been researched carefully, but any interaction they are supposed to have had with the (fictional) Violet Frogg is, of course, entirely invented.

All the world's a stage,
And all the men and women merely players.
They have their exits and their entrances,
And one man in his time plays many parts.

As You Like It, Act II Scene VII

§

A girl should be two things: who and what she wants

Coco Chanel

By the same author

NON-FICTION
Australia: A personal story series
The Worst Country in the World
A Country To Be Reckoned With
Australia and How To Find It

FICTION
Modern Women: The Roaring Twenties series
The Awakening of Claudia Faraday
The Purpose of Prudence de Vere
Entertaining Edwardians series
Mrs Morphett's Macaroons
The Humbling of Meredith Martin

All We Need Is Love (an anthology)

Prologue: Lady Armstrong's conundrum

Kenley Manor, Renwick, East Sussex, 1903

'I am beginning to think,' announced Lady Armstrong one morning out of the blue, 'there is something *rather odd* about our housekeeper.'

'What do you mean?' asked her husband from behind his newspaper.

'She is not the sort of person you'd expect, in that sort of position.'

'You've only just noticed this?'

'I suppose I thought it from the start.' Lady Armstrong paused, and looked out of the window for a moment across the expanse of lawn at Kenley Manor.

'To begin with she is far too attractive to be a humble housekeeper.'

'Do housekeepers have to be ugly these days?'

'And refined. And intelligent.'

'Dear me, it gets worse and worse,' murmured her husband.

'I heard her talking to Olivia the other day about the suffragists. The *suffragists,* of all things.'

'What's wrong with them?'

'Nothing wrong with them, nothing at all. It just made me wonder if we may not have an activist on our hands.'

Lord Armstrong lowered his newspaper for a moment.

'Well, we can't have that, can we?' He looked at his wife from beneath his eyebrows, which were excessively bushy.

Lady Armstrong ignored him.

'Does she do the job?' he asked, as he resumed his newspaper.

His wife did not reply for a moment, then: 'Yes, perfectly. That's partly the point. She's almost too perfect. And I can't help wondering how such a perfect housekeeper was able to step into Mrs Simpson's shoes so immediately.'

'Who's Mrs Simpson?'

'Oh Horace, for goodness' sake!' Lady Armstrong sighed. 'What would a simple housekeeper know about the suffragists? It's all very odd and I think I need to find out.'

'What are you trying to say? That Mrs Humphreys is a fraud?'

'No, not at all. I just don't feel she's who she claims to be.'

'Which is?'

'Whatever it was she said on her . . . I don't really remember now.'

'Did you read her references?' asked her husband, though he already knew the answer.

'She came highly recommended.'

'Recommended by whom?'

'I don't remember.'

Angelica Armstrong had a sharp mind but a selective memory. She judged people as she saw them rather than by what other people said about them. Truth to tell she could not remember who had recommended the housekeeper to her in the first place. The then current incumbent Mrs Simpson had had to leave very suddenly and her ladyship was, not to exaggerate, desperate. That at least was her excuse for not checking references.

Besides, she fancied herself as a good judge of character and in the case of Violet Humphreys, she took to her immediately. She liked her obvious intelligence, the almost mischievous twinkle in her eyes. There was a lightness about her that indicated a woman who did not take life too seriously. In different circumstances she might have enjoyed conversations with the new housekeeper on subjects other than what the family were eating for dinner. Mrs Humphreys was also one of the few people who was able to communicate on a proper level with Lady Armstrong's wilful daughter Olivia.

'She and Olivia are thick as thieves,' said her Ladyship.

'Is that wrong?' her husband remarked.

'No, but as I said it's – strange. She has all the makings of a governess, she knows all there is to know about classical history. So why isn't she teaching rather than housekeeping?'

There was a pause.

'Am I talking to the walls here?'

'What?' Her husband lowered his newspaper again and smiled at his wife. His eyebrows gave an impression of gruffness, which was misleading.

'I thought you were just thinking aloud, my dear,' he said. 'I didn't realise you required a response. Yes, I'm sure you're right, as you always are.' And he went back to *The Times*.

Lady Armstrong sighed again and stared into her lap.

'Nonetheless,' she began, and stopped. 'Nonetheless I feel I ought to do some investigating. It's not that I don't trust her, I do, absolutely. Absolutely.'

There was a silence. The clock ticked.

'Interesting,' resumed Lady Armstrong. 'I think I'll have a word with Olivia.'

LIFE ONE

1873-91

Miss Violet Frogg

1: The Frogg family

You might expect that a woman with a name like Violet Magenta Rose would have been born to parents with a sense of humour, or at least some artistic sensibility. But you'd have been wrong on both counts.

Violet's father was a vicar and her mother a vicar's wife. They lived in a cramped and slightly damp vicarage adjoining St Peter's Church in Newbridgeworth, a little-known dormitory town north-east of London within commuting distance of the City and inhabited largely by junior clerks and bank tellers.

Reverend Frogg and his wife were creatures of unbreakable routine. They ate at regular hours no matter what day of the week; parishioners were permitted to visit between 11 am and 12.30 pm on weekdays only; after lunch the elder Froggs would take a constitutional along the high street to the park, around the lake and back again; following which the Reverend would pay visits to needy parishioners while Mrs Frogg went home and napped. This routine could only be broken by exceptional circumstances such as serious illness, family crisis or ecclesiastic emergency.

The only respite for Violet was school, which she enjoyed as she was a bright girl and she had an enquiring mind – paradoxically perhaps the result of her uninspiring home life. At school she was nicknamed 'Frogspawn', which was the first time she became conscious of her ridiculous name and her small stature. It was said in good humour and she took it in the same spirit. She learned quickly that if you don't take yourself too seriously nothing much can touch you.

Violet had an older brother named Victor, who was eight years her senior and therefore, in her eyes, a generation and a whole world away. He had been sent to boarding school soon after she was born, and during his brief spells at home he did his best to ignore her. So Violet spent much of the time at home on her own. Conversation over the dinner table largely consisted of the Reverend relating some of the sadder biographies of his parishioners, which thanks to his over-developed sense of discretion and a certain natural ability he managed to render deathly dull. Most of the stories concerned illness of one sort or another, a subject which fascinated the Reverend rather more than it did the rest of his family. After dinner he retired to his study and his wife took up her needlepoint and Violet . . . well, Violet, who had no propensity for embroidery at all, would sit there trying to make conversation. Eventually she gave up and spent the evenings in her room studying classical history.

As Violet grew older, and bigger, so the house around her appeared to shrink, along with her aspirations. She felt hemmed in, literally and figuratively. She did not realise quite how tedious her home life was, however, until she was invited to stay with a school friend called Veronica Ann, known as 'Vee' to her friends. Vee's parents were something else. Father was a furniture designer (of the *avant garde,* so Violet was informed) and her mother taught music. They were fun, lively, unpredictable and altogether bohemian before their time, as was their daughter; and despite the best efforts of their housekeeper – oh yes, they were not too bohemian to have servants –

the house was chaotic, noisy, and an all-round mess.

Vee herself was a large girl with untidy hair and a tendency to trip over the furniture. The friendship was built on the attraction of opposites, you could say: Vee was big and clumsy and Violet was small and neat. Being girls, of course, they envied one another and longed to swap places.

The moment of truth arrived when it was time for Violet to leave school. In other times and in different circumstances a girl with a brain like hers might have continued her education at university, but unfortunately the school she'd attended had limited expectations. Their stock in trade, as it were, was to produce well-mannered, meek young ladies with refined voices, modest dress sense and a total lack of personal ambition. Ideal wives, in other words. The word university was never even mentioned. When she brought up the topic at home her father gazed at his daughter over his glasses as if he had no idea what she was talking about.

Violet was not enough of a rebel to take matters into her own hands and leave home without her parents' approval. Instead she took on the odd teaching job, which at least got her away from the house for a few hours at a time. But it was satisfying only up to a point and after a year or two of this she found herself returning home each day with an increasingly heavy heart.

There was only one way out of it: marriage.

But how does a single woman of eighteen with very little social life acquire a husband?

She confided in her friend Veronica Ann, with whom she had all but lost touch ever since they left school. Vee was married now, with a child on the way, which rendered her larger and clumsier than ever. She told Violet she knew just the chap.

Vee arranged the meeting over dinner. In addition to

Veronica Ann and her batty husband Cecil, a magistrate – batty was his own description – there was a distant cousin of Cecil's called Anthony. It was typical of Vee to introduce people by their first names only. Anthony was handsome in a kind of swashbuckling way ('raffish' was how Violet would later describe him); immensely tall, with thick black hair, probing eyes and a very loud laugh. He seemed to find life and everything in it screamingly funny. On being introduced to Violet he bowed, kissed her hand, gazed into her eyes and said, 'Why are you so very small?'

To which Violet responded, after a short, startled pause: 'Because I was brought up in a very small house with very small rooms.'

Anthony chuckled.

'And I have to live up to my nickname,' she added.

'Which is?'

'Frogspawn.' Violet fluttered her eyelashes at him and he laughed.

He referred to the girls as 'the two Vees' – 'Which must make you,' he added, 'one double-u' – which made Violet laugh until she almost cried (she was, at that age, very eager to please). He was a junior civil servant in the Foreign Office and over dinner he told jokes about his colleagues which were just this side of spiteful, yet too puerile to be truly offensive. He made fun of everyone, himself included – himself especially – and when he sensed he was getting a little too close to the knuckle he would turn to Violet and say, 'You're not offended, Frogspawn, are you? You don't mind if I call you Frogspawn?'

'Not in the least. Just so long as you don't object if I call you . . .' she paused. 'Did you have a nickname? I imagine you did.'

'Nipple.'

'I beg your pardon?'

'Perhaps you'd prefer to call me Neep. That's how I was known at school.'

If Violet had thought that by marrying she would be able to get rid of her ridiculous surname she had chosen the wrong person in Anthony Arthur Walpole Turnip.

~

And yet it was the surnames that sealed it for them. Over the course of the next few months they met several times, usually at Vee's house. They continued to share jokes about their names. Anthony claimed that it was his family name that made him the man he was. 'You can't have a name like Turnip and not have a sense of humour,' he pronounced. 'And the same goes for Frogg. Don't you agree, Frogspawn?'

Thus it was that after a remarkably short time he proposed, and Violet, at the age of eighteen, accepted.

The wedding was, by decree from the Reverend Frogg, a modest affair, and attended by immediate family and friends only. Violet wore a becoming (yet understated) dress with just the *suggestion* of a train and the *smallest* hint of lace. Veronica Ann acted as matron-of-honour and her husband Cecil as best man. Brother Victor spent the day smirking and sporadically yawning. Mrs Frogg shed tears. Anthony Turnip's parents over-compensated for their shock at having to be there in the first place by exuding delight at everything from the flowers (a couple of thin vases of chrysanthemums arranged by the ladies of the church) to the food (cold ham and salad and no alcohol), and smiling far too indulgently at the little thing who was in the process of becoming their daughter-in-law. The ceremony was conducted by the Reverend Frogg himself, who did not crack a smile throughout.

And so, after a brief honeymoon in Normandy, Mr and Mrs Anthony Turnip settled down together in a large house in Bloomsbury.

LIFE TWO

1891-96

Mrs Anthony Turnip

2: Humphreys Street, Bloomsbury, W

There were four floors of it, plus a basement, and after the cramped quarters she'd been used to, to Violet the new marital home in Humphreys Street was a palace. The moment she arrived she was running up and down the staircase, from top to bottom and back up again, like a small child. Her favourite room of all was the bathroom, which contained the biggest and most elegant bath she had ever seen and a brand new flushing water closet, made of porcelain and beautifully decorated with dolphins. She spent several minutes, while her new and bemused husband looked on, pulling on the chain and watching the water swirl around in the bowl of the lavatory before miraculously disappearing down an invisible pipe, only for the bowl to miraculously fill with water again.

What utter joy.

It appeared the house had been a gift to Anthony from a childless uncle, and it had been lived in by one Turnip or another for generations. The walls were chock-full of family portraits – you would wonder there were so many Turnips in the world – and every horizontal surface was littered with onyx and ivory and silver-framed photographs of yet more Turnips. It was a Turnip house through and through, but Violet did not mind in the least; in fact she welcomed it. Anything that took her as far away from her old life as possible had to be a good thing.

And there were servants, many of them: a personal maid, Amy, for her, and a valet called James, for Anthony, doubling as under-housekeeper and butler respectively. In addition there was a cook and a housekeeper, two maids-of-all-work and sundry others Violet could barely keep count of. Where the money came from to support all of these people she had no idea, nor did she concern herself with wondering.

To begin with it was daunting, to say the least, to have a housekeeper present herself first thing in the morning for instructions. 'Oh, do what you've done before,' was her general response. 'Only just a bit more when it comes to food.' She giggled. 'As there's one more of us now.'

She was still a young thing, after all.

And how strange it was to have someone dress you, do your hair, take care of your laundry, run a bath for you and altogether encroach on your most personal arrangements. And to know you were responsible for the hiring and firing of same servants if and when necessary. But it's odd how quickly one gets used to things. Once she'd rid herself of a niggling feeling of guilt at her good fortune Violet settled into an enjoyable routine of entertaining, being entertained, shopping, going for long walks in parks, taking tea with friends, attending the theatre and museums – the British in particular – and spending relaxing evenings at home with her beloved.

There was the usual trepidation in the bedroom, especially on the wedding night. Vee had prepared her to some extent.

'It's a bit awkward,' she'd said, 'at first. And it can be uncomfortable. But after a while you sort of get used to it and then it can be rollicking fun!'

It took a while for Violet to reach the rollicking fun bit. Anthony certainly seemed to suffer no qualms about it, very much the opposite. It was enough for Violet to know that at least one of them was getting something out of it, though she would have preferred it if there were – how should one put it – more of a gentle lead up to the main event, to allow the participants to as it were tune up before getting down to business. But that was not Anthony's way and she learned early on not to make a fuss.

It was a happy enough existence. Life was fun, and carefree. As she grew gradually bolder Violet felt able to indulge her love of play by leaving little messages for her nearest and dearest hidden in cupboards, or behind cushions, written on lavender-scented paper. Silly little things, sweet nothings. Her husband was amused, and touched, at least to begin with.

She acquired, in secret, the services of a dressmaker. It was a secret not so much from her husband – who loved to see Violet dressed beautifully and liked nothing better than to show off his pretty wife to his friends – as from her old self, Miss Frogg; daughter of Reverend and Mrs Frogg, the parents who had brought her up to value frugality over almost everything else (except faith, love and charity of course), and allowed her one new dress a year, and that in the plainest of colours and designs. The sheer extravagance of being allowed to fill an entire wardrobe with whatever she fancied made her quite giddy with guilt.

Compared with her years back in Newbridgeworth Violet felt she was on permanent holiday.

But who wants to be on permanent holiday?

The most contented women of the 1890s were generally supposed to be happily married mothers and women of what Anthony would call, unkindly, 'limited brain'. (Violet did wonder on occasion if he didn't consider all women to be of limited brain.) For someone like Violet, entertainment and shopping was all well and good, but once one had 'done' the museums and galleries until one knew them so well one could offer tours of them to the general public, there was still a good part of the day to fill. Days, weeks and months would go by with nothing to show for them. At times she felt she was marking time on a treadmill that, as treadmills will do if one marks time on them, just kept on turning round and around *ad infinitum*.

Children did not appear. She assumed, being a woman, that it was her fault. She was doing it wrong. Or she wasn't enjoying it enough. Each month when the inevitable arrived Anthony would show his disappointment, or disapproval, by removing himself to another bedroom. As time went on so these removals became more and more prolonged, so Violet ended up spending more time alone in her bed than with her husband. That at least helped to remove some of the tension that was beginning to creep between the beautifully laundered sheets of the marital bed.

Then life took an unexpected, and welcome, turn. At tea with her friend Linda Longhurst Violet was introduced to a lady called Miss Dorothy Moss. Miss Moss was quite unlike the usual sort of person one met on these occasions. To begin with she was unmarried, very obviously so. She was also a passionate suffragist.

Now Violet had heard of the suffragists, who hadn't, but she had only a vague notion of them as a bunch of earnest upper-class women who were lobbying for the right of women to be able to vote. She had tried to bring up the subject at home with her beloved but all she got in return was a grunt. But here was a lady, Miss Moss, a remarkable lady in some respects, not least because she ignored the unspoken rule that afternoon-tea conversation should focus on the strictly trivial, and launched unbidden into a lecture on the rights of women.

'There is a feeling abroad,' she pronounced, sitting bolt

upright in her chair, 'that all women are good for is prettifying drawing rooms and pushing out children. Which is arrant nonsense. We should be out there, instead of sitting around like a bunch of stuffed monkeys, talking nonsense. We should be out there getting our voices heard. We are more than half the population of this benighted country and it's high time we had a say in the way it's being run. You, Mrs Turnip,' she swung violently round in her chair to address Violet directly, making her jump, 'you have a head on your shoulders, you should come to one of our meetings. We could do with some young blood. What are you doing tomorrow afternoon at three o'clock?'

'I, er, well . . .'

So that is how Violet Turnip found herself sitting in Caxton Hall the following afternoon, along with around forty or so other well-bred ladies, Miss Moss among them, and a smattering of men, listening as speaker after speaker was invited to address the assembly. Some were strident, some spoke so softly you could barely hear them. All of them were cultured, erudite, informed, and impressive in their different ways. Many of them were educators of one sort or another – the Principal of Cheltenham Ladies' College among them – and had written books and pamphlets on the importance of female learning. There was even a lady doctor, and a couple of actresses. Every single one of them left a deep impression on Violet. It was overwhelming. It was inspiring. Never before had she heard people talking with such logic, and humour, and passion. Never before had she quite realised how so many women were already an established part of the workforce.

'Well, Miss Moss!' she said afterwards. She felt quite flushed. 'That was . . .'

'Dorothy, please. I can't be doing with the Misses and the Mrs, they're unnecessary labels.'

'Misses and misses?'

'As if one's title defines one. As if a person of a certain age, who is unmarried, and likely to remain so,' she turned to look straight at Violet to emphasise the point, 'is an old maid.'

'I don't think people think that, do they?'

'Of course they do. *You* do. It's plain on your face.'

'Oh dear.' Violet was quite distressed.

'You have me down as a determined spinster, always was, always will be, with no time for frippery or femininity or anything else that begins with an f. Don't deny it. Unmarried, unmarryable, proud of it. And you'd be absolutely right.'

And then to Violet's surprise, and alarm, Miss Moss threw back her head and howled with laughter.

'So, tell me your thoughts.'

They were seated in a tea house in Victoria Street. Miss Moss – Dorothy – drank her tea from a mug, a tin mug such as workmen use, which she appeared to carry around with her.

'It was inspiring,' Violet replied. 'Absolutely inspiring.' She stirred her tea. 'I've never heard so many people speak with such power, and intelligence, and knowledge of history. I'd never realised how many women there are who are already making their mark professionally. It's so obvious, women must have the vote! Women of the calibre of – what's her name, the doctor?'

'Elizabeth Garrett Anderson.'

'Who fought so hard to be accepted, and succeeded, and there she is.' Violet took a drink of her tea. 'It's what I've been looking for.'

'Indeed.' Dorothy watched her companion over the rim of her mug.

And then by way of explanation of her last remark Violet proceeded to tell the story of her life, or a truncated version of it, from her drab upbringing and the great escape from the provincial dreariness of Newbridgeworth to the luxurious comfort of Bloomsbury and the security and companionship of a handsome husband, who . . .

'What's handsome got to do with it?' Dorothy interrupted.

'I beg your pardon?'

'Is that how you define your husband? Is that the most important thing about him?'

'I, well . . .'

'It's the first adjective you came up with. The only adjective you came up with.'

'Before you interrupted me,' said Violet.

Dorothy nodded in acknowledgement. 'Go on.'

'I . . . I seem to have lost the thread.'

'You are married to a handsome husband. Is that why you married him? Because he was handsome?'

'Well, no. And yes. It helps. I can't pretend it doesn't matter. It's nice to look across the room and see a handsome face smiling back at you.' Violet toyed with her teaspoon. She was feeling less and less sure of anything the longer the conversation continued.

'That,' said her companion, with emphasis, 'is entirely the problem. Handsome men are not to be trusted. Men with charm likewise. They think they can twist us around their little finger. The more charming they are, the more handsome, the worse it is for us women.'

'If you say so.' Violet was beginning to lose heart. She glanced at the clock on the wall.

'You mark my words – do you have to be somewhere?'

'No, I . . .'

'Take my word for it. The only successful marriages are between meetings of minds. Looks fade. Charm comes and goes. Minds go on forever.' Dorothy took a gulp of her tea. Then before Violet could interject, 'What does your husband think of women's suffrage?'

'He won't discuss it. I think he believes women have enough to do in the home.'

'Told you!' Dorothy slapped a hand onto the table, causing the tea things to rattle. And then once again, without warning, she leaned back in her chair and howled with mirth.

'My dear,' she continued, 'and no, everything is quite all right, thank you' – this to the concerned waitress – 'what you need is the strength of your convictions.' She leaned across the table and tapped the back of Violet's hand. 'You have to not mind me. Everyone knows what a harpy I am. I'm the one they send to sound people out. People like you, with brains, but with no conviction. You have to learn to stand up to the likes of me. If you can't do that, what chance have you against that handsome, charming husband of yours?'

What chance indeed.

It was obviously – it had felt like – an initiation. Violet arrived home feeling both shattered and exhilarated. After dinner that evening she made an attempt to describe her afternoon to her husband, but something – his lack of response maybe, or her excess of emotion – rendered her near tongue-tied.

'So what,' he drawled, 'was it that you found so inspiring?'

'All of them. It. Did you know, on the Isle of Man women already have the vote? And New Zealand is about to have the same?'

'Bully for them.'

'They made such *sense*. You wouldn't believe how clever they were, how articulate.'

'You're probably right there. I wouldn't believe it.'

'You should come to the next meeting, I can find out when it is. It's perfectly all right for men to attend, in fact they welcome it.'

'That's awfully good of them.'

'I mean it, Anthony. I'm sure you'd find them as inspiring as I did. And you could join in the debate.'

'Really?' Anthony raised one eyebrow and then the other, a trick he was rather fond of and which had once been guaranteed to make Violet laugh. 'Well fancy that.' And he picked up the evening newspaper again.

There followed a long silence, during which Violet gazed blankly into the fireplace.

Had she escaped from a stifling family only to find herself in an equally stifling marriage?

3: The suffragists

The following day, instead of taking her usual walk through the streets of Bloomsbury to Russell Square and back again – she had without realising it become a creature of habit, just like her parents – Violet sat herself down in the drawing room for a serious think.

She realised, albeit belatedly, that she did not love her husband. She was not sure she had ever loved her husband. She had married him on a whim, because he made her laugh, and because, yes, he was handsome, and charming, and because she was desperate to escape her family home. The notion of love had never, truth to tell, entered her head.

But that was all right. Plenty of marriages survived – thrived even – without love. There had to be something of course, something mutual, like trust, or Dorothy's meeting of minds. In Violet's case the only thing that sprang to mind were jokes. It was the jokes that had kept them going initially, and while laughter is not to be sneezed at, so to speak, it takes more than a mutual sense of humour to form a proper relationship. Violet's mind, which her schooling and her parents had tried so hard to repress, was starting to atrophy through lack of use. The after-dinner conversation around the fireplace that used to be the highlight of the day had dwindled now to a series of eager attempts on her part to introduce a new and interesting topic and half-hearted responses from her husband. Hardly a meeting of minds.

Children would have helped, obviously. Even with nannies, and the little things being kept out of sight for most of the day and only presented to the doting parents on request, children were at the least a distraction, and at most an all-absorbing delight. Violet loved children. She loved their unpredictability, their uncomplicated, self-centred zest for life, their total lack of restraint or self-consciousness. It dismayed her, when she looked back, to think she was once like that. Were all children once like that? she wondered, until something or someone – a parent or a teacher – battered the life out of them and forced them into the straitjacket called Proper Behaviour?

However it seemed that some people had escaped the straitjacket and one of them was Dorothy Moss. Violet was both fascinated and appalled by the woman. She admired her, she was curious about her, but God forbid she did not want to be like her.

They were an intimidating lot on the whole, the suffragists. They were all thoroughly educated and terrifyingly clever. But they were not all desperately serious. One of the actresses – Lolly Mulligan or something – had the room in stitches impersonating some of the more pompous members of parliament. She would like to be friends with Miss Mulligan.

She would, she resolved, attend the meetings and see what happened. She was excited.

~

'There is someone to see you, Mrs Turnip.'

How unexpected. Violet rarely had visitors in the daytime.

'Who would that be, Amy?'

Violet's personal maid hesitated. 'She calls herself Dorothy. She did not give another name. I told her you were busy as I know you're not fond of people turning up unexpectedly, but she did not seem inclined to believe me.'

'Then show her in.'

'I knew it.' Dorothy Moss was already speaking as she entered the room. Without so much as a look around she continued, 'Stuck here with nothing much to do, eh?'

'Oh, hello, Miss Moss. What a surprise.'

The visitor took a seat without being invited. 'There's another gathering coming up tomorrow evening, thought you'd like to know.'

'Oh? Where?'

'At Millicent Fawcett's house. Nine o'clock.'

'I'm not sure that I can . . .' Violet hesitated.

'That you can what? Leave your husband all alone in the evening? Come now, how often does he stay out late working, or carousing at his club, or who knows what else?'

'What are you implying, Dorothy?'

'Nothing. I never imply things. Are you with us?'

Once again Violet felt she was being tested, and she resented it. If she declined it inferred she was afraid of her husband, or at least that she was kowtowing to him. If she accepted she'd feel as if she was being bludgeoned, which of course she was. The idea that she might be allowed to consult with her other half and report back was obviously not worthy of consideration by the likes of Dorothy.

'I will let you know,' she said, with as much coldness as she could muster.

'You'll be asking permission, you mean.' Dorothy's expression was remarkably expressionless at times.

'No. I will be consulting. It's only fair, and courteous.'

Dorothy continued to stare at her for a long moment.

'Good for you,' she said finally. And she got to her feet and left.

Violet did consult, and to her relief Anthony merely shrugged, muttered something about having dinner at his club, and that was about it.

The meeting was one of many, and regular. They took place in people's houses – smart houses, Kensington houses. Violet loved every minute. She made friends. She made particular chums with Lolly Mulligan, the actress, who was every bit as funny off the podium as on.

'It is not a case so much of women so to speak encroaching on the dominion of men as it were that concerns me,' she mimicked in her best Gladstone-esque tones. 'What concerns me is that their – how can one put this – their purity, their fragility, all the very qualities that give them the wherewithal to twist us mere men around their dainty fingers – where was I? – Oh yes. Will be compromised. Which is another way of saying,' she continued in her own voice, 'that the only people considered suitable to run this country are foul-mouthed, corrupt, unrefined brutes. Men, in other words. Not,' she continued quickly, 'that I don't like 'em. I love 'em. I loves 'em very much.' She had, like many actresses, a tendency to drop in and out of accents, and personalities. 'Not like some others I could name,' she continued, with a wink.

She didn't need to mention the name Dorothy.

'So,' Miss Mulligan went on. When she got the bit between her teeth it was difficult to stop her. 'What he's really saying is,' and here she adopted the exaggerated tones of a duchess, 'Were the superior species to deign to cock so much as half an ear to the inferior species – can you cock half an ear? – they might, just *might* take notice of what the inferior species has to say. In other words *we*, the gentle, lower, stupid sex, can only wield influence through the medium of the upper, cleverer, and altogether better-informed sex.'

Then, dropping the accent, she said, 'Do you suppose Dorothy had a bad experience, once, at the hands of a man?'

'I don't know, I've never given it a thought. Why do you suppose that?'

'This man-hating thing. I know I make jokes but, you know, life would be ever so dull without them. Who else could we make fun of?' Miss Mulligan laughed, and then stopped. 'Sorry. You have to tell me to shut up. Otherwise . . .' She thought for a split second. 'I'm not sure she's had any experience with men - she'd terrify the life out of them. Poor Dorothy.'

There followed a thoughtful pause, during which each pondered on their own vision of Dorothy.

They were sitting in Violet's drawing room. She had not invited many of her new suffragist friends back to her house, she felt a bit shy about it. But Lolly was different. She was many things but she was not intimidating.

'Nice place you got here,' said Miss Mulligan. She got up and began wandering around the room, fingering things here and there, stopping to gaze at the portraits on the wall of Anthony's forebears. To be truthful Violet had quite forgotten who they all were. Those family portraits were beginning to oppress her.

'Thank you,' said Violet.

She knew very little about her visitor. Despite her apparently extravert nature she rarely talked about her background.

'Where do you live, Miss Mulligan?' she asked.

'Lolly. Here and there.' She was studying the silver-framed photographs on a side table. 'Yours or his?' she asked.

'His.'

'All of them?'

'All of them.'

'Hmm,' said Lolly. Then, 'I don't like my family much either.'

'Oh? Can I ask why not?'

Lolly shrugged. She continued to meander, trailing her hand on the furniture, back and forth from the sofa to the bay window, now and again leaning against the edge of a chair.

She was red-haired – dyed, probably, or at least enhanced – pale-skinned and thin. She had a delicate face that belied her boisterous personality, and she was dressed with no regard to current fashion whatsoever in an ankle-length, asymmetrically-layered rust-coloured skirt – possibly home-made – and a patterned blouse with a couple of shawls in varying shades of orange and brown draped languidly around her shoulders. There was not a hint of the ramrod stiff, corseted uprightness of the typical Victorian woman. The overall effect was distinctly odd yet, Violet had to admit, in its own way distinctly stylish, and certainly unique.

'You live here and there?' Violet prompted.

'What? Oh. Yes. No fixed abode, you could say.'

'That sounds dangerous.'

'I suppose it is. But it makes for an interesting life, doesn't it? Oh my word.' Lolly stopped dead and looked up at the grandfather clock. 'Is that the time? I must fly. Terribly sorry.'

'That's a shame.'

'Thank you so much. Sorry to rush off. My cloak?'

'Of course.' Violet picked up a small bell and rang it.

'You have a bell!' Lolly pointed, like a small child. 'You really have a summonsing bell! How absolutely beyond!'

'"Beyond"?'

'Don't mind me. I make things up. It's been really interesting talking to you Mrs T. Will I see you at the next meeting?'

'Whenever that is, quite probably yes.'

'Here perhaps?' Then as Amy appeared with her cloak. 'Thank you so much, er . . .'

'Amy,' said Amy, and dropped a curtsey.

'Oh my!' Lolly hooted with laughter, to Amy's consternation. 'That's a new one. I've never been curtseyed at before.' She curtseyed back, gave a merry laugh and went.

4: Cracks

She was all a-flutter. It was the first meeting she had hosted at her home and it needed to be perfect. It was set for 8 o'clock, by which time the attendees would have already dined. But light refreshments had to be supplied. And there was no knowing how many people would turn up. And what was the best layout – around the dining table, like a board meeting? Or in the less formal surrounds of the drawing room, with guests scattered here and there, far more comfortable but also fragmented? It was necessary, Violet felt, for there to be one conversation, one person talking at a time, one topic.

And who was to be in charge? Should there be an agenda and if so, who was responsible for making sure it was stuck to? Was it automatically assumed that the hostess should also act as chairwoman?

'I'm as nervous as a kitten,' Violet announced to Amy, unnecessarily.

'Why madam, may I ask?'

'Well, there's so much responsibility. Not just as a hostess but as a . . . you know.'

Amy did not know. She stood there politely, hands clasped before her, waiting for enlightenment.

'Would you like to attend, Amy? You should, you know.'

'"Should", madam?' Amy gave her mistress a cockeyed

look. They both knew that what Violet was really looking for was not the education of her personal maid so much as moral support.

'It concerns you every bit as much as me,' Violet went on. 'It concerns all of us, men as well as women.'

'I'd feel ever so out of place, madam,' said Amy. 'But you can tell me all about it, if you like. I'd be interested to know what happens at these meetings.'

'It's a very good question, Amy. What *does* happen?'

'I know how women can talk, Mrs Turnip, and how they can go on for hours and hours without meaning very much. Or doing very much.'

'You've hit a sort of nail on a sort of head, Amy.'

She had been so concerned about the detail – the seating plan, the organisation, the usual anxieties of hosting – she had not addressed, not now and not really up until now, exactly what these meetings were about. Exactly what they achieved, or even what they set out to achieve.

The suffragists were lobbyists. Their immediate aim was to keep the topic of women's suffrage in the public eye and debated in Parliament. This last required a knowledge of parliamentary procedure that Violet had not yet come to proper grips with. She knew it had something to do with Private Members' Bills, which meant co-opting sympathetic MPs and then hoping they could make their voices heard above the babble of endless debates on shipping regulations or street lighting. The whole thing seemed to have more to do with luck than anything else. An odd way to run a country when you thought about it.

However, it was easy to become too absorbed in the smaller things – just as Violet had been stressing over her seating plan – while losing sight of the ultimate aim, which was to secure a majority agreement in Parliament in favour of women's right to vote.

There were arguments among the suffragists about the definition of 'women': whether this included all women, or just unmarried women – married women being regarded as an adjunct of their spouses, and therefore already represented, albeit by proxy. Or should it mean women with property, or those over thirty, or what? This argument occupied far more time and energy than was justified in Violet's view, and threatened to weaken their overall case. It gave fuel to those critics, both male and female, who declared that until they could agree between them on exactly what it was they wanted the suffragists did not deserve to be taken seriously.

'What I would really like,' said Violet eventually, 'is for you to be there Amy, in some capacity. Pouring coffee, if you like, but listening, and there all the time, even when there is no coffee to be poured. I would really like your opinion. I mean it.'

Amy shrugged, then smiled. 'I'm at your service, madam,' she said.

It needed an outside eye, Violet considered, from an impartial source. Amy was a sensible soul who was not easily taken in. She had the appearance of looking on at the world in a sardonic, detached sort of a way, like a spectator at a play. Sometimes the most sensible and balanced person in the room is the lady's maid.

'Are you happy with your lot, Amy?' Violet asked.

There was a pause, during which Amy tried very hard not to smile.

'What's brought this on, madam, may I ask?'

'You seem . . .' Violet regarded Amy thoughtfully. 'Sometimes I think you seem more content than anyone I know.'

'Ooh.' Amy wiggled her shoulders. 'Fancy that then!'

'Because you don't want anything. That's how it looks to me, Amy. You're not striving for something. That's the secret of contentment. Don't you agree?'

Amy put a finger to her lips and made a big show of considering this.

'I would like to be taller,' she announced. 'With a smaller nose, and sharper cheekbones, and . . .'

'That's enough of that, Amy!' Violet laughed, sighed, dismissed her maid, and sat for a while longer staring into space.

~

'Please come,' she implored.

It had taken some courage to broach the subject in the first place, and she knew the answer even as she asked the question, but it had to be asked.

'Why?' said Anthony. 'What's the point?'

'So you can understand what we're doing, and why.'

'I think I understand enough already without having to sit for interminable hours listening to a bunch of women chattering on.'

Anthony had now risen in rank in the Foreign Office so he was a senior member of the civil service and therefore in a position to wield some influence on the powers that be. Violet had been under pressure for some time from her fellow campaigners to get him on their side, so he could employ that influence in aid of the cause.

But if ever there was a time when the government's mantra – to wit that women were far better able to influence events by way of feminine persuasion of their husbands – could be disproved, this was it. The best thing she could do for suffragism, Violet realised, would be to get her husband on board. The fact that he wouldn't even discuss the matter was yet another failure on her part.

'Would you do it for me? Just this once? You might find it amusing.' She tried to smile. 'There are some very entertaining women in the group, you'd be surprised.' She started to tell her husband about Lolly Mulligan, who could do such wonderful impressions and who really should be on the stage, she was so . . . Oh but wait, she *was* on the stage, they really ought to see her perform one of these days. And anyway, it would be a change from spending yet another evening as his club. And he would be so welcome. There were friends of hers who'd love to meet him, they'd heard so much about him. Why not give it a try, what did he have to lose?

She was burbling, and they both knew it, and they both knew it was to no effect.

~

The meeting turned out to be quite small, to Violet's relief. Small enough that they could congregate in the drawing room and stay in one group, with one topic of conversation. There was very little that was new. They were simply covering the same old ground, and Violet felt her spirits flagging. From time to time she glanced over at Amy, who was standing docilely by the coffee trolley, occasionally topping up the cups and offering cakes and refusing to catch Violet's eye, or to show any expression whatever.

And then a voice rose above the others and declared in confident tones, 'What this movement needs is a kick up the backside! Action, in other words! Action, not words!'

They all turned to stare. She was a newcomer to the group, a small and slightly dumpy young woman with a mass of curly hair. She was sitting with her arms folded and a merrily defiant expression on her face.

She had been introduced to Violet earlier as Miss Brooks. 'Prudence, for my sins. Prudence by name, not by nature.' She was new to the campaign, she had been introduced – or press-ganged, as she put it – by none other than Mrs Fawcett herself.

Violet took to her immediately. She, Prudence-by-name-not-by-nature, had put her finger on something that had been bothering Violet for a while. The movement, these women with their perfect manners and their unshakable belief in the logical rightness of their cause, was stuck in a rut, and its members were far too well-bred to haul themselves out of it.

'Exactly what do you mean by action?' This was Lady Dalloway, without question the best-bred member of the whole troupe, and the most hardened traditionalist.

'Action,' said Miss Brooks. 'Creating a ruckus.'

'A "ruckus".' Lady Dalloway rolled the word around her tongue as if it were faintly unclean. 'So you think a group of women running around behaving like hooligans and "creating a ruckus" will have a better chance of persuading the men of Parliament that they are mature and intelligent enough to be granted the vote than reasoned debate and lobbying?' There was a murmur of approval around the room.

Miss Brooks shrugged. 'It's not as if it's got you anywhere yet, has it? We should up the stakes, raise our voices, turn ourselves into headline news. Let the world know about us!'

Lady Dalloway frowned. Some of the other women, watching her, followed suit. Violet looked at Amy but Amy was looking at the ground.

'Persistence is all, my dear,' said Lady Dalloway graciously. 'Persistence, and consistence. We will wear them down eventually.'

Miss Brooks puffed out her cheeks and sighed noisily. 'If you say so.'

It was at that point that Violet heard the front door open and close. She rose quickly and left the room.

'Anthony!' she breathed.

'Still here, are they?' He took out his watch. 'It's after midnight, shouldn't you ladies be tucked up in bed?'

'Please, come and join us.'

He didn't immediately reply. He was preoccupied with removing his coat and hat and handing them to James, the valet.

'They've heard so much about you. Just come and say hello. Just that.'

'I'm going to bed,' said her husband, and made for the stairs.

'Why?' Violet's tone was harsh enough to stop him in his tracks. He paused on the second stair and turned to look at her. 'Are you afraid of us?'

'*Afraid* of you? I'm *terrified* of you, don't you see? I am *terrified* that the softer sex are wasting their time discussing things they *know nothing about.*'

'Then come and argue your case. They're sensible women, they won't jump down your throat.' She wasn't sure about Prudence Brooks. She thought he might meet his match in Miss Brooks.

He paused, placed one hand into a pocket and looked down at his feet. He seemed to give his next comment some thought before he said, 'If you held a gun to my head and a lit bomb to my rear end, the answer would still be no.' He gestured wearily. 'I'm tired. Goodnight.'

Violet watched him ascend the stairs and disappear from sight.

She was aware of the door of the drawing room opening behind her. The women were leaving. How much of the conversation they had heard they did not divulge. One or two of them gave her arm a squeeze, as if to say, 'We know what you have to put up with.' Prudence Brooks gave her a big wink.

And then there was no one left but herself and Amy.

'So?' said Violet.

'Yes, madam?' replied Amy.

'What did you make of it?'

Amy hesitated a moment before responding. 'I'm glad

to know my place, madam.'

'Meaning?'

'I'm glad to know my place, and to be happy there.' She smiled, gave her mistress a small – and possibly sardonic – curtsey, and began to pile the coffee cups onto a tray.

'And that's all you have to say? Lucky you,' Violet murmured to herself. To Amy she said: 'Goodnight, Amy. And thank you for staying around.'

'My pleasure, madam.'

Violet made the mistake of tackling Anthony about it when she eventually reached the bedroom.

She felt humiliated. There could not have been one person in that room who had not heard at least the gist of their conversation. She felt she had let the whole group down, the whole movement even, by allowing them to think she had some kind of hold over her husband. She needed to make him rethink. However unlikely, and absurd, she needed him on her side. She felt terribly alone and betrayed, and angry, at herself and at other unknown and undefined targets.

'Why won't you listen to me?' she cried.

He sat up in bed and looked right at her. There was no anger in his eyes, she'd have preferred it if there had been. There was a kind of weary sympathy, the sort of look you put on with an elderly relative who has lost her senses and needs to be gently, and patronisingly, reassured.

'Dear sweet wife, I have listened to you. I have listened and listened until my ears are at risk of falling off altogether.'

And he lay down again and turned away from her.

'We have never had a proper conversation.' She was becoming tearful now. 'Not about this, not about anything of importance. Not for years.'

He groaned, loudly. And then she said what she had

been trying so hard not to say: 'Do you have any idea how humiliated I was? Do you have any idea what those women must think of me now?'

'Ah!' He shot up in bed again. 'So that's what it's about. What do the women think. A very important conundrum, I admit. There is nothing more dismaying, or belittling, than knowing your friends think badly of you.' And he lay back down again.

'Just promise me,' said Violet. She wished she could shut up but something was compelling her on. 'Promise me that you and I can sit down and have a proper talk, a civilised discussion. Tomorrow. That's all. Please.'

'Goodnight,' said Anthony.

That was the night Violet first began to harm herself. There were feelings welling up inside her that were so overpowering, feelings she'd never had before; a desperate, nightmarish desire to hurt something. Him. Someone. Anyone.

She could not hurt him. So she hurt herself instead.

5: The impudence of Prudence Brooks

Then Prudence Brooks came to stay.

It had been a long day in the cause of suffrage. They'd been printing leaflets at a house around the corner from Humphreys Street, it was late into the evening and they were exhausted. And so Violet, out of the blue, invited Prudence to stay the night, to save her the journey back to her place in . . . wherever it was.

'Clerkenwell,' said Prue. 'Not far. But I'd be happy to, thank you.'

Prudence was good company. Like Lolly, she appeared to regard the whole suffrage movement as a lark. They shared jokes about the terrifying likes of Lady Dalloway, who clearly considered her rank, if not her age, gave her some kind of authority over the lower orders of Violet and Prudence and Lolly and the rest. Like Lolly, Prudence made fun of some of their fellow suffragists, their primness, their insistence on *not treading on anyone's toes.* Violet wasn't sure that Prue cared that deeply about the movement, or about politics or suffrage in general, but that didn't seem to matter. She had the confidence and the ability to get to the heart of the business, any business. She was not hamstrung by doubts or propriety or concern for her reputation. She was forthright, dogmatic, indiscreet, enthusiastic, rude, and an all-round delightful companion.

Prue stayed for several days. Once the leaflets were

printed they had to be distributed through letterboxes, which took time and a good deal of legwork, but it was a lot more fun with her friend at her side. It was Prue's idea to stick some of them onto trees with drawing pins, an illegal activity which had to be done at night.

Violet was nervous about introducing Prudence to Anthony, but she needn't have worried. Her husband took to her immediately. They shared the same sense of humour, and she was a far better audience for his sometimes childish, often unrepeatable jokes. Better still, she didn't try to batter him over the head with her ideas on female suffrage. The subject barely arose in conversation, and when it did it invariably had to do with some prank that had got out of hand; like the time when Prue was chased around the block by a policeman for pasting posters onto the wall of the police station. I could learn from this woman, Violet thought.

Prudence didn't talk much about her home life. But she did talk about her exploits working in the theatre as a self-styled dresser for the actress Mrs Patrick Campbell – a position she appeared to fall into almost by accident.

'This theatre business, what a poser,' she was wont to say, time and again. 'People standing on stage and talking too loudly at one another? Melodramatic malarkey, if you ask me. And Mrs Pat herself, such the *grande dame* and all that, but you should see her when she's in her cups.' Turning to Anthony she said, 'You'd love her. She has the coarsest sense of humour of anyone I've ever met, including you.' She then went on to regale them with anecdotes about Mrs Pat. How on the first night of one of her plays in the middle of a scene of high drama the elastic of Mrs Pat's skirt gave out and she was revealed in all her knickerbocker glory; and how without batting an eyelid she picked up the skirt and carried on with such aplomb she got a resounding round of applause on her exit. How she used to try out her parts in her dressing room to her dog, who she considered a far better critic than anyone on two legs. The dog went everywhere with her, including her bed. It was a wonder she didn't bring it on stage with her. And for all that she purported to take her profession seriously she was apt to fool around on stage on occasion in an attempt to put fellow actors off their lines.

'For someone who detests the stage so much you seem very enthusiastic about it,' said Anthony.

Prue nodded in acknowledgement, then carried on. There was a time, she said, when Mrs Pat was so bored with a part she'd been playing for too long that she took to throwing chocolates at the scenery. 'They're just children, all of them,' she concluded.

'I love the theatre,' ventured Violet. 'And I love Mrs Pat, I think she's glorious.'

'I do too,' said Prue. 'Truly. I was in love with her once.'

There was a bit of a silence.

'When I was very young. About three years ago.'

The silence continued, but for the odd clink of knife upon plate.

'Are you a lesbian?' asked Anthony, eventually.

Prue thought for a moment. 'Yes! No. Yes, maybe. Would you like me to be?'

Anthony chuckled. 'I don't think I've ever met one.'

'I'm still working it out,' Prue continued. 'There's no question I've felt passionate love for women, at least for Mrs Pat. Not for you Violet, no offence.'

'Fascinating,' said Anthony.

There was no question that life at home was a lot more pleasant with Prudence around.

~

Prue's life as she described it was a series of happy accidents. She met Mrs Pat through her 'dalliance', as she

46

put it, with a stage hand who was working backstage at the Adelphi Theatre, who in turn she happened to come across when she was hanging around the West End. What she was doing hanging around the West End in the first place, on her own, and far too young, she didn't go into. But it appeared her parents neither knew nor cared what their daughter got up to.

Her association with the suffragists was a result of another chance meeting, this time with Mrs Fawcett herself, in a teashop off Regent's Street where she, Prue, was working as a waitress.

'What were you doing working as a waitress in a teashop?' Violet looked positively alarmed.

'A long story.' It transpired Prue's father had lost his job, so for the first time in her life Prue had felt the need to go out in the world and earn 'some pennies'. Being too well-bred for manual work and too uneducated to be a governess, she finally managed to get taken on as a waitress at a teashop, and only then because the manager considered her 'refined manner' – as he described it – would attract the right sort of customers, such as Mrs Fawcett.

After a few days Prue announced she had to go home, not least for a change of clothes. Violet grabbed her arm and, to her own surprise, pleaded with her not to go.

'I can come back if you like,' Prue told her.

And she did. Barely twenty-fours later she was there, on the doorstep, looking flustered, and even quite distressed. It turned out her mother, in order to make ends meet, was taking in mending – she a frail fifty-something who'd never so much as threaded a needle in her life before – and she was using Prue's bedroom as a working space. So Prue felt it was really time she did her bit to contribute to the household expenses.

'If it's money that's the problem we can help you!'

Violet exclaimed.

'Absolutely not, thanks all the same,' said Prue. Then, 'Why are you wearing a glove?'

In her excitement at seeing her friend again Violet had quite forgotten about the glove.

'Chilblains,' she said.

There was a pause, during which Prudence stared at her friend and her friend stared around the room, before they both burst out laughing.

Violet removed the glove to reveal the scratches on her hand. She described the rows that took place in the bedroom, late at night and invariably after she'd returned in the early hours from a meeting or a leafleting session with the suffragists. Her handsome husband accused her of neglecting her duties as a wife and wasting her time on a cause that had a tinker's chance of succeeding. He went on to quiz her on current affairs, starting with the names of members of the Cabinet, which was not a problem, Violet giggled. But when it came to interrogating her on affairs of state and what had taken place in Parliament that very afternoon, that's when she faltered.

'He told me if I spent less time talking nonsense with my lady friends and more time paying attention to what is actually happening in the world, I might consider myself worthy of the vote.' She paused. 'And he has a point.'

'I can't see how not knowing the ins and outs of the Enclosure Acts' – Violet chuckled at this – 'means a person is too ignorant to have a say in things. And nothing – *nothing* – gives a man the right to stab his wife in the hand.'

'It wasn't him that did this, it was me. With nail scissors. It was him or me, you see.' Violet wasn't smiling now. 'And I thought it would be safer to be me. I didn't think I had a violent bone in my body. I used to rescue wounded birds when I was a girl. I once brought a cat into the house that had been kicked by a horse and it died right there in the sitting room, in front of my mother and me.' She began to weep. 'I would never, ever hurt anything or anyone. Never!'

'So what are you going to do?' asked Prudence, after a shocked moment.

Violet looked down at her hand. 'It'll heal,' she said, replacing her glove. 'I'm told it's better if it's protected but not covered in bandages.'

'I meant about Anthony.'

'You won't say anything? You absolutely promise? I'm afraid it would ruin everything if you did.'

'Of course I won't.'

'He blames me for not having children.' Violet's tears began to well again. 'He thinks it's because I don't like the . . .' she stopped.

'The what? Sexual intercourse?'

'Yes. It's not that I don't like it, it's . . .'

'You don't like sex.'

Violet hung her head.

'It's probably his fault you don't like sex. It's a two-way thing, after all. Does he help you to climax?'

Violet looked up, shocked. 'To what?'

'I thought as much,' said Prue.

~

It was not long after that that Prudence was banished from the Turnip home.

Violet never did discover exactly what went on between Prue and Anthony while she was out of the room that evening. She was gone for only five minutes or so and when she returned to the drawing room her friend was leaning back in her chair looking triumphant while her husband sat opposite her with a face like thunder.

'What happened?' she enquired.

Without a word Anthony rose from his seat and exited

the room.

'What did you say to him?' cried Violet.

'Not much,' said Prue. 'I asked him his opinion on the suffragist movement, and he said what was the point of it when we couldn't even agree on anything amongst ourselves? I said isn't that why there's an opposition party in Parliament, because men didn't always agree on anything? That's all.'

'You must have said something else.'

'Well, maybe I made a comment about the size of men's . . . brains.'

Violet continued to stare at Prue, who examined her fingernails.

'I seriously think you should leave him, Vi,' said Prue.

'*Leave* him?'

'He's absolutely no good for you at all. Do you really want to spend the rest of your life with a man like that?'

'He's not a bad man, Prue.'

'He is a bad man, Vi. He's a bad man not just because he bullies you but because you blame yourself for it. And you have a brain twice the size of his. It's in his nature and he's not going to change. You could have fifty more years of this – is that what you really want?'

'But I can't leave him!'

'Why not?'

'I'd have – nothing!'

'You'd have your self-respect.' Prue was staring at Violet now with an intensity she'd never seen in her before.

Violet looked down at her feet.

'I'm going to bed,' she said.

~

At breakfast the following morning once Anthony had left for work Violet, studying her plate, told her friend that her husband had declared he did not want her in the house any more. 'Ever,' she added, with emphasis.

Prue nodded and took a bite of her toast. 'Before you know it he'll make sure you have no friends left,' she said.

Violet didn't respond.

'Think about what I said last night,' Prue went on, with her mouth full.

'You're not married,' Violet pronounced. 'You have never made the vows, you don't know . . .'

'I know an unhappy person when I see one. Vows be damned.' Violet drew in her breath sharply. 'Don't be shocked. What's the point of supporting the suffrage movement if you can't even control your own life? Isn't that what the whole movement is about?'

Violet had no answer to this. She was feeling altogether too miserable to care one way or another.

Then Prue leant over and touched her on the arm. 'Dearest Vi,' she said, with uncharacteristic softness. 'You are a very special person. You are clever, and kind, and beautiful.'

'But . . .'

'Don't you dare deny it! And there is so much you can offer the world. But the longer you carry on with this self-absorbed, brainless bigot – yes, that is what he is – the more miserable you're going to get. Not,' she reached for the marmalade dish, 'that it's any of my business. But I've said my piece, more than my piece, I will shut up now.' She spread the marmalade and lifted a piece of toast to her mouth.

'Actually, I will say something else,' she said, toast suspended halfway. 'Sex is the best thing in the world. With the right person.'

And she winked at Violet and took a large bite.

6: The scandal of divorce

Of all the sentiments her dear, if opinionated, friend had expressed it was this last one that astounded Violet the most.

Sex was the best thing in the world?

Violet was fond of her husband. She liked to touch him. Sometimes in bed, lying awake and watching him as he slept she experienced an overwhelming feeling of tenderness. She wanted to reach out and stroke him, and on occasion she did, and he would turn away with a grunt of irritation as if to say – I am trying to sleep, don't bother me, woman.

And the sexual intercourse thing. There wasn't much tenderness there. It was more of an animal thing, entirely physical. He would crouch over her, straddling her, his face very close to hers, his *appendage* (she didn't know what else to call it) dangling above her stomach. Sometimes he would grab her hand and place the thing in it and order her to pull on it – not stroke it, which she wouldn't have objected to – but yank it, hard, as hard as she could. She did her best. She pulled so hard on occasion she was afraid it might come off in her hand. And then when he – or it – was ready, he would plunge it into her, and his body would arch above her and his face contort. And he would go on plunging, plunging, minutes on end, his body writhing and his face still contorting, her body bouncing up and down and the springs of the mattress beneath them squeaking fit to bust, and she . . . well frankly she was just waiting for the whole thing to be over. And when it was, he would let out a groan loud enough to wake the whole household. And his body would go into spasm for an entire minute before he relaxed, withdrew from her and lay on his back, panting like a long-distance runner, before turning on his side and going immediately to sleep.

How could that be the best thing in the world?

She would have liked to have asked Prue exactly what it was that made the whole business so wonderful. But Prue was banished now. And besides, there were some topics that even close friends did not talk about. No one had ever discussed sex with Violet before, certainly not her mother.

On the other hand, it obviously gave Anthony huge pleasure, and that had to be something. Sometimes in the morning, when he was short of time, he would reach out for her and kiss her, on the mouth, hard, and again he would grab hold of her hand and place it on his genitals and rub it up and down until she felt a wetness. She didn't know what this wetness was, though it certainly left a stain on the bedsheets, which was somewhat embarrassing.

On other occasions he would take one of her breasts into his mouth, whole as it were, and suck on it, which was mildly pleasurable, until the sucking turned into biting, which caused her to yelp with pain. She did wonder at times if she was really no more than a doll, with all the female attributes more or less in the right place, and she could have been anyone and it would make no difference.

Maybe all men were not like that. Who was to know?

One way or another, life could be a lot worse. She had a

comfortable home, and friends, and she was free to come and go as she pleased, in the daytime at least. She wanted for nothing. And if she had to forego the whole suffrage business, so be it. She would make friends elsewhere. She would find something else to stimulate her mind.

She would see out the year with the suffragists, and then look around for something else to occupy her.

~

It so happened that at that time there was in the news a much-publicised divorce case between Marquess and Marchioness Dalhousie (not their real names).

Divorce cases were held in open court, so any Tom, Dick or Mary could attend. They were, naturally, the source of much gossip among the *hoi polloi*, the suffragists not excepted. This case was of particular interest to the gossip-mongers as it was the marchioness who was divorcing the marquess, which made the whole business that much more contentious.

Opinion among the suffragists was divided. Where one might have expected the women to have sided wholeheartedly with the marchioness, on the grounds that she was a woman, and that she would not willingly have submitted herself to so much public shame without very good cause, that was not the case at all.

Violet was surprised, and intrigued, to see who of her suffragist friends came down on the side of whom. Lady Dalloway, predictably perhaps, was on the side of the marquess. Marriage, she declared in her cut-glass tones, was sacrosanct, and a woman who decided she had married the wrong man had only herself to blame. If she were stupid enough not to find out what she was getting herself into before she married then she was a fool, and it was her duty to stick by her husband through thick and thin.

'Even if he beats her?' asked one young woman.

Lady D frowned. 'She should have discovered that before she married him.'

That led into a lengthy argument about how far in a relationship a woman could go in order to find out as much as she could about a man before marrying him. Sleeping together was obviously out of the question, living together likewise. At a pinch, spending the night in the same house, in separate bedrooms, so long as there were others around to act as chaperones, was just about acceptable.

'So,' sparked up another young thing, 'if a woman discovers after she's married that she's married a brute, she's to put up with it? For the rest of her life?'

'She should have . . .'

'But how could she find out about the man she has married if she isn't allowed to have sexual intercourse with him before the wedding?'

'A woman's intuition,' Lady D replied firmly.

'Well, we all know how men can change after they get married,' said someone. There was a chorus of approval for this.

'Even so . . .'

Lady Dalloway was beginning to be drowned out. The idea that a woman should know everything about a man before she married him, even though they were not allowed to share a bed together – and let's face it, it was in bed that much of the wrongdoing and cruelty took place – did not hold water among the younger suffragists.

The conversation then got around to the double standards enjoyed by the male of the species, from the kings of England down – but not, significantly, by their own beloved Queen, who was as faithful and loyal as a lap dog – who had one rule for their own sexual shenanigans and another for their spouses'. There was talk of Thackeray, who pointed the finger at politicians who condemned the tyrannies of foreign royalty while behaving like 'household tyrants' themselves.

'And while we're on the subject,' piped up a stern-looking woman in a print dress, 'what possible justification is there for a divorce law which makes it far harder for a woman to divorce a man than vice versa?'

Violet kept quiet throughout the argument and concentrated on not catching Prudence's eye, which she was aware was fixed firmly on her. She was surprised at how the room was split. Not all the younger unmarried women supported the divorcée. Dorothy, to Violet's astonishment, sided with the marquess for much the same reasons as Lady Dalloway.

Then Prudence stood up and spoke. 'A woman who puts up with a brutal husband is a fool. What is the point of us fighting for the rights of women to have our voices heard if we are still expected to keep quiet in our own households? It goes against the whole grain of the movement, it's nonsense.'

Someone clapped, half-heartedly.

'We are never going to get on an equal footing with men so long as we're expected to play second fiddle to them,' she went on. 'They don't like us, they can divorce us. We don't like them, we have to put up with it. Are we happy with that?'

She looked around the room, glaring at each person in turn.

'Hear hear,' said someone.

'Are you married, dear?' asked one elderly woman, who was not Lady Dalloway.

'No,' said Prudence. Then she smiled. 'I'm not so much of an idiot.'

This caused consternation among the assemblage, some of them laughing out loud, others booing, or snorting, or expressing their disapproval in other animalistic ways.

Violet was astonished at times at how coarse and unruly these otherwise perfectly-behaved ladies could be.

'We should be fighting for the top, not the bottom. We should be aiming to be better than them, not vying to be the lowest,' said a mousy-looking woman who reminded Violet, alarmingly, of her mother.

'Oh, for God's sake,' said Prue. 'Let's be realistic. Life is a battle and if we want to win it we need to get our hands dirty from time to time.'

'There is no need for that,' came a voice from a corner.

'You would think,' Prue continued, 'the suffragists would be a radical lot. But we're not. In many ways we're more conservative than the common person in the street. That's conservative with a small "c". And a large one,' she added as an afterthought.

'I think you've said enough, Miss Brooks,' said Lady Dalloway. 'Thank you so much.'

'Yes, I think I have too.' So Prue took her seat again and stared at the wall.

I love these people, thought Violet. I love them for their passion and their prejudices and their disagreements. I love them for their conservatism and for their radicalism and above all for the *arguments*. However heated the debate there was very rarely any rancour afterwards. Where else am I going to find friends like these?

7: Marital conflict

If Lady Dalloway was correct in asserting that a woman should know all there is to know about a man before marrying him, Violet had obviously failed.

Nobody really knows what love is until they experience it. Violet was still young. After five years of marriage she was only twenty-three, and a relatively green twenty-three at that. Despite her marriage she was far less worldly-wise than Prue, who she guessed to be a few years younger than her. Prue knew the world, she knew love – albeit infatuated love with the glamorous Mrs Pat – and she had experienced sexual pleasure. She had disregarded all the rules young ladies were expected to abide by in the last decade of the nineteenth century, and she was all the better for it.

Violet had hoped she might grow to love her husband, in time. It was not at all uncommon. Once the initial shyness and excitement had gone, and you got used to a person, you understood their routines and their habits, their likes and dislikes, you could settle into a kind of comfortable harmony. Reading each other's thoughts. Finishing one another's sentences. There was love to be found in predictability, and security, and a deep knowledge of the other person. Maybe it was the truest love of all.

But after five years of marriage this did not seem to be

happening. There was less and less communication between Violet and Anthony as the years went by. Even the rows had fizzled out. There was less sex too – that at least was a relief – and most crucially of all, there was less interest. Anthony did not want to hear what Violet had been up to in the daytime, and truth to tell she wasn't particularly curious to hear about his day either. Any talk of the suffragists was ignored. It was only a matter of time before he would lay down the law about what he described as her 'senseless' hobby. So when it did come she was not in the least surprised.

'It's time you cut yourself off from those awful women,' he said one day over dinner.

They still dined together. It was about the only time they did spend together. After dinner and at weekends, if he was at home and not spending the evening at his club, he would retire to his study to work – and here Violet was reminded, with sadness, of her father. How many men retire to their studies to work of an evening in order to avoid their wives?

'Why?' said Violet.

'They're time-wasters,' said her husband. 'They've been agitating for female suffrage for decades and look where it's got them. Nowhere.'

'Is it their fault, if nobody listens to them?'

'They don't have a case. There are too many people in this country with the vote as it is. It's unwieldy.'

'What do you mean?'

'The politicians in this Parliament are the best in the world,' he said. 'The best minds, the sharpest intellects, the most experienced policy-makers a person could ever wish to see. Lawyers, doctors, professors, men of the cloth – every inch of British life and experience is there.'

'From one class only. Representing themselves.' Violet felt a surge of anger.

'But you, you women, seem to think you know better. What is wrong with the government of this country? Tell me. Tell me one thing you would want to change, if you had the vote.'

He was toying with his empty glass, his fourth of the evening.

'The divorce law.'

There was a chilly pause.

'Why? Why that?'

'Tell me why you think a husband can divorce his wife for adultery but a wife cannot do the same.'

Anthony reached for the wine decanter and refilled his glass.

'Without having to prove cruelty on top,' she went on. 'Though I'd have thought adultery was cruel enough.'

'There you go then,' said Anthony. His face was flushed and he was drinking too fast.

'You don't have to agree with them,' Violet went on. 'But I'm not giving them up. I love them. They're the best thing in my life. They're the only good thing in my life.'

That came out unexpectedly. Anthony was still studying his wine glass. He drank half of its contents down in one gulp before he said, quietly, 'What are you trying to tell me?'

'I'm trying to tell you I want a divorce.'

That was unexpected too, or at least unplanned. It was followed by a very long silence during which Anthony sat perfectly still, his hand holding the wine glass, eyes fixed on the tablecloth in front of him.

'Why?'

'I've given you the reasons why. We don't see eye to eye on anything, not any longer. If we ever did.'

'I haven't been a good husband to you?'

She didn't respond to this.

'I haven't provided for you, given you a home, given

you everything you need? Been loyal, and faithful?'

'Of course you have.'

'Then what' – he slammed the glass down onto the table – 'what possible grounds do you have for wanting a divorce?'

'I told you,' she said.

'Of all the people I know,' he went on, as if he hadn't heard her, 'all the men, married men playing fast and loose with other women, staying out all evening, coming home drunk, and abusive. Neglectful. Cruel. Often physically so. Have – I – ever – done – any – of – those – things? Have I?'

He was shouting now.

'Not until now, no,' said Violet.

She was not frightened. She had not planned this conversation, nor the direction of it. Had she done so she would have tried to pick a moment when her husband had not downed nearly a whole decanter of wine.

But the human psyche does strange things, when you least expect it to. Now the rabbit was out of the hat, and the die was cast, there was no turning back. Violet found herself smiling as she thought how only a year ago they made a game out of how many clichés you could include in one sentence.

'What are you smiling about?'

'I was thinking how we used to play games, stupid games, do you remember? Word games.'

'What's that got to do with anything?'

'It's just one of the things we used to do but no longer.'

'And whose fault is that?'

That was it, that was the entire problem. Fault.

'It's nobody's fault,' she said. 'Not everything has to be somebody's fault.' She reached out to touch her husband's hand and he jerked it away. 'Do you love me, Anthony? Please, be truthful.'

He swallowed, looked down and back up again before he spoke. 'I did, once. You were funny, and witty and beautiful, and clever. Very clever. Far cleverer than me. I thought that was enough. But you're frigid. You can't bear me to touch you. And so long as you feel like that we'll never have children – how could we? Do I repulse you so much?'

'No, of course you don't!'

'I think I do. And do you know what that does to a man's self-esteem? To know he's lying next to a wife who cannot stand the sight of him? Are you not surprised I haven't looked elsewhere? Lord knows I'd have every right to!'

'You don't repulse me, Anthony, that's not what it is.'

'Then what is it?'

There were altogether too many truths bursting into the light right now.

'You're not – please don't drink any more – it's not to do with being repulsed.'

Anthony emptied another glass. His speech was beginning to slur.

'Then whad?' he said.

'There's no tenderness.'

'Huh?'

'You're like – it's like animals mating. It's not what I expected,' she finished, lamely.

Anthony sat there, slumped over the table His face was flushed and angry. And the one thing Violet wanted to do, which was to touch him, to stroke his face, or simply to place an arm around his shoulders, she did not do as she knew he would simply shake her off.

It was *impasse*.

They continued to sit there together, in silence, until Violet could bear it no longer. Finally she said, 'I'll be gone in a week.'

She paused for a moment for him to object, but he said nothing. So she got to her feet and walked out of the room.

~

It's one of life's oddities that an all-out row can be the saving of a relationship. Paradoxically Violet felt closer to her husband then than she had for years. Indifference is the greatest enemy of happy marriage, she thought. They had never shouted at one another before in the whole of their time together, and in its own peculiar way it was wonderful. She felt purged.

It could have been the making of them. Now things were out in the open they could start afresh. She truly felt they'd broken through a barrier and from now on, with a bit of luck and the odd tweak in the mechanism of their married life, everything would be different. It was within their grasp. She could hold him and show him some of the tenderness he had never shown her, by way of illustration of what was missing in her life. They would laugh together, as they used to.

Except of course that he did not come to bed. Not that night nor any of the succeeding nights. She was fooling herself. Like it or not, it was a *fait accompli.*

8: The end of a chapter

Violet appraised herself in the full-length mirror in her bedroom.

Item: one body, on the small size, though well-proportioned. Dressed stylishly, yet sufficiently understated to secure the approval of her parents, had they been present, and with enough ornamentation to please her husband.

Item: two eyes, pale blue and a little large for the face, with lids to them.

Item: expressions, variable, depending on circumstances, often cleverly masked.

Item: character, undefined and changeable, depending on who she was trying to impress on the one hand or not to offend on the other.

Item: demeanour. A child-like belief that all is for the best in the best of all possible worlds, and the adult realisation that this is not the case. And a further recognition that at the precise point when Violet felt she was mature enough to withstand a marriage and all the compromises it entailed, it was over.

~

She wrote to Prudence. And the following day her friend arrived on her doorstep with a very expensive bottle of champagne, which they drank together in Violet's drawing room.

'I don't usually drink this early in the day,' said Vi.

'You don't usually leave your husband,' said Prue. Then: 'Chin-chin!' She raised her glass high in the air, took a swig and nearly choked. 'Oof!' she said. 'I'd forgotten how the stuff gets up your nose.' She sneezed loudly and took another swig to calm herself down. 'Here's to adventures to come.'

Violet lifted her glass and smiled wanly.

'Now,' Prue continued, 'we need to find you somewhere to live. Unfortunately there's not much I can do there – I don't even have a room of my own at the moment. What I can offer you is support and advice, for what it's worth.' She smiled broadly, raised her glass again and said, 'Here's to freedom.'

Freedom. It was what Violet had always wanted. It was why she left the family home, but was that why she wanted to leave her marriage too? Freedom looked pretty daunting from where she was sitting right now.

They drank on. Prue chatted away but Violet was only half listening. Her friend seemed to be mapping out all the opportunities that lay ahead: a safe place to stay, an interesting job, her own money, a liaison or two – the possibilities were endless. She was a good friend in a crisis. But the longer the afternoon went on and shadows deepened the sleepier Violet became. In the end Prue half carried her up to her bedroom and gave her a peck on the cheek before she left. And Violet slept through the whole evening until the following morning.

The next person she told was Lolly Mulligan. They sat opposite one another in a coffee house and Lolly held her hand across the table and gazed at her with her enormous brown eyes throughout the telling.

'I can't offer you a roof over your head, darling,' she said. 'Well, obviously, no fixed abode and all that. But I do have an idea.'

'Oh? Please tell me.'

'You won't like it.'

'Won't I?'

'No.'

'I don't suppose I have a lot of choice. So?'

'Dorothy Moss. She has a spare room. I know because I've stayed there. She's wildly eccentric, I don't need to tell you that, but she's quite kind underneath it all. She will make your life a merry misery but there you are.'

'Dorothy?' Violet repeated, nonplussed.

'I will speak to her. If you'd like me to, that is.'

'Thank you, Lolly.'

Then, as she continued toying with Violet's hand, Lolly launched into a re-enactment of her latest adventure running the gauntlet of yet another Lothario of a producer who promised her a part in his latest *oeuvre* in return for certain favours. It seems Lolly found it impossible to obtain acting work without having to be chased around the desk by some 'fat, over-sexed, balding letch,' as she put it. The stories, while always entertaining, were much the same, and the fact that most of the protagonists were Scottish was mostly due, Violet surmised, to Lolly's skill with the Scottish accent.

'Did you get the part?' asked Violet.

'Oh. Well. Noo. No.'

'You seem to know a lot of Scottish people,' said Violet.

'Do I? Well, what d'ye noo?' Lolly laughed merrily. Then she became serious for a moment. She still had Violet's hand clamped between hers.

'Which reminds me,' she said. 'I may just know of a job going.'

'What kind of job?'

Lolly moved her head from side to side. 'Well, can't tell you yet, darling. And I'm not sure it's your *thing,* but, you know . . .'

'Beggars cannot be choosers.'

'Oh let's not go *that* far.' Lolly released Violet's hand finally and sat back in her chair.

'Thank you, Lolly,' said Violet. 'I really appreciate it.'

'My pleasure, dear heart,' said Lolly, and giggled.

~

Violet saw very little of her husband through the week. He stayed out late every night – at his club presumably – and spent the nights in another bedroom. The only time they were physically together was at breakfast-time, when he buried himself in the newspaper and did not say a word to her.

The week went by fast. There were practical matters to be sorted out – Amy, for one, Violet's loyal, shrewd maid, who'd been with them throughout their married life.

'Amy will need three months' pay,' she said to her husband one morning over breakfast.

'I'm not giving you a penny,' he said, without lifting his face from *The Times*.

'It's in her contract, it's an understanding. We can't just throw her out onto the street.'

'You should have thought about that before.'

Violet had a few pounds set aside, most of it the remains of a wedding gift from her father. It was just about enough to cover three months' wages for a lady's maid, or a few nights in a hotel, but not both.

To Amy, she said, 'I'm going away for some time Amy. I am so sorry I couldn't let you know sooner.'

'That's all right, madam,' said Amy, as ever mistress of the deadpan expression.

'I meant, I have to give you notice.'

'I understand, madam.'

Violet had been addressing Amy in the mirror of her dressing table, as ladies so often do with their maids. Now she turned to look at her directly before adding, 'I may not be coming back.'

'I understood that too, madam.'

It came as a shock to Violet to realise that her clever, secretive young maid was ahead of her.

'How?'

Amy cleared her throat before speaking. 'I did realise there was some friction between yourself and Mr Turnip, madam. That's all.'

'So you knew I was going to leave him?'

'I didn't know anything, madam. But let's say it didn't come as a total surprise.'

'It came as a surprise to him.'

'Of course. Men don't always have their antennae so well-attuned, do they?'

Violet laughed. 'Amy, dearest Amy, you are far too clever to be a lady's maid.'

Amy smiled. 'Cleverness is all a part of it, madam.'

'There must be a way you can put your cleverness to better use than as a lady's maid.'

'I have no ambition, Mrs Turnip. I am very easily contented. As you know.'

Violet gazed at Amy for a moment. She took a deep breath before she said, 'You are due three months' wages. I will get it to you, in time, but not immediately. Will that be difficult for you?'

'Not at all.'

'And I'm sure Mr Turnip wouldn't object if you stayed here until you found another position.'

'There's no need for that, madam. I already have another position.'

Violet's eyes widened. 'But you've only . . . How could you have found one so quickly?'

'They've been asking me to come and work for them for a year, madam. A Mr and Mrs Richardson. They live in Chelsea. They have three daughters.'

'They've been asking you?'

'I didn't take up the offer madam, because I wanted to remain here.' Amy's smile was bland, but genuine. 'I've liked it here. I shall miss it. I shall miss the both of you.'

Violet felt close to tears.

'I shall miss you too, Amy. Very much.'

'And who knows, madam, maybe one day in the future our paths will cross again.'

~

When it came to time for Violet to leave she felt almost more tearful saying goodbye to her maid than she would have done to her husband, had he been there, which of course he was not.

She paused on the pavement outside the four-storey house to look back at it. It seemed, now if not before, unbelievably salubrious. Amy, just Amy, stood in the doorway with her hands clasped before her, smiling. In the street the cab driver was loading the last of Violet's luggage into the vehicle. Beside her stood Prue.

'Ready?' she said.

'As I'll ever be,' said Violet.

Amy was still standing there as the cab drew away from the kerb.

9: The vagaries of Dorothy Moss

Dorothy's house was a two-storey cottage in a cobbled mews in South Kensington, recently converted from stables. (She claimed you could still smell the horses.) By comparison with Humphreys Street it was a doll's house: pretty enough from the outside, though the odd shrub or flower pot would have helped, and everything, from the windows to the staircase, on a miniature scale.

On arrival, Prue quickly made her excuses and left. 'I can't stand the woman,' she muttered to Violet on the doorstep. 'Sorry, have to leave you to it, good luck', before walking briskly away.

Dorothy greeted Violet at the front door looking surprisingly diffident, even nervous. She ushered her guest into her front room before instructing the cab driver to take the luggage upstairs to 'the bedroom at the back'. Once that was done and the driver had left, with a gratuity which Dorothy had ready, she closed the front door, bustled into the room and said to Violet, 'Sit down, sit down. What can I get you? Tea?'

'Tea would be lovely, thank you,' said Violet. She looked around the room. 'Where shall I sit?'

'Anywhere, anywhere,' said Dorothy.

Violet seated herself tentatively on one end of the sofa.

'I don't have servants.' Dorothy raised her voice as she disappeared into her kitchen. 'I can't be doing with other people around the house. Besides, it's too small. Do you take sugar?'

'No, thank you.'

Dorothy's 'front room' was, by contemporary standards, austere. There were no knick-knacks, no ornamentation, nothing that did not serve an essential purpose. The furniture was a mix of mismatched pieces, all of it old and rather shabby. There was a sofa with wooden arms, its seat covered in faded brocade, an ancient and much-worn armchair with a patterned cover, a heavy wooden chest of drawers, two upright chairs and the odd occasional table. There was nothing personal in the room at all – no photographs, no paintings, no clue as to its inhabitant. After years of living with Anthony's forebears glaring down at her from every wall of the house this was, to Violet, a bit of a relief.

Dorothy appeared with the tea tray and placed it onto one of the tables, which wobbled. She muttered as she poured the tea into, Violet couldn't help but notice, mismatched cups.

'Milk?'

'Please.'

She poured the milk straight from the bottle – there was no jug to be seen – and some of it went into Violet's saucer, for which Dorothy apologised, flustered, then made a big play of returning the spilt milk from the saucer to the cup and wiping it with a napkin before at last handing it to her guest.

Eventually she sat down on the armchair opposite Violet, took a deep breath and said: 'This is my doing, isn't it?'

'What is?'

'This, you leaving your husband. I feel responsible. If it weren't for my introducing you to the suffragists – it was that that did it for you, wasn't it? That and my remarks about him.'

Violet laughed. 'No, of course not! It had nothing to do with you, Dorothy. Not directly.' She took a sip of her tea. It was extremely strong and she had to stop herself from grimacing.

'Nonetheless. It was not what I intended.' Dorothy was staring at Violet through her glasses almost anxiously.

'It is very good of you to take me in,' said Violet. 'And of course I must pay you something.'

'Out of the question,' said Dorothy. 'I don't suppose you have anything anyway, if I guess rightly. I feel responsible, no matter what you say, so having you here is the least I can do. Can you cook?'

'Not really.'

'Well, you can learn. That would be useful. In fact, that would be the most useful thing you could do for me. I am a bad cook. Food means nothing to me except to keep me alive. Otherwise, I don't want anything from you, nothing at all.' She gestured dismissively. 'I will leave you to yourself for the most part, and vice versa if you don't mind, that way we should get along nicely. There is a desk in your bedroom for your work – that's if you have work. Do you?'

Violet shook her head and tried not to smile.

'I forget, ladies don't work. I work all the time, either here or in the museum.' Dorothy wafted a hand vaguely in the direction of the window and the great outside. 'I rise at seven in the morning, and if I'm at home I lunch at noon and dine at whatever time it happens to be.'

She paused.

'We may eat together if that suits. I am happy to have conversations with you over the dinner table, but please do not think me rude if I choose to read the newspaper instead. I am used to being on my own and doing precisely as I please.' She was addressing the floor now.

The conversation seemed to be costing her some effort.

She looked up finally as she moved onto safer ground. 'There are plentiful shops nearby and they all deliver. There's a china pot in the kitchen with change. And if you need any more money just ask.'

'I couldn't possibly . . .'

'Of course you could. What else are you going to do?'

She explained the house was a result of an inheritance from her father, and she lived comfortably, if frugally, on the remainder of the inheritance and the wages she received from her work at the museum. 'If you are prepared to cook, that is payment enough as far as I am concerned.'

Violet inclined her head. 'Then that suits me very well. Thank you Dorothy.'

Dorothy grunted.

'Though please understand I will be looking for a position as soon as possible,' Violet added. 'I'm not sure as what at present, but . . . As a matter of fact Lolly Mulligan told me she might know of something.'

'Lolly Mulligan?' Dorothy scoffed. 'That flibbertigibbet! I wouldn't take anything she says without a large dollop of salt. She's an actress.'

Lolly's character thus summed up, signed and sealed in a couple of sentences, Dorothy got to her feet and made for the door and the staircase, which led steeply to the upper floor. 'I'll show you your room.'

It was at the back of the house, and again as might be expected it was more of a work room, or even a monk's cell, than a lady's bedroom. There was a simple single bed, with a chenille bedspread, a chair, a wardrobe, a chest of drawers, a washstand and a table – presumably the desk that Dorothy had referred to. A small window overlooked gardens belonging to the much larger edifices behind. Apart from the bedspread and the curtains, which were made of threadbare blue cotton, there was no fabric or upholstery in the room at all. Neither was there a mirror. The only mirror in the entire place, as Violet was to discover, was in the hallway.

Violet's luggage sat in the middle of the room, dwarfing it.

'I'll leave you to get settled,' said Dorothy. And she left.

~

The following morning Prudence arrived at the front door.

'Is she in?' she whispered.

'No,' Violet whispered back, stepping aside to let her in.

'Thank God for that.'

Prue made straight for the front room and sat down.

'So,' she said, removing her gloves, 'how goes it?'

'A bit early to tell. It's small, but it's comfortable enough. And there's a bathroom, but with no hot water.'

'You'll get used to that. And how are you and the old witch getting along?'

'She's made it perfectly clear she likes to keep herself to herself, which suits me too.' Violet took a seat on the armchair, which was more comfortable than it looked. 'Why do you dislike her so much?'

'We're too alike.' Prue drummed her fingers on the wooden arm of the sofa. 'We're both forthright, say what we think, offend people left right and centre. She can be remarkably rude at times, but then so can I.' She laughed loudly. 'But she's a good soul underneath, I suppose, and a lifesaver in your case.'

'She seems to think she's responsible for my leaving my husband. I think she feels almost guilty.'

'Does she now? Well, that's no bad thing at all. Is she asking for rent?'

'No, she refused my offer point blank.'

'Good, excellent. Don't discourage her. If she thinks she's guilty, let her.'

'She asked me to cook for us instead.'

'Ooh, that's a challenge, I'll say. Can you cook?'

'I haven't cooked anything since I left home. The family home, that is.'

Prue laughed heartily. 'There you go! Another adventure. Later on we'll do the rounds of the local shops, see how the land lies.' She gazed around the room. 'Strange taste she has, or you could say she has no taste at all. And no pictures. No photos of family.'

'I was thinking much the same thing myself.'

'She's a dark horse all right.' Then, after a moment's thought, Prue stood up and made for the staircase. 'Let's snoop,' she said.

She was out of the room before Violet could stop her, marching up the stairs and peering first into one room and then another, and finally, arriving at the closed door of Dorothy's bedroom, at which she knocked, paused for a split second and entered.

It was not unlike Violet's bedroom in its starkness. It was dominated by the 'desk', which was piled high with papers and books. The window opened on to a miniature balcony that overlooked the street and onto which, Violet was to learn, Dorothy never ventured.

'Well, blow me down, it's more of an office than a bedroom,' Prudence pronounced.

'Do you think you should be doing this?' Violet hesitated in the doorway.

'Obviously not. But I've been wanting to do it for a while.' Prue wandered around the room, taking everything in, peeking into drawers and cupboards, until finally: 'Aha!' she said.

'What?'

From a drawer in a bedside table Prudence pulled out a

framed photograph. It was of a man of about fifty. He was a gentleman of some substance, with an ostentatious moustache. He stood ramrod straight in his three-piece suit, hat in hand, gazing superciliously at the camera.

Violet peered over Prudence's shoulder. 'Her father?' she ventured.

'Maybe. But why would you keep a photograph of your father in a drawer?'

'Why would you keep any photograph in a drawer?'

'Because,' said Prue, placing her finger on her lip Sherlock Holmes-style, 'you don't want to be reminded of him. Yet you cannot bring yourself to throw him away.' She replaced the photograph and closed the drawer. 'I am counting on you, Vi, to uncover his identity.'

Violet laughed. 'Why should I be interested? I can't exactly ask her, "Who's the man in the photograph in the drawer in your room I didn't go into today?"'

Prue began rummaging in the wardrobe. 'Heavens to Betsy, her clothes – they're antiques! There can't be anything here that's less than twenty years old.'

'Are you surprised?'

'Not in the least. Well.' Prue closed the wardrobe door and stood with her hands on her hips. 'That looks to be it. No more photographs. No more clues.'

'Why are you so interested in Dorothy's private life?' Violet asked as they descended the stairs and returned to the front room.

'Because I am naturally nosy. And because despite what I said before, Dorothy intrigues me. If you look at her closely she's actually quite attractive, but she goes to enormous lengths to hide it. It's as if she's deliberately trying to repel people. She'd be – what – forty or so? She must have had a man in her life. Or a woman.' She sat herself back down on the sofa. 'So I'm relying on you to dig the dirt.'

'I'm not making any promises.'

'And the next thing,' said Prue, 'is to find you a new identity.'

'A new what? Whatever for?'

'You can't go about as the absconding wife of a senior civil servant. They'll soon track you down. He'll track you down for sure.'

'I don't think he cares one way or another.'

'Not about you maybe, but about his reputation. He's a cuckold. Not technically, if you see what I mean, unless there's something you haven't told me. He's lost his wife, and he's lost face. He may seek revenge.'

'Don't be ridiculous!'

'Nonetheless,' Prue spread her hands, 'a new identity will mark the beginning of your new life as a new woman. It will make you feel better, cut yourself off from the past completely. So, what do you think?'

There was a baffled pause.

'You can keep your Christian name,' Prue added.

'Thank you very much.'

'But you can choose your family name, and not many people get to do that.' Prue's logic was idiosyncratic. 'So, where to begin? A touch of aristocracy perhaps, but not double-barrelled. Maybe a hint of the foreign. Spanish. Japanese. No. Let's not get too complicated.'

'Humphreys.'

'Humphreys?'

'After the street we lived in.'

'Don't be absurd, woman, he'll guess that immediately.'

It took a while, as they went through the gamut of surnames, beginning with their friends and proceeding to politicians and other well-known distinguished people of the time – writers, journalists, scientists, academics. It was a ridiculous game, and Violet could not see the point of it but she enjoyed it all the same.

'It needs,' said Prue, 'to be quite a common name – not common as in *common* if you know what I mean. A not unusual name, so it's tricky to track you down.'

'Smith?'

'Not quite. But getting close.'

In the end Prue plumped for Graham.

'Graham?'

'It's neutral,' she said. 'It doesn't tie you to anything or anywhere in particular. It's a common enough name, so should someone want to investigate your past they would find too many Grahams to be able to pinpoint you. You are a widow,' she went on. 'Your husband died in a riding accident after two years of marriage and you have no children. He was – what was he, let's have a think – he was a banker, yes. No, that would mean you'd be well off. He was a writer. A failed writer, which is why no one has ever heard of him and he left you penniless.'

Violet continued to sit there while her friend prattled on, inventing her entire character and background down to the smallest detail of siblings and parents, even pets and grandparents. She wasn't really listening – Prue was quite happy to talk even when she knew no one was paying her any attention. It passed the time. And it was mildly amusing.

But most importantly, in a peculiar sort of a way, Prudence had a point. A certain degree of reinvention would not go amiss. If it helped Violet to cope with, or even look forward to the future as a new woman then it was no bad thing. It was, after all, the first day of the beginning of her new life. Her third life, you could say.

LIFE THREE

1896-1902

Mrs Violet Graham

10: Introducing Mrs Graham

And so Mrs Anthony Turnip became Mrs Violet Graham, and the freshly-minted Mrs G discovered there were many and huge adjustments to be made in her new life, the most immediately obvious of which was that she was free to do whatever she wanted whenever she wanted to do it.

That took some getting used to. If there is no one to wake you in the morning, why should you get up at any particular time? If there is no one to help you dress, or do your hair or other essential tasks, how are you supposed to cope? A person gets used to things. True, Violet had managed without a personal maid at the vicarage, although there had always been some help in the house. Here there was none at all. All the daily chores the admittedly spoilt Mrs Turnip had had done for her were now her own responsibility. It would not be too far-fetched to admit she missed her personal maid more than she missed her husband.

How much, thought Violet, is the general timetable and layout of a typical day dictated by the servants of the household? Could it not be said that what they made up for in time they also took back? Half an hour to dress a lady and do her hair, the next half hour spent passing on instructions to the housekeeper? Not to mention the fact that a lady with servants was always accountable. There were few minutes in the day when someone – her husband, her maid, the housekeeper, a friend – did not know where she was or what she was doing.

And now she could go wherever she fancied and no one would know. Or care.

Freedom. Time. She had both, as much as she wanted.

Then there were her new surroundings, which were not only a quarter the size of what she had been used to in recent years but were in no way to her taste. The bedroom most of all needed a woman's touch. A dressing table with a mirror was the first priority, followed by a rug so that Mrs Graham's delicate feet had something soft to place themselves upon of a cold morning.

Next, and above all, there was her landlady, whose habits were both eccentric and unpredictable. One day Dorothy would be so verbose Violet could hardly get a word in edgeways, the next she would clam up like a bolted door. She had a strange, hooting laugh, which would burst forth at unexpected times – at dinner, for instance, at something she happened to see in the newspaper. Such a person is not easy to live with, especially when they are one's hostess and one is staying in her house gratis.

In order to familiarise herself with the day-to-day business of shopping and cooking Violet acquired a copy of the housewife's bible, *Mrs Beeton's Book of Household Management*, which she studied, over time, from cover to cover. It was the most terrifying book she had ever read. It set out, in detail, precisely what was expected of a lady of standing and how she should run her house and her servants; how, when and in what circumstances she might pay a social visit on a friend or acquaintance, and – most important of all – when she should remove her hat. There were rules for entertaining guests and how to manage the dreaded "great ordeal" of *the half-hour before dinner*, during which the hostess should on no account show the slightest sign of agitation but make "light and cheerful conversation" with her guests; and so on.

It shocked Violet to realise what responsibilities she had unwittingly once had as the lady of the house, mistress of her domain, whose behaviour set the standards for the rest of the household. The lady of the house rose early, so did the servants. The lady was solemn, the servants likewise. She was gay, the servants felt it permissible to smile. All this, and she had had no idea.

She had lived within a prescribed framework, without being fully aware of it. All that was now gone. Mrs Graham had no responsibilities. She could spend the day exactly as she pleased, within reason. She had that frightening thing: total freedom.

And there was the cooking. Violet quickly acquainted herself with the local grocery shops, and she had no qualms at all about asking the butcher for advice on the various cuts of meat and how to cook them. Here, again, Mrs Beeton was helpful, if not crucial. Her standards were way beyond anything a relative newcomer such as Mrs Graham might achieve. She had been known to have fiddled around in the kitchen of the Frogg family home occasionally, but that was a long time ago and they were only her parents and didn't really count. Whatever she produced – and it was by her own admission distinctly hit-and-miss – it seemed good enough for Dorothy, who didn't appear to mind, or to particularly notice what she ate.

Meanwhile Violet scoured the newspapers for teaching work and found herself a few hours here and there tutoring local children. It was not a job she enjoyed, and the hours were irregular, but it earned her enough to pay for most of the food and regain some of her self-respect.

Word soon spread at suffragist meetings, of course,

that Violet Turnip had left her husband. Most of the ladies were too polite to comment, though she did catch the odd glance of curiosity in her direction when they thought she wasn't looking. One or two approached Violet directly, thumped her on the arm and congratulated her. Some took hold of her hand and stroked it, as if she were a pet that had just lost its mother. Lady Dalloway looked down at her from her great height and said, 'Well I must say, I am surprised,' and that was it.

Prudence, meanwhile, was nowhere to be seen. She had, predictably, gone 'a step too far', as the suffragist ladies delicately put it. One afternoon as they were peacefully lobbying outside Parliament, without warning she had thrust her way through the phalanx of policemen, broken into the House of Lords, clambered onto a chair and shouted, 'Votes for women!' before being immediately manhandled away from the scene by the very same policemen she had just shoved aside. To her and everyone else's astonishment Prue was not thrown into prison, as she had intended, but made to languish for several hours in a police station before being escorted home and placed under house arrest (as she had put it) for a fortnight and forbidden to leave it under any circumstances.

'Good for you,' Violet said quietly to herself.

~

It came as a bit of a surprise to Violet to discover that her landlady liked to drink. For the most part she liked it in moderation, as in a glass of wine, or maybe two, with dinner. But on occasion, when she had had a particularly good day, she liked it rather more than that, and two or even three glasses of wine were followed after dinner by a tot of brandy, or grenadine. It was at times like these when Dorothy was at her most garrulous.

Her conversation focused invariably on the politics of the day and her opinions of politicians past, present and future. Violet listened dutifully, if not with total attention, occasionally chipping in with a 'Good gracious!' or 'Well, fancy that!' It was no surprise to hear Dorothy had no time for the Tories and considered the Liberals a weedy lot, lacking backbone, imagination and foresight – all the qualities, she declared, that come naturally to a woman.

'Would you want to be a member of parliament yourself?' Violet asked.

'No,' said Dorothy immediately. 'I don't have the personality.'

'I thought you despised personality.'

'I never said I despised personality. Did I? If I did, I meant I distrusted it in a personal sense. In a professional sense it's another thing altogether.'

'Then who, of all the lady suffragists, do you imagine might make a politician?'

Dorothy placed her knife and fork on her plate and sat back in her chair.

'What's needed,' she pronounced, 'is a woman of high intelligence, naturally, that goes without saying, and knowledge, ditto, but above all of dedication and total commitment. It would not suit a married woman.'

'Oh?'

'Married women have too many household duties. Or they think they have. Or more to the point, their *husbands* tell them they have. Especially if they have children,'

'That cuts out a lot of women.'

'Maybe. But there are plenty left. Barbara Wolsey might do, she's a bright soul, but a boring speaker. How she can drone on. Lady Dalloway would certainly command attention but she's too much of a traditionalist, and she is far too used to ruling the roost.'

'Is that a bad thing?'

Dorothy leaned forward and, setting her elbows on the table – something Violet's parents would never have allowed her to do – she proceeded to work her way through the suffragists, assessing each of them in forensic detail and in her unique, opinionated fashion.

And as she spoke it occurred to Violet that you can tell a lot about a person by the way they talk about other people; and that, interestingly, the women Dorothy most disparaged were women who were not unlike herself. Lady Dalloway was a case in point. From which one might well conclude that Dorothy did not have such a high opinion of herself and was a good deal less self-assured than she appeared.

'Did you ever think of getting married yourself?' Violet asked, as casually as she dared.

Dorothy did not answer for a moment. Then: 'Why do you ask?'

'I'm just curious. No reason really.'

It put a halt to the conversation, as if Violet had poured cold water all over it. After several moments of complete silence Dorothy got up from her seat and with a muttered, 'I'll see you tomorrow,' she left the room.

~

The weeks went by and winter became spring, and Violet looked out from her tiny bedroom window at the trees in the expansive gardens of the neighbouring houses bursting into blossom. It lifted her spirits, and it reminded her it was time she thought seriously about her future.

The shortage of money was, despite her part-time tutoring, a big drawback. Occasionally the suffragists helped out with those they thought were 'down on their uppers'. It purported to be payment for the women who worked especially long hours compiling and distributing leaflets. It helped, but it was nothing more than pin money. Besides, life in Dorothy's dollhouse was beginning to wear Violet down.

She thought about becoming a full-time teacher, or

even a live-in governess, though the thought dismayed her. That left clerical work, for which she was not trained, or lady's companion, which dismayed her even more. Of Lolly Mulligan, and her hint of a promise of a job, there was no sign.

She was not a lot she could do.

She heard nothing from Anthony, nor from their mutual friends, which included Veronica Ann and husband Cecil. Violet was a social pariah. She had broken the rules and betrayed the entire social structure of Victorian society as laid down by Mrs Beeton herself. She had absolutely no doubt that in her old circles her name was never mentioned, that as far as they were concerned she'd been wiped off the face of the earth.

11: Dorothy's secret

The evening began so well.

Dorothy had arrived home in a state of high excitement. It appeared her beloved museum was to be officially opened the following year by none other than Queen Victoria herself, at which point its name would be changed from the South Kensington Museum to the Victoria and Albert.

She celebrated by breaking the habit of a lifetime and taking a glass of sherry before dinner. Throughout dinner itself she talked non-stop about her museum, pausing now and again to take a drink, or indeed a gulp, of her wine; of its expansion, its commendation from none other than the Queen herself ('the old battleaxe', Dorothy couldn't help herself adding), how from its humble beginnings it was set to become the most important institution of its kind in Britain. In the world even. Open to everyone. A haven for artefacts from around the world, available for everyone to view, and totally free. And how she, Dorothy Moss, was one of a select few whose task it was to make arrangements for the royal opening, to decide which exhibits to put on display, and so on and so on. You'd think from the way she chattered on that she'd been single-handedly responsible for the museum's existence.

When dinner was over and the wine decanter was empty – a solo achievement on Dorothy's behalf – she rose unsteadily to her feet, and in the course of attempting to seat herself in an armchair she missed it completely and ended up flat on her back on the floor, hooting with laughter.

Violet was first alarmed, then surprised, and then relieved that such an indignity had failed to dampen Dorothy's spirits. She'd never seen her in such a childlike mood. She helped her to her feet and guided her into her chair, with care and some difficulty, and by the time Dorothy's backside was properly deposited in its intended destination both ladies were crying with laughter.

As Dorothy removed her glasses and wiped them on her skirt Violet was reminded of something Prue had once said about her.

'Do you know Dorothy, you have the most beautiful eyes,' said Violet.

They were a vivid blue, not huge like Lolly Mulligan's, but soft, and supremely feminine. Her entire face, without the thick-lensed, heavy-framed glasses, was transformed. She looked twenty years younger.

Dorothy burst into laughter all over again. She replaced her glasses and sat there, her shoulders still heaving, staring into her lap.

Violet had a sudden thought: 'Would you let me do your hair?'

'What?' Dorothy looked up. Her eyes were still watering. She blinked and pushed her spectacles further up her nose.

'Please. Just once. For fun.'

'My hair?' She laughed, and pulled at it. 'Not much to be done with it, I'm afraid.'

'But let me try, would you?'

Dorothy giggled. 'If you like.'

So upstairs they went, Dorothy first, unsteadily, hanging onto the banisters for dear life, Violet following and giving her a nudge when she faltered.

She sat Dorothy down at her dressing table and began to dismantle her bun.

Dorothy's hair was long and mousy with a touch of grey, and she wore it in a tight bun that gradually unravelled as the day went on. When a wisp of hair parted company from the rest she would shove it out of the way and roughly pin it, so by the end of the day there were almost as many pins as there was hair.

It reached halfway down her back, and it was surprisingly thick and unsurprisingly tangled. So Violet wielded her hairbrush and as gently as she could, she drew it slowly yet firmly through the length of Dorothy's hair, pausing to unpick the tangles as she went. After several minutes of this the tangles were gone. Dorothy sat there perfectly still, glasses off, eyes closed.

'Can't remember the last time anyone brushed my hair,' she said sleepily.

'It's soothing, isn't it?' said Violet. 'I used to love it when Amy brushed my hair. I could sit there for hours.'

'Who's Amy?'

'My maid.'

'Never had a personal maid,' said Dorothy. 'Wouldn't know what to do with one if I did.'

She then related, unprompted, as Violet continued to brush in long, firm sweeps, how she was brought up in Stow on the Wold, one of four children, two boys, two girls, and she the youngest. Her father worked in the rubber trade so he was rarely around.

'And how did you end up in London?' Violet asked. She looked at Dorothy in the mirror, exactly as Amy had looked at her all those times, considering how best the lady of the house might wish to wear her hair today.

'I went to a further education college for ladies,' said Dorothy. 'Studied history.'

'And did you get a degree?'

'No. I had to leave before the course ended.'

'Oh, why was that?' Violet put the hairbrush down, and reaching into a drawer she took out a small tin of pomade, dipped her fingertip into it and rubbed it between her palms before applying it to Dorothy's hair in long, even strokes. That done, she took hold of her hair in both hands and held it about her face, framing it. Then, deciding her client could do with a softer look she took from another drawer a *frizette*, which she deftly – she had learned this from Amy – placed behind the hair at the front, above the forehead, folding the hair over it so as to form gentle waves.

She moved it this way and that to achieve the right effect, and it was not until she was satisfied, and reached for pins to hold it in place, that she realised Dorothy had not answered her question.

'Dorothy?'

'Uh? Oh, yes. It's a long story.'

And then, without further prompting, she told it.

As a child she was a sprightly little thing with boundless energy, and everyone adored her. She was the particular favourite of a friend of her father's, a few years younger than him but still old enough to be her father. His name was George.

She paused, and then went on. Her eyes were still closed.

George and she would play together whenever he visited the house. He would tell her she was a soldier and his knee was her horse, and he would bounce her up and down on it until she giggled so hard she fell off. On one occasion she giggled so much she nearly disgraced herself.

As time went by she no longer sat on his lap, but they still liked to spend time together, chatting and laughing. He told her she was beautiful, and she blushed. Then it came time for her to leave school and she told her parents she wanted to join a ladies' further education college in Kensington to study history. Her parents demurred. They thought as all parents thought that she'd be better off learning how to cook and run a house and all the other trappings of Victorian womanhood. It was George who persuaded them to let her go. 'She has an exceptional brain,' he told them. 'It would be a shame to let it go to waste.'

She loved George for that. And then she realised she loved George not just for that. She loved him, full stop, even if he was almost her father's age. She wanted to marry him. But not yet. First, she had to get her degree.

A week or so before she was due to leave for London George invited her to his house one afternoon. It was the first time she'd been there on her own and she was nervous and not a little excited. Soon after she arrived he took her in his arms, as she had dreamt he would, and kissed her. And then he started to fondle her and before she knew what was happening they were in the bedroom, on the bed, and he was on top of her and . . . here Dorothy hesitated . . . making love to her. Really. Making love to her. And this continued throughout the afternoon and Dorothy felt waves of love and exhilaration she had never experienced in her life before.

It happened again, twice more, and each time was more thrilling than the last, and she felt her whole body bursting into life. And then, too soon, it was time for her to leave and go to London, and she clung to him and told him she loved him, and he swore he loved her too and it would not be too long before they saw one another again and, well, who knows?

A few weeks later she found out she was pregnant, so she wrote immediately to George to ask what she should do. She would like to have the child, which would mean they would have to get married, as soon as possible. He did not reply. He did not reply to her second letter either.

When she came home for the holidays she went immediately to see him. His face was stern and his manner distant. He told her he did not want her child and that they should cease seeing one another immediately. She cried, and pleaded, and made an all-round fool of herself, but he was adamant.

She went back to the college, with no idea what to do. A month later she miscarried, in the privy, on her own. She may have known little of the facts of life but there was no mistaking a miscarriage.

Word got out, in the college. She was called to see the headmistress and dismissed immediately. '"It's a shame," said the woman. "You showed much promise. But we have a reputation to maintain and we cannot permit anyone of loose morals . . ." And so on and so on and so on,' said Dorothy.

She continued to sit there, with her eyes closed, for several moments. 'So that's why I had to leave college early,' she concluded.

Then for the first time she opened her eyes and looked at herself in the mirror. Her long hair was now draped in lustrous folds around her face and in gentle coils around her forehead, pinned to perfection. A picture of elegance and grace.

'You are so beautiful,' said Violet.

Dorothy burst into tears.

~

And that was it. What's said cannot be unsaid. And while Violet felt at last she had broken through the carapace Dorothy had built around herself – and who would have thought such a person had experienced such passion, and sexual passion to boot? – Dorothy herself took a very different view. She had shown her weakness, she had revealed her darkest secrets, and now there was this Thing hanging between them.

It was never mentioned again, by either of them. But life was not the same. If ever Violet needed a reason to move on, Dorothy's confession provided it.

The question was – move on to where?

12: Violet's initiation

And then, just when Violet was beginning to give up hope, Lolly Mulligan popped up again.

'I warned you, you won't like it, but the job is there if you want it,' she said.

They were having coffee together in a tiny Italian place in Soho, one of Lolly's regular haunts apparently. She was dressed in a multi-coloured, multi-layered outfit that made her look like a gypsy, with – there was no mistaking it – a pair of loose trousers. *Trousers.*

Violet was distracted by them for a moment, before she said, 'Why are you so insistent I won't like it?'

'It's a rough old business, the theatre. Full of lowlifes.'

'What you do you mean?'

Lolly took a deep breath. 'Drunks, letches, all sorts. Desperate people. Violent even, some of them. Not all of them. But, well, not the sort of people you've been used to shall we say.'

'I'm sure it's nothing like as a bad as it sounds,' said Violet.

'It's a crazy world,' said Lolly, with some relish. 'And the crazy thing is it attracts the craziest people, people who are least able to cope with the craziness. The sort of people who end up wandering the pavement singing strange songs and talking to themselves.'

'You make it sound like an asylum.'

'That's exactly what it is!' Lolly bounced up and down in agreement. 'I promise you, you wouldn't like it.' She shook her head with some vehemence. 'Not a respectable woman like you.'

'Oh my,' said Violet. 'You make it sound like an accusation.'

'Well let's face it, you've led a pretty sheltered life, hain't yer?' She grinned.

'Have I? I suppose it depends who you're comparing me to.'

'Personally, I wouldn't give yer a week in the job. Two mebbe. Still, if you feel you're up to the challenge,' Lolly shook her teaspoon at Violet by way of emphasis, 'I'll have a word.'

'Thank you, Lolly, I'd appreciate that.'

Well, that puts me in my place, thought Violet. How revealing, to see yourself as others see you. She was bristling slightly. To be accused – as she saw it – of leading a sheltered life. And besides, the world of theatre could not be as Lolly described it. It made no sense that those dapper and elegant young things that adorned London's West End stage were all rogues and vagabonds behind the scenes.

Anyway, the gauntlet had been flung, and she was going to pick it up, come what may.

'How are you getting on with the old bag?' asked Lolly.

Violet was momentarily nonplussed. 'Dorothy? All right.'

'Find out anything about her?'

'In what sense?'

'In any sense.'

'No, not really.' Violet was a bad liar. She tried to shift the conversation back to where it began. 'So, this job, what happens next?'

'I bet she had a lover,' said Lolly. 'Who deserted her.

It's hard to imagine Dorothy with a lover. But it has to be. Unless she's a lesbian.' She cocked an eyebrow.

Violet chuckled. 'I've seen no sign of it.'

'She doesn't think much of me, she reckons I'm a silly little thing. Which is true, I am.'

'Not quite as silly as you make out, I believe.'

'Well, I am a silly little thing. I haven't got a proper brain, not one I can do anything with. I listen to things and then I can't remember a word of them afterwards. And I get bored easily. I join causes, like the suffragists, and then . . .' She shrugged.

'You live off your wits, that's not silly.'

'Do I? Yes, I suppose I do.'

'And you are very pretty.' It was true. It wasn't just her enormous eyes, and the languidly sensuous way she carried herself. There was a vitality about Lolly that Violet positively envied.

'Why, thank you kindly, ma'am,' said Lolly, in what Violet took to be a Southern drawl. 'And that's another thing about actors,' she went on. 'Whatever the conversation starts out as it always, *always*, ends up being about them. Us. We simply cannot resist talking about ourselves.'

'There are worse things.' Violet thought of Dorothy and her tight lips.

'Did you know Henry Irving got a knighthood?'

Once again Lolly's butterfly brain flummoxed Violet for a moment.

'Who?'

'Henry Irving. You must know who he is.'

'He's an actor, yes of course I know. A knighthood?'

'So you see,' said Lolly, 'we are becoming respectable at long last.' She grimaced. 'I may have to look for another profession.'

~

A week later Violet presented herself, with some trepidation, outside the door of an office in Panton Street belonging to a Mr Frank Sharp, amanuensis, or right-hand man, to none other than Mr Herbert Beerbohm Tree, London's leading actor-manager.

She'd been there a few minutes when the door to the office flew open and out burst a young woman of around twenty, a pretty little thing with a mass of golden curls. She stopped dead when she saw Violet, then burst into tears and ran off down the corridor.

It was not a good start. If that's how potential employees of Mr Frank Sharp ended up after an interview it did not bode well.

Still, she was there, so she gave it a minute and then she tapped on the door, and on the word 'Come!' she entered the room.

A middle-aged man with unruly, greying hair was seated behind a desk, his head in his hands.

'Mr Sharp?'

The man looked up and motioned her to a chair.

'I have been' he began, with some deliberation, 'in this business for getting on for twenty years now. And I still have not the first idea what goes on inside the head of an actor. This woman,' he gestured towards the door, 'she comes to me a week ago, goes on at me for a whole hour with a list of grievances. She is being bullied. She is being told off for being late for rehearsals, *consistently* late for rehearsals. She says her fellow actors mock her behind her back and call her names. That they tell her she cannot act to save her life. That they are making her life a total misery. That she is given only small roles to play. I say, "Very well, leave it with me, I'll see what I can do". I go to the Chief, I explain the problem to him, briefly. He says, "Go ahead Frank, deal with it as you see fit". So I terminate her contract, with the correct amount of notice and pay, and I find a replacement. And then . . .' He tilted his chair back and addressed the ceiling. 'She comes to me in hysterics, and yells, "What did you do that for? I didn't ask you to sack me!"'

He brought his chair forward again so it landed with a thump. And for the first time he looked at Violet directly.

'What am I supposed to do? Eh?'

'Well, I . . .'

'She tells me she hates working here, that her whole life is wretched, and then she goes and gets hysterics when I try to help her.' He threw his hands into the air.

'Perhaps she was just looking for sympathy,' Violet ventured.

'Sympathy? What's the good of sympathy? She had a problem, I solved it for her. What else am I supposed to do?'

'There is a difference between someone who is unhappy and wants someone to complain to, and a person who wants to end a contract.'

'What difference? Does she think it'd make any difference if I went down there and wagged my finger at her fellow actors and said, "Look here, chaps, you're making this girl's life a misery, stop it at once?"'

He stood up, shoved his hands in his pockets and began pacing the room.

'Perhaps she didn't want you to do anything in particular,' said Violet. 'She just needed to get things off her chest.'

'What?' He stopped in his tracks to stare at Violet.

'Men and women have different ways of dealing with things,' Violet found herself saying. 'The man wants to solve the problem. The woman just wants a shoulder to cry on.'

'A shoulder!' He sat down and drew a deep breath. 'Well, I tell you something, Miss . . .'

'Tur – er, Graham. Mrs.'

'Mrs Graham. You seem to understand actors a lot better than I do.'

'Not just actors. Women in general. But actors, yes, they're probably more vulnerable, and volatile, than most.'

Violet had no idea where all this worldly wisdom was coming from, but it seemed to calm him down. 'I've come about the position,' she said. 'Lolly Mulligan sent me.'

'Frank Sharp,' said the man, and smiled wearily. He placed his forearms on the desk and appraised Violet properly for the first time. 'You want to work here. For me.'

'Yes, I do.'

'Why on earth would an intelligent woman like you want to work in a place like this?'

Violet laughed. 'That's what Lolly said.'

'My job,' said Sharp, 'is as right-hand man to the great Chief himself, Mr Herbert Beerbohm Tree. He is a great man, a delightful man in his own way, but he has no interest in *detail*.' He ran a hand through his hair. 'Mr Tree is a self-confessed genius, and geniuses, I can only imagine, not being one myself, are too far above the rest of us to be concerned with *detail*. They have visions, so they say. It is their purpose, their talent, to have *visions* and to get other people to realise them. And the greater the genius, the greater the vision. Imagine the Emperor of China casually announcing to his underlings, out of the blue one day, "I fancy a Great Wall, stretching right across the country, to keep out the undesirables. Go ahead, build it for me, there's a good underling."'

There was a short pause. Sharp brooded.

'The Chief is one of a species called the "actor-manager,"' he went on, with a stress on the 'tor'. 'The ac*tor*-manager is what you might call a contradiction in terms. The ac*tor* lives in a make-believe world of fairies and goblins and all manner of nonsense, which renders him childish and unstable. The manager relies on business acumen, which requires a steady mind and no imagination at all. The two don't mix.'

Violet smiled.

'In the Chief's case, I couldn't comment on his acting but as a manager he is . . .' he made a gesture of hopelessness.

'Might I ask,' Violet began tentatively, after a moment's hiatus, 'what pleasure you get from your work? If any?'

Sharp turned to look at her sharply, as it were. 'I know what you're getting at. You're saying I'm like the little blonde thing, all curls and complaints. And you'd be right.' He laughed ruefully. 'Funnily enough, that's not a question anyone has asked me before. Not least myself.' He shook his head and pushed his chair back. 'So, down to business. I am the one who does all the unpleasant stuff the Chief doesn't want to soil his hands with. And I'm looking for someone who does all the unpleasant stuff *I* don't want to soil my hands with. Such as dealing with temperamental actors. A dogsbody, in other words. It's not a job for the squeamish, or the fragile. The hours will be long and unpredictable, the pay will be respectable, demands and expectations will be off the scale. If that's the sort of position you think you want to take on, it's yours.'

And that is how Violet Frogg Turnip Graham came to find herself plunged into the murky world of the West End theatre.

13: The working woman

Violet was given a small room a few doors away from her new boss in their offices in Panton Street, around the corner from the Haymarket Theatre. The room had been used as a store-room, so she spent her first morning trying to clear enough space for a desk. She arrived back from her lunch break to find a large and fearsome-looking object staring at her defiantly from her otherwise empty desk, which she recognised, with a mixture of terror and fascination, as a typewriter.

Violet had never encountered a typewriter before, though she'd heard them talked of. For several minutes she sat gazing at it in wonder and trepidation. It offered up no clues as to its origins, or to its method of use. She found a sheaf of paper among a pile in a corner, extracted one sheet from it, and after some toing and froing she managed to insert it successfully into the machine – as she must have once seen demonstrated, though she had no recollection of it. Then, with the aid of the knob at the side of the machine she succeeded in rolling the paper clockwise so that it protruded in what looked like the right place, and began to type.

At first all that happened was the keys, on which she was tapping gently, congregated together halfway up, stuck to one another in an unseemly huddle, and she had to delicately unpick them until they fell back with a clunk onto their resting place. They required, she realised, considerably more force than she was giving them. The next time she fairly hammered on them, and they flew up to strike the paper so hard they practically penetrated right through it.

It was like learning to play a wind instrument. Too hard and the sound distorts. Too soft and nothing much happens.

So Violet spent her first afternoon playing with her new toy. Still on occasion the keys stuck halfway up. Many times her finger missed the keys altogether and found itself wedged between them, which caused not inconsiderable pain. She learned how to use the carriage return handle so she could progress to the next line, though it frustrated her that her typing was not visible until she'd moved the paper up, and all of it was in lower case. Further examination and experimentation revealed the space bar, which produced spaces between the words, the shift key, which transformed her letters into capitals – hoorah! – and the tab key, which indented automatically for her. By the end of the afternoon Violet was tapping merrily away producing nonsense rhymes, with capital letters, spaces, punctuation and sentence breaks, and eventually numbers, thanks again to her old friend the shift key. Not all the letters were in the right places however, and there did not immediately seem to be a way of correcting them short of starting all over again with a fresh sheet of paper.

This merry diversion absorbed Violet so completely throughout the afternoon she forgot she was meant to be there for a reason. Of her boss, or of anyone else, there was no sign. Eventually, when it came close to 6 o'clock, she trotted along the corridor and knocked on his door.

Sharp looked up in some surprise, as if he had forgotten all about her, which no doubt he had.

'Oh hello, er, Mrs Graham. How are you getting on?'

'Very well,' said Violet. 'I have mastered the typewriter. Or rather, we have reached a mutually friendly agreement.'

'Good.'

'So. I await your instructions, Mr Sharp.'

'Frank,' he said. He took out his watch. 'I'll see you in the morning then, Mrs Graham. Or is it all right to call you Vivien?'

'Quite all right, Frank,' said Violet with the smallest flutter of her eyelashes. 'Though I prefer Violet.'

'Violet. Yes. Of course. Yes. Well then.' And he nodded at her by way of what she assumed was dismissal.

~

The honeymoon lasted one day.

The next day the visitors started arriving. A trickle, to begin with, that turned into a stream as the day progressed.

They were actors, for the most part, all with grievances, mostly to do with casting. *She* was not contracted to play maids, *he* refused to play a character with a regional accent. *He* had been given the wrong dressing-room, *she* refused to wear the 'hideous' gown that had been allotted her. Violet sat and listened patiently and then explained, very apologetically, that it was really 'not her department' and they should seek advice elsewhere. The actors responded with differing degrees of annoyance and resentment and departed considerably more aggrieved than when they had arrived.

After a few hours of this Frank appeared in her doorway.

'"Not your department",' he said.

'I beg your pardon?' said Violet.

'Maybe I did not make myself clear,' he said, with badly concealed irritation. 'Everything is your department.'

And he went.

Violet sat perfectly still for a long moment.

She wanted to go home. She also rather wanted to cry. Neither option being possible she stayed put and gritted her teeth.

Her next visitor was a strapping young woman, immensely tall and powerfully built. She loomed over the desk at Violet and explained, with some violence, that she'd been threatened with the sack for socking a fellow actress in the face for 'doing bits of business' during her best speech.

'I'm sorry,' said Violet. 'Can you explain "doing bits of business"?'

The woman heaved a sigh. 'Fiddling with props. Making faces. They weren't listening to a word I said. Don't you know what "business" is?'

'I see,' said Violet, though she didn't really. 'And what is it you want me to do about it?'

'Tell her,' said the unnamed woman (she had not yet introduced herself). 'Give her a piece of your mind. Tell her to act the professional for once.'

'You say you socked her in the face?'

'It was more of a slap.'

'Perhaps you could tell her yourself,' Violet ventured.

'You think I haven't already?' The woman drew herself up to her considerable, and intimidating, height.

'What did you say your name was?' Violet asked.

'Miss Meredith Martin.'

'And this – the other actress? The one you slapped?'

'Gigi Worth. Worthless, I call her.'

'Maybe you could send this Miss Gigi Worth to me.'

Miss Martin glared at Violet for a moment, then she turned and left.

It was not until the following afternoon that Miss

Worth arrived at Violet's room, her face heavy with resentment. She was a good deal shorter than her nemesis but every bit as antagonistic. Violet, so out of her depth she felt she was drowning, explained as calmly as she could that it was 'not professional' to distract attention away from a fellow actress while she was speaking, and that perhaps Miss Martin had had a genuine grievance. And while it was utterly reprehensible of her to resort to physical violence, perhaps in future the only solution would be not to "do the business" while Miss Martin was speaking, and then perhaps . . .

She was aware as she burbled on that the lopsided smile on the face of Miss Worth was becoming broader and broader as she listened, with barely-concealed contempt, to the idiotic utterings emitting from someone who, it was blatantly obvious, had no idea what she was talking about. When Violet was done Miss Worth just nodded slowly and left the room, still grinning crookedly, without a word.

'You'll have to do better than that,' Violet told herself.

It was a baptism by fire. It was all Violet could do to stop herself running from the room there and then.

But she had a job to do, and do it she would. She summoned the Misses Martin and Worth to her room together in order, she told them, to resolve this thing once and for all.

They sat down across the desk from her, one at each corner of it, like contenders at a tennis match with the desk the net and the two women lined up against her. Violet was aware of two pairs of eyes studying her with equal disdain.

'You ever worked in the theatre before, ducky?' drawled Miss Worth.

'No, as a matter of fact I haven't.' Violet tried not to bristle at the 'ducky'.

They two women sniggered and glanced at one another.

'Thought as much,' said Miss Worth. 'It's a rough old business, not everyone survives it.'

'You seem to have survived it,' said Violet.

'We're tough old boots,' said Miss Martin.

'Can come as a shock if yer ain't born to it,' said Miss Worth.

'Not a fit place for ladies,' said Miss Martin.

'Not that we was all born to it,' said Miss Worth.

'Did you ever visit the music hall, Mrs . . .?' asked Miss Martin.

'Graham. No, I don't believe I ever did.'

'"Ai don't believe Ai ever did",' said Miss Worth. 'Well, that's a shame, for sure.'

'Very interesting places, music halls,' said Miss Martin. 'But perhaps they're a little too . . .' She turned to Miss Worth.

'Vulgar,' said Miss Worth.

'I was going to say low . . .'

'Coarse.'

' . . . entertainment. It's where some of us cut our teeth,' said Miss Martin.

'Some of us.'

'Not all of us. Some of us are from better stock.'

'Her dad's a brigadier,' said Miss Worth, with a jerk of the head in Miss Martin's direction.

'And her father started out in the circus,' said Miss Martin, with a jerk of the head in Miss Worth's direction. 'Or so she likes to make out.'

'Circus, music hall. He done them all.'

'But you don't want to believe everything she says.'

'Cut me teeth on the trapeze, I did.'

It was like some bizarre double-act. Violet looked on in bafflement. She wondered if they'd rehearsed it – the cut-glass Miss Martin and the earthy Miss Worth, if that's what they really were.

After a few more moments of this she cleared her throat loudly and said: 'Forgive me interrupting your act, but we are here for a reason and we don't seem to be addressing it.'

The two ladies stopped dead and stared at her.

'What reason was that then?' asked Miss Worth.

Violet gave a sigh. 'Miss Martin, as you may remember, came to me complaining that you, Miss Worth was – what did you call it? – doing 'business' during one of her speeches.'

The two women continued to stare at her.

'Well? Was that the case or was it not?'

They looked at one another, and then back at Violet, in perfect synchronicity. Neither of them seemed inclined to respond.

She may have been outwitted, and made fun of, but the one thing Violet's instinct told her to do above all was to keep her cool.

'If that was not the case then I don't see any point in prolonging this.' She leaned back in her chair dismissively.

The two women continued to sit there for a moment, still staring at her, like children whose game has been interrupted.

And then, again in perfect synchronicity, they got to their feet and walked to the door, and together in the doorway they turned to look back at Violet, grinned, and exited.

Violet was impressed, despite herself. While it may not have been the result she was hoping for – and she half wondered whether the original complaint hadn't been a put-up job all along – she quickly realised there was no rule book, no one solution to fit all situations in a world she knew nothing about. If this had been a form of initiation then so be it.

Not all of her 'customers' – as that is how she was beginning to see them – were quite so demanding. Some of them just wanted to sound off. Others needed what Prue would have termed a kick up the backside.

Yet others simply needed reassurance.

There arrived at her door one day an actor whom Violet guessed to be in his mid-sixties, which made him one of the oldest members of the company. She recognised him vaguely as he wore makeup, offstage as well as on, and a black wig. He introduced himself as Mr Jeffrey Notting.

His problem, he explained politely, and with some circumlocution, was that he was being given parts to play that he felt he was quite unsuited for, and which had never been his intention to perform when he joined the company.

'What sort of parts?' Violet enquired.

Mr Notting mumbled a bit before 'Older men,' he said.

He rambled on some more, and Violet listened without speaking until he appeared to be finished, at which point she found herself saying what, presumably, no one else had had the courage to say.

She moved her chair so she was no longer separated from Mr Notting by her desk, and lowered her voice. She told him, as gently as she could, that as one of the more venerable members of the company he might regard it as a privilege to be offered the parts of older men. That while he did look remarkably well for his age, the wearing of makeup offstage was, she suggested, unnecessary. And not just unnecessary but, she dared to add, it risked making him look *older* than he was which, she felt sure, was not his intention. That should he grasp the nettle and forego both the makeup and the wig his fellow actors might regard him with renewed respect, as their senior and their better. That rather than trying to compete with his younger colleagues to play characters in their thirties and forties, as a man in, she surmised, his sixties (Mr Notting winced at that) he would have a monopoly on those wonderful character roles of elderly statesmen and grand old men; which, she felt sure, he would perform to the manner born.

There followed a long silence once Violet had finished speaking, during which she noticed, to her alarm, a tear descend the cheek of the gentle Mr Notting; something that, normally speaking, would have been largely invisible were it not for the fact that it was streaked in black greasepaint.

Then, very slowly, Mr Notting reached up and removed his wig and ran a hand gingerly over his thinning hair. After which, with a brief nod, he got up from his chair and left the room.

(The next time Violet came upon Mr Notting he was *sans* makeup and wig, and, as she had rightly imagined, looking not just younger than his sixty-odd years but several times more chipper. He greeted her with a shy smile.)

Then there was Reggie Billing, stage name 'Shuffles' – 'On account that's what I do, see, I do the soft shoe. Want to see?' And he would demonstrate, right there in the room in front of her, this elderly man so quick and light on his feet he quite took Violet's breath away. 'Want to try? Come on, give it a go, I'll show yer.' And so he did. And Violet found herself dancing the two-step with old man Shuffles as if they'd danced together all their lives.

Shuffles was a regular visitor. He'd knock and enter without so much as a by-your-leave, park his backside on a chair and off he'd go. Violet learnt his entire life history from the day he first appeared on stage as a 'nipper' – 'born into it, you see, born into panto at the Lane' – to his days on tour in the provinces, 'where the nearest you got to the manager was the sight of him scarpering down the stairs with the takings'. Weeks on the road, literally – 'train fare? No fear' – twenty-mile hikes followed by one-night stands. 'And if you was lucky you got paid a bit. If you was really lucky you got paid what they promised you.'

Oddly enough she never saw Shuffles anywhere else in the building, and when she enquired about him to other actors nobody seemed to know who he was; though one or two conjectured they'd seen him entertaining the queues outside the theatre before a show.

There were actors who didn't turn up to rehearsals, and so it was 'Send for Mrs Graham', and Violet was sent to comb the local hostelries. She was hesitant about this, they were not the sort of places a young woman would normally be seen in. It was only the thought of not being allowed back into the building without the absconder that gave her enough courage. Sure enough, she found him eventually, propping up the bar. 'Rehearsals?' he would scoff. 'I don't need rehearsals, I know my lines backwards.' Violet learned to simply stand there and wait until the guilty party found her presence so annoying he relented and followed her back to the theatre with the worst grace possible.

In time the successes began to outnumber the failures, and Violet even found herself the recipient of visits from actors with nothing to complain about. Most of them were young men who simply liked to pass the time in the company of a pretty young woman with dark hair and pale blue eyes. She received several proposals of marriage and one or two offers of a less respectable nature. She fielded them all with humour and grace. She also learned to toughen up. She even found herself at times resorting to mild sarcasm. If an actor came to her complaining the play he was in had no right to be seen on a stage, *any stage*, she told him that short of rewriting the thing herself there was little she could do to help him other than to suggest he use his own considerable skills in performance to make it look as if it was masterpiece; that if a girl didn't like what she was being made to wear she had to remember it was not she who was wearing it, it was her character. The next time she saw Miss Martin and Miss Worth she smiled at them and said, 'No fisticuffs lately, then?' and they gave her a watery smile back.

She saw very little of Mr Sharp – Frank. While he very rarely *thanked* her for anything, let alone congratulated her for making his life so much more manageable – to the extent that he was able to absent himself more and more frequently in order to indulge his passion for what stage management told her was 'the Turf' – he had the wit to leave her largely to her own devices. And that suited her perfectly.

14: Settling in

On quiet days Violet would wander across the road to the Haymarket Theatre and sneak into the darkened stalls to watch rehearsals. She was both enchanted and amused by the interminable arguments between the actors and what she took to be the writer, who may or may not have been nominally in charge but who spent most of the time being ordered to explain himself, or vainly trying to stop the actors 'improving' on the words he had, as he told them, sweated over for months, if not years. Here and there, on the rare occasion when the actors managed to perform an entire scene without interruption and with total concentration; when there were no petulant looks passing between them and no yelling or offstage hammering from an oblivious stage crew, there was magic. Undeniable magic, she could sense it. Without costumes or make-up, rehearsing for one play on the set of another, under the harsh house lights, Violet felt transported.

From time to time an actor, young or older and inevitably male, would sit himself down beside her and ask her what part she was playing; and when she laughed and said she was not an actress they would say, 'Stage management then?' When she shook her head at that they would look at her in confusion. 'I am the company lackey,' she would say, which usually shut them up. And it was true.

~

Frank showed his satisfaction at her work by passing on more and more tasks to his long-suffering assistant. Violet learned how to draw up a contract and compose a letter to a would-be patron. She even took over the business of paying the actors' salaries and calling them to rehearsals. After a couple of months or so she had learned a lot about the strange new world she found herself in, namely:

All actors are insecure and all too aware of their dispensability. Their over-inflated sense of their own importance is a mask behind which they hide their anxieties.

Heterosexual actors, particularly if they are passably handsome, think they have a God-given right to seduce every female they come across. If you are a passably pretty female and an actor does not try to seduce you, chances are he is not heterosexual.

Not all talented actors are watchable. Not all watchable actors are talented.

All writers have a persecution complex.

All actors think they are better writers than the writer.

Construction crews will always baulk at the demands made of them and protest they are impossible to achieve, and then go ahead and achieve them.

Stage managers are the most crucial and under-appreciated group in a theatre company and nobody takes the slightest notice of them until they make a mistake.

Ways to annoy your fellow actors: i) Upstaging; ii) Altering your lines just enough to throw them; iii) Entering or exiting from an unexpected part of the stage; iv) Jumping on a fellow actor's laughs; v) Introducing bits of physical business when another actor is speaking (*vide* Misses Martin and Worth).

The combination of all these feelings of insecurity, bad temper, superiority, inferiority and envy is what creates a great theatre company.

Theatre is not like any other business in the world. The only people who understand it are the audience.

Some of these observations Violet gleaned from experience, and some from Archie, the stage carpenter. Archie was one of the few members of the stage crew who never complained. He was smiley and happily married and just got on with his job quietly and so efficiently that he was able, in his spare time, of which he had plenty, to create little wooden models of famous London landmarks, which he sold in swanky souvenir shops in Piccadilly for what he called a tidy sum. On first nights he would present the actors with miniatures of themselves, in costume, again carved from wood. Violet would visit Archie in his workshop now and again and sit and watch as he whittled and carved and sanded and polished, and she listened as he expounded on his experiences of working in the theatre in general and the Chief in particular.

'He has a wife,' said Archie, 'and she likes to think of herself as an actress.' He paused to study the model figure he was working on – which was, Violet noted, an elegantly dressed woman. 'Which causes no end of strife between her and the Chief. And I'm not saying' he placed the model down on his work bench and stared at it,'she's no good. She's just . . .'

'Just what?'

'She's a bit too much of a lady, if you see what I mean.'

'Too much of a lady for what?' Violet asked.

Archie turned to look at her and scratched his head. 'I'm no critic but it strikes me, if you're going to be a *proper* actress – letting your emotions show and all that – you've got to be able to let your hair down. So to speak. Be a bit less of a lady.'

'Yes, yes I see.'

'At the same time, she has a lot to put up with, being married to the Chief.'

'In what way?'

'Well, he's not here at the moment, he's in America. And she's just had a baby.'

'So?'

'So. You haven't met him yet then?'

Violet shook her head.

'When you do, you watch yourself.'

'Meaning?'

'Meaning watch yourself.' He winked at her and picked up his model of what Violet took to be none other than Mrs Tree herself, and began polishing her tenderly.

It certainly was not like any other business in the world. After just a few months Violet was beginning to feel settled in her job. She found herself for the first time looking forward to going to work.

It was time she found somewhere else to live.

15: Moving on

Breaking the news to Dorothy that she was moving out was easier than Violet expected. She even thought she detected a look of relief on her face.

The atmosphere between the two women had been cool to the point of downright frosty ever since Dorothy's 'confession'. Though the subject of her past was never referred to again, by either side, it was there in the room with them all the time. It followed them about. It hung from the ceiling looking down at them, monitoring their every word and gesture. And while Violet in a wild attempt at over-compensation became ever brighter, and friendlier, so Dorothy retreated further and further into her shell. It was like living with a ghost of a person, who moved about, and occasionally spoke, but who cast a dark, cold shadow wherever she went.

At least it smoothed the parting of the ways. Dorothy made all the right noises – 'If it doesn't work out for any reason, I'm still here' – but she spoke the words with no attempt at sincerity. She smiled wanly and did her best not to flinch as Violet kissed her on the cheek. And that was that.

It was Archie who had told Violet about the set of rooms near Camden Town. They comprised the first floor of a three-storey house in a quiet street off Hampstead Road. What had once been a single dwelling for a well-to-do family had been converted into flats for working people. It was not the most salubrious part of town maybe, but the rooms were of a good size, and clean, if a touch shabby, the landlady seemed kind, and the rent was reasonable. The bedroom was twice the size of Violet's cubby-hole in South Kensington, and there was a sitting room attached. Most surprisingly there was also a kitchen, if you could describe it as such, set into an alcove at one end of the sitting room and containing a small sink and the tiniest gas stove Violet had ever seen. Which meant, to her relief, that she could 'do' for herself.

The first thing Violet did on unpacking was to give Archie's beautifully-carved likeness of herself pride of place on the mantelpiece. Once the bulk of the unpacking was done she sat down on the least worn of the two armchairs and contemplated her new life.

It was just over a year since she had left her husband and the elegant four-storey house in Bloomsbury. And now here she was, in a set of rooms in Crighton Street in far-from-fashionable Camden Town, a hop and a skip from Bloomsbury as the crow flies, yet a million miles away in society's terms. In society's terms she had slipped several rungs down the ladder, from respectable upper-middle-class wife to working woman. In theatrical parlance she had moved from the stalls to the pit. In the last decade of the nineteenth century this was not something many young women were likely, or willing, to do.

Violet did not miss her past life. Looking back, she wondered now how she could have borne it for so long. Privileged it may have been, to be living in a large house in a fashionable area of London, with servants at your bidding, the best tables in the smartest restaurants, the most expensive seats for the most popular West End plays at your disposal. But then there was the sword of

Damocles that hung over the head of a society lady waiting to descend upon her at the first sign of a *faux pas*, such as the removal of a hat at the wrong time; or her admission that her favourite leisure activity was reading up on classical history or studying the plays of Shakespeare and Marlowe.

Worst of all of the rules laid down by the likes of Mrs Beeton and others was the insistence on maintaining a façade. So no matter how wretched your life might be – your husband was unfaithful or your mother had just died or your child was dangerously ill – woe betide the lady or gentleman who showed the smallest hint of it to the outside world.

That was privilege?

And now here were these actors, who wore their hearts on their sleeves and thought nothing of pouring out their most intimate secrets to a total stranger. Whose lives were built on emotion, the rawer the better. Yes, they bickered and fought, like children. They were not afraid to show wonder or excitement, or loss and tragedy and grief, immediately and unreservedly, like children. True, they could drive a person mad with their self-centred, melodramatic reaction to the most trivial happening. But what a joy it was to be among them.

Violet could do anything she wanted, with whomever, in whatever way she chose. Now there was no longer anyone standing at her shoulder telling her which picture she should admire, or which building was considered aesthetically acceptable, by way of example, she looked forward to discovering who she really was.

She felt terrifyingly modern.

It was not just Violet's world that was shifting, it was the world around her; one could sense it distinctly. The stern old Queen would soon be replaced by her handsome and colourful son. So the suffragists may not have achieved their aims, not yet – no thanks to opposition from the Queen herself – but there was no doubt it would happen sooner or later. Women, Violet surmised, were so much more adaptable than men. The whole notion of change was disturbing to a man – and why wouldn't it be? He'd had it his own way for so long, why would he want to alter anything? Yet it was only a matter of time before women were not only given the vote, but were able to stand for Parliament, and even – who knows, one day – to become Prime Minister?

The country was in a state of flux, and it was utterly thrilling.

She was passing through the Haymarket Theatre one morning when she came upon a group of people backstage huddled around a tall, elegant woman. The object of attention appeared to be not so much the woman herself but something she was holding, which turned out to be a very small baby which she was passing from one person to another. Before she had time to step out of the way Violet found herself in possession of the tiniest human being she had ever seen. As she looked down at the miniature object it stretched, yawned, opened its eyes and, she swore, smiled right at her. It was as if a tiny dart had penetrated the deepest recesses of her heart.

'She likes you,' said Mrs Tree, smiling, as she retrieved the baby.

That was her introduction to the famous, or infamous, stylish, elegant, emotionally-limited Mrs Tree.

Would a child have made a difference to her own marriage? Well yes, of course, all the difference in the world. But it didn't happen. And if it had, and she had continued to be unhappy, how could she leave a marriage knowing the father still had sole rights to the child?

Then there was her assumed name, and what it signified. A reinvention, or a lie? Or both? A running away from or a running to?

She did not feel entirely happy about the deceit. Yet at the same time it gave her permission, as it were, to be born again, to free herself from her past. She had gone from dowdy Miss Violet Frogg to socialite Mrs Anthony Turnip to independent, hard-working Mrs Violet Graham, all in the space of twenty-four years. Who knows what other lives and identities lay ahead? She could try them out for size and see which one fitted best.

16: The majestical Tree

Violet was witnessing aspects of London she'd never experienced before. The street traders: the baked-potato seller, the coal carrier, the tin-smith, young boys and girls (too young) selling matches on street corners. The perpetual cacophony of itinerant bands and hurdy-gurdies. Packed pavements, busy roads, two-storey horse 'buses overflowing with passengers and young lads weaving suicidally through the horses' hooves. Barely controlled chaos.

Of course they had always been there but she had simply never looked at them. If you are the kind of person whose carriage picks you up at the doorstep of your smart house in Bloomsbury and deposits you on the doorstep of the theatre/restaurant/shop/friend's house, how could you possibly know what really goes on in an ordinary street in London? More to the point, why would you want to?

But now Violet was having to hustle her way through those crowded pavements in all sorts of weathers to clamber onto one of those two-storey omnibuses, to sit elbow to elbow and thigh to thigh with shop girls and bank clerks, and a total stranger would think nothing of starting up a conversation with you. It took some getting used to, and if you didn't mind the stench – of sweat or beer or a particularly potent brand of tobacco – and the way everyone was crammed in together, it was quite enjoyable in a colourful kind of a way.

As she was arriving at Panton Street one morning she saw a brougham pull up at the stage door of the Haymarket Theatre and out of it stepped Lolly Mulligan. Violet was about to call out to her but she hurried too quickly into the building. Fancy that, thought Violet. She must be cavorting with the nobs. Good for her.

It was on the same day that as she was working at her desk there came a knock on the door and a tall man with ginger hair and no eyebrows peered in, looked around, said, 'Um,' and disappeared again. Three seconds later, in a perfect illustration of the double-take, the door opened again and the man stepped into the room and approached Violet's desk with his hand outstretched.

'I don't believe we've met,' he said. 'My name is Herbert. Herbert Tree – no, please don't get up.'

Violet resumed her seat and shook the proffered hand. 'Violet Graham.'

'How do you do Miss – Mrs? – Graham.'

'Mrs. How do you do, Mr Tree.'

'And you are . . . ?' Tree twirled a hand in the air.

'I am Mr Sharp's assistant.'

'Are you now? So, Frank has got himself an assistant? Excellent idea. I am out of touch. I've been in America, you see.'

'Yes, I know.'

'So.' Tree put his hands in his pockets and rocked back and forwards on his heels for a moment. He smiled at Violet. 'How is it, working for the old curmudgeon?'

'Who, Fr – Mr Sharp? I'm getting along all right, I think.'

'He's passing on all the nasty little jobs he doesn't want to deal with, I've no doubt.'

'That's precisely it.' Violet smiled.

'Which I have in turn handed down to him.'

'I believe so.'

'Not a job for the faint-hearted.'

Violet laughed.

'He's a strange soul, old Frank. Been with us for years. He loves his horses, did you know that?'

'I did, yes.'

'He loves his horses more than anything else in the world, I believe. He certainly loves them more than he loves actors. Has he told you how much he dislikes actors?'

'He made that very clear right from the start,' said Violet.

'Yes. You want to ask what he's doing working here, don't you?'

'You wonder how he ended up working in a theatre ...'

They spoke together, and then they laughed together.

'Did you work in the theatre before this, Mrs Graham?' Tree asked.

'No, never. I was just a patron, on the other side of the curtain.'

Tree's pale eyebrows twitched. 'How are you finding it?'

'Different. Unpredictable. Sometimes frantic. Never two days the same.'

'Hmm,' said Tree. Then, with a nod towards the typewriter, 'You've got one of those things, I see. I could never get on with them. Machines and I don't seem to live happily together. I kept getting my fingers stuck between the keys.'

'So did I. You have to use just the right amount of force. It took me a while but I think I've just about mastered him now.' Violet gave the machine a patronising pat.

'You've beaten him into submission, bravo!' Tree swivelled on his heels and surveyed the room. 'So . . .'

'Were you looking for someone, sir?'

'Herbert, please. Yes, I believe I was. Though I'm damned if I can remember who. Excuse my language, Mrs Graham.'

'Violet, please.'

'Oh, may I?' He smiled warmly at her, then he removed his hands from his pockets and said, 'Anyway, I suppose I ought to get on with whatever it was I was getting on with.' He turned to go, and in the doorway he stopped and said, 'Perhaps we might have lunch one day?'

'Oh! Yes, that would be lovely.'

'I will see you soon, Violet. Good luck with the . . .' he gestured towards the typewriter.

'Thank you.' And he was gone.

Violet sat there for a moment with a smile on her face. She was remembering Archie's 'Watch yourself'.

Watch yourself indeed.

Not long after that Violet had another visitor. There was a knock on the door and she entered without waiting to be invited and plonked herself down on a chair. It was Lolly. She was wearing a calf-length peasant skirt, a blouse that looked as if it came straight from Bohemia, and an eyepatch.

'Hello Lolly,' said Violet. 'I haven't seen you for ages, what have you been doing?'

'This and that,' said Lolly.

Violet nodded at her eyepatch. 'Is that part of a costume, or did you walk into a door?'

'I tripped.'

'Really?' said Violet. 'I saw you this morning getting out of a brougham. I was about to call out to you but then I thought – Well, Lolly looks as if she's struck lucky. Hobnobbing with the nobs.'

Lolly didn't reply. She was sitting with her legs crossed, one leg swinging.

'What's up Lolly?' Violet asked.

'Not much,' Lolly shrugged.

'Then what are you doing here?'

The leg stopped swinging. 'I've been hearing things about you,' said Lolly.

'That sounds ominous. What sort of things?'

'You had a little to-and-fro with Merry and Gaye, so it's said.'

'And who would Merry and Gaye be?'

'Meredith Martin and Gigi Worth. One tall, one short.' She gesticulated accordingly.

'Oh, them. What have you heard?'

'If you can survive Merry and Gaye you can survive anything,' said Lolly gnomishly.

Then just as Violet was contemplating whether or not to pursue the subject – she was curious, but she suspected Lolly was little more than a tease – the girl herself suddenly sat up and said: 'You met the big Chief yet?'

'As it happens yes, just half an hour ago.'

'Did he flirt with you?'

'I wouldn't call it flirting.' Violet smiled, though she tried not to.

'Aaah,' said Lolly. 'He did flirt with you, of course he did. Did he ask you to lunch?'

'Well . . .'

'He *did* ask you to lunch. Oh Vi!' Lolly stood up and struck a pose. 'Like my skirt? It's from Hungary.'

'It's very exotic. It looks lovely on you.'

Lolly sat down again with a bump.

'So, what's happening in your life, Lolly?'

Lolly slouched in her chair, stretched out her legs in front of her and contemplated her feet, which were encased in what looked like a pair of clogs. 'Not very much at the moment actually. Life is quite humdrum. How are the suffragists?'

'I haven't seen them for a while,' said Violet. 'I do feel

bad about it but the work here is hard, and often goes on into the evening. All this' – she gestured, at the room, her desk – 'has rather taken over my life.'

'Lucky you.'

'Tell me,' said Violet, 'what parts have you played on stage, Lolly?'

Lolly took a deep breath, and then: 'Miranda in The Tempest, Viola in Twelfth Night, Ophelia in Hamlet, Beatrice in The Candle and the Flame, Miss Truss in The Spider's Web, Leola in The Castle of Santa Maria. Do you want me to go on?'

'But where?'

'All over. You only have to ask anyone.'

'But I'm asking you. How do you know Mr Tree, for instance?'

Lolly went back to studying her feet.

'It's a long story.'

'Tell me.'

'I don't really remember.'

Violet stared at Lolly for a long time. 'You don't remember,' she said.

'I'm glad you like the job,' said Lolly eventually. She leaned back in her chair. 'I didn't think you would. But it's done you a power of good, I can see.'

'You must come and visit me at my new place,' said Violet. 'With Prue perhaps.'

'With Prue perhaps? Why yes, that would be lovely, darling.'

'I will cook for you.'

'Cook?' Lolly's eyes widened. 'My, you are a clever one, ain't yer?'

Then quite suddenly Lolly got up and went, with a cheery, 'I'll be seeing you, Vi!'

And so the mystery of Lolly Mulligan remained.

~

She was on her way home that evening when she had a distinct feeling of being followed. At first it was just the sound of footsteps, behind her. She turned down a side street and the footsteps followed. She crossed the road and looked back as she did so, as if checking for traffic. She saw a middle-aged man with greying hair and a beard. She quickened her pace, and turned the corner. He was still there. She thought to duck into a doorway, or stop to remove something from her shoe to let him pass, but instead she decided to hurry on to the safety of her front door. As she paused at the bottom of the steps to look for her keys he came up right behind her, removed his hat and said, 'Excuse me'. Then, producing his own set of keys, he unlocked the front door and held it open for her to enter.

'Oh!' She did her best to hide her embarrassment. 'Thank you.'

'You live here too?' he said, as he closed the door behind them.

'Yes, as of a few weeks ago.'

'I am surprised we have not met before.' He gave a little bow. 'Welcome. My name is Mr Kapps, with a K. I own a drapery shop in Drury Lane.'

'How do you do, Mr Kapps. Violet Graham. Mrs,' she added, for good measure.

'I have been living here for six months, Mrs Graham.' He spoke with a slight accent – German perhaps? 'I am an escapee, from Vienna. Not' he added quickly, 'a real escapee. I am an intentional interloper, you could say.'

They were standing together in the hallway.

'Well,' said Violet after a moment.

'You might think me very forward,' said Mr Kapps, 'but it would be very delightful for me if we might take tea together some time, in my rooms. I do not have many friends here Mrs Graham, and I do like to polish my

English.'

'Well,' said Violet again.

'I am being too forward, please forgive me. I have to learn English backwardness, as well as the language. Good evening to you, Mrs Graham. No doubt we will crash into one another again, on the doorstep perhaps.'

'Bump.'

'I beg your pardon?'

'Bump into one another. That is the expression you mean, I think.'

'Bump! Excellent. Thank you so much.'

'And I think,' Violet went on, 'when you said "English backwardness", I think perhaps you meant reticence? Reserve? English reserve?'

'Reticence, and reserve?'

'Meaning that we English are,' she hunted for the word, 'not as forward as perhaps a European might be.'

'Indeed.'

'Which is not to say,' Violet burbled on, 'that we are not friendly. It's that perhaps we just don't show it.'

'I understand completely, Mrs Graham. I am so obliged. And if we were to crash into one another again, on the doorstep or other place, kindly do not feel too backward to correct my faulty English.'

Violet laughed. 'I certainly will, Mr Kapps.'

He smiled and nodded a goodbye, and Violet watched as he slowly made his way up the stairs.

17: Prudence & Lolly

'**W**ell, this is homely.' Prue took a quick look around the room as she divested herself of her hat and gloves and sat down.

'It's a start,' said Violet. 'Can I tempt you with a sherry?'

'You can.'

She had bought new curtains and a couple of brightly-embroidered cushions, and that was about all she had had time for. Now that she had to do everything herself – clean out and refill the fire grate each morning, wash her clothes and put them through the mangle, let alone shop and cook, in addition to going to work every day, there was very little time left over for home improvements. Or for a social life. Prue was in fact her first visitor.

'I met your Mr Kapps on the stairs,' said Prue. 'With a K.'

'Oh?' Violet handed Prue her sherry.

'Thank you. He invited me to tea, to improve his English, he said.'

'He didn't!'

'Why? What's wrong? He's not a sex fiend, is he? He doesn't look like one.'

'No. Nothing's wrong at all. Did you accept?'

Prue shrugged. 'I said why not? Or something to that ilk. Cheers.'

How typical of Prue to plunge in where angels, and Violet herself, feared to tread.

'So,' Prue sat back in her chair and crossed her ankles. 'What's happening? Tell me about your job. What is it you actually *do*?'

'I am responsible for making sure actors are called for rehearsal at the right time, that stage management and stage crew know what's expected of them and are on top of things. I see that everyone is paid. I type letters, on Frank's behalf. Solve problems. If there's a dispute of any kind, between actors say, or between actors and stage management, or writers, I do my best to fix it.'

'Doesn't sound like the dream job to me,' said Prue.

'Put like that no, it doesn't.' Violet smiled. 'But I like it. It suits me. I'm doing something useful at least.'

'Hmm,' said Prue. Then, 'I worked for Stella Campbell a few years ago, did I tell you? Mrs Pat. As her dresser. Ridiculous business, the theatre.'

'Yes, you did tell me.'

'I went to visit her a while ago, backstage. She has an army of bodyguards now. There was once a time when a person could just swan in and knock on her door and there she was. Not any more.' Prue sniffed. 'She's become too high and haughty for words, in my opinion.'

'Because she didn't want to see you?'

'Oh, she saw me all right, I made sure of it. She used to tell me everything. I was her closest confidante at one time. And now . . .' Prue made a grand gesture. 'She was like a goddess, dispensing wisdom from a great height. She made me feel like a child. I said to her, "Stella, this is me, remember? Silly old Toffee-head!" It was her pet name for me. I tell you, the theatre does no good to anyone.'

'What do you mean?'

'If you live in a world of fantasy it's easy to lose touch with the real world.'

'Theatre *is* the real world.'

'No it isn't. That's the whole point about theatre. It is not the real world. It doesn't pretend to be.'

'You're talking about what happens on stage,' said Violet. 'You're not taking into account the hard work that goes on behind the scenes to get that fantasy onto the stage. You can't think all theatre people have their head in the clouds. Nothing would ever get done if they did.'

Prue looked at Violet and pulled a face. 'You really have it under your skin, don't you?'

Violet smiled. 'Yes, I suppose I do.' Then she said: 'I hear you got yourself into a spot of bother with the police.'

'What a lot of nonsense. I was just trying to give the whole suffragist movement a kick up the backside. Action not words!' She punched the air. 'It's the only way anything will get done.'

'Good for you.'

'Not really. All I managed to achieve was house arrest for a fortnight.'

At that moment there was a knock on the door and Lolly flew in.

'So sorry I'm late. Hello there, girls. Phew!' She stood for a moment with her back against the door, breathing heavily.

'That was quite an entrance,' Prue remarked.

Lolly flung off her cape and what appeared to be a beret. 'What a day!' She was wearing much as she'd worn the last time Violet had seen her. Of the eyepatch, or whatever it was meant to be hiding, there was no sign.

'No eyepatch?'

'What?' Lolly touched her eye absently. 'No, no. All done with. So, ladies, what's new?' Then before they had a chance to answer she turned to Violet. 'I met your neighbour Mr Kapps just now. What a lovely man, so polite. He complimented me on my get-up.'

'Not you as well!'

'Why?' Lolly looked almost disappointed. 'You mean he does that to every woman?' She pouted. 'Oh well, never mind. A compliment is a compliment, even from an old man. Thank you.' She accepted the proffered glass of sherry and flopped into an armchair, one leg characteristically folded beneath her.

'Mr Kapps seems to spend all his time on the stairs,' remarked Prue. 'I wonder why.'

'Oh, he wasn't on the stairs,' said Lolly. Then, raising her glass – 'Cheers, ladies!' – she took a sip.

'Then where was he?'

'I knocked on the wrong door.'

'Didn't Mrs Sargent tell you which were my rooms?' Violet asked.

'Probably,' said Lolly vaguely. 'But you know me, scatterbrain.' Then, glancing around, she said, 'Nice place, Violet. Not quite like your old one, but nice all the same.'

'Thank you,' said Violet.

'It must be strange, coming from that mansion to this.'

'Via Dorothy, remember,' said Violet.

'Of course, via Dorothy. It must be a relief, after Dorothy.'

'Talking of whom,' Prue sat forwards on her chair, 'give us the dirt, Vi. She must have told you something.'

'About what?'

'Don't be obtuse. The man in the photograph.'

'What photograph?' piped up Lolly.

'Nothing.' Violet sat with pursed lips.

'She did,' said Prue, 'obviously.' She was watching Violet closely. 'You're a terrible liar, Vi. Out with it.'

'There are some things,' Violet said, rather primly, 'that should remain secret.'

That was a mistake. Prue was now sitting so far forwards in her chair she was in danger of tipping right out of it. 'All right. Let's try this,' she said. 'You don't have to say anything, just nod for yes and shake for no, how's that?' She didn't wait for a response. 'She fell in love with an older man who threw her over for an older woman.' Violet shook her head. 'She fell in love with an older man who threw her over.'

Violet looked into her lap. 'I'm not joining in this silly game,' she said. But it was too late.

'We have it!' Prue raised her glass in triumph. Then, 'Here's to Dorothy, and to older men, God bless them.'

'If you breathe one word of any of this outside this room, I . . .' Violet stopped.

Prue tilted her head to one side. 'You . . . ? I think we have our answer. And no, we won't breathe a word of anything you haven't told us, will we, Lolly?'

Lolly frowned in puzzlement.

'Talking of which,' and in a rather too deliberate attempt to change the subject, Violet swivelled to address Lolly directly. 'How have you been Lolly, since I last saw you? I thought you seemed a bit out of sorts.'

'Did I?' said Lolly.

'What happened with the eyepatch? It looks as if it's cleared up very quickly, whatever it was.'

'What eyepatch?' demanded Prue.

'Vi doesn't believe I'm an actress.' Lolly pulled a pitiful face.

'I never said that!'

'You did, more or less.'

'I just asked you where you'd worked, and what parts you'd played. I'd love to see you perform, wouldn't you, Prue?'

Prue nodded. 'If you say so.'

'Very well,' said Lolly. She got to her feet.

'What, you mean here and now?'

And without further prompting, Lolly walked to the

middle of the room, thrust out a hip and placed one hand upon it, held out the palm of the other, and began:

> '*I left no ring with her, what means this lady?*
> *Fortune forbid my outside have not charmed her!*
> *She made good view of me, indeed so much*
> *That straight methought her eyes had lost her*
>   *tongue.*
> *For she did speak in starts, distractedly.*
> *She loves me, sure!*
> (She gave a brief, shrill laugh)
> *The cunning of her passion*
> *Invites me in this churlish messenger.*
> *None of my lord's ring! Why, he sent her none!*
> *I am the man.* (She slapped her chest)
> *If it be so, as 'tis,*
> *Poor lady, she had better love a dream!*
> (She continued with a change of tone)
> *Disguise, I see thou art a wickedness*
> *Wherein the pregnant enemy does much.*
> *How is it for the proper false*
> *In women's waxen hearts to set their forms?*
> *Alas, our frailty is the cause, not we,*
> *For such as we are made of, such we be.*
> (A thoughtful pause)
> *How will this fadge? My master loves her dearly,*
> *And I, poor monster, fond as much on him,*
> *And she, mistaken, seems to dote on me!*
> *What will become of this?*
> (She walked in a circle)
> *As I am man,*
> *My state is desperate for my master's love.*
> *As I am woman, now, alas the day,*
> *What thriftless sighs shall poor Olivia breathe!*
> (She addressed the ceiling)

Oh time, thou must untangle this, not I.
It is too hard a knot for me to untie.'

And with that, Lolly gave a little bow and resumed her chair.

'Was that Shakespeare?' asked Prue, after a moment.

'Of course. *Twelfth Night.'*

'Huh. It sounded almost like ordinary speech. If everyone spoke it like that I might understand what all the fuss is about.'

Violet was struck dumb. It was an unorthodox rendering, to say the least, and startlingly realistic. There was very little sign of *acting*, it was as if Lolly was voicing thoughts that came into her head at that very moment.

'So this girl is pretending to be a man, and the woman she is wooing on behalf of the man she is in love with, who doesn't love him, falls in love instead with the girl, thinking she's a man. Is that it?' said Prue.

Lolly spent a moment unravelling Prue's convoluted exposition, before nodding. 'That's exactly it.'

Prue snorted. 'And this woman really believes the girl is a man, even though she is standing right in front of her, nose to nose.'

'This is theatre, Prue,' said Violet. 'Suspension of disbelief.'

Prue snorted again.

'What did you think, Vi?' Lolly looked positively anxious.

'I thought it was miraculous,' said Violet simply. 'I've never seen it done like that before. It was very unusual, and modern, and quite extraordinary. I really can't think of anything else to say. Well done, Lolly.'

'Oh good. So you do believe me now, do you?'

'I do, I really do.'

There was no doubting Lolly now.

The rest of the evening was spent in convivial conversation while they ate braised beef with boiled potatoes and carrots sautéed in butter and sugar (thank you, Mrs Beeton), on topics ranging from the 'insufferable' suffragists, as described by Prue; and what was to be done about Prue's friend Claudia, such a beauty she could have any man she wanted, who was about to embark on a *disastrous* marriage to the dullest man in the universe.

'Nothing,' said Violet. 'If she could have any man she wants she's obviously chosen the right man for her, dull or otherwise. There's nothing you can do. There's nothing anyone should want to do. Marriage is nothing to do with anyone except the married couple.' Then, seeing the others were staring at her, 'In my opinion,' she added.

'Well, as the only one among us with experience of such a thing I suppose you should know,' said Prue. 'Talking of which,' she continued with her mouth full, 'have you heard from the beast from Bloomsbury?'

'Anthony was not a beast, I won't have him called that.'

'Oh my.' Prue placed her fork on her plate and leant over to touch Violet's arm. 'Let's not get too het up, shall we? It was a joke. And you haven't answered my question.' She pointed at her plate. 'Excellent food by the way. What is it, mutton?'

'Beef,' said Violet. She sat there, her food half touched. 'I know you were joking but I don't want it bandied around that my husband was a bad man. He was not. He was good to me in many ways and I will always feel terrible about what I did.'

'Do you regret leaving?'

'No, not for a moment. But that doesn't mean I don't feel guilty about it.'

'Feeling guilty about something you don't regret makes no sense.'

'I've no doubt you're right.' Violet took up her knife

and fork again. 'And to answer your question, no, I haven't heard from him.'

'Good. That shows you did the right thing. He was probably glad to get rid of you.'

'You say the nicest things, Prue.'

'I do, don't I?' Prue replied.

Later on, Lolly entertained the two ladies with an anecdote about her 'admirer', as she put it, who followed her everywhere. She'd seen him on more than one occasion, lurking outside the theatre or wherever she happened to be that day. He was short and bald and had difficulty keeping up with her, so she led him a merry dance through the streets of London, darting in and out of alleyways and occasionally doubling back on herself, just to confuse him. On one occasion she stopped to stare into the window of the most compromising shop she could find, which sold female undergarments. As she gazed at the near-naked models he bent to tie his shoelace. And when she continued to stand there for a ridiculous amount of time he bent to tie his other shoelace, at which point she took off like a rocket, around the corner and across a busy road; and he, running to catch up with her, very *very* nearly got run over by a taxicab.

The other two ladies gazed at Lolly with horror.

'You should report him to the police,' said Violet.

'Why? He's totally harmless.' Lolly tossed her head. 'So eventually I stopped dead in the middle of the pavement and turned round to say hello, and he looked as scared as a wounded cat and walked away very fast.'

'Are you sure he was an admirer?' asked Violet.

'What else would he be?' said Lolly.

'He could be . . . I don't know.'

'A stalker,' said Prue. 'You should do something about it.'

'I have done something about it.' Lolly smiled blithely.

~

When it came time for Violet's guests to leave, Lolly hung back for a moment.

'May I ask you something, Vi?' she said.

'Of course.'

Lolly shifted awkwardly from one foot to the other. 'If it came to it,' she said, 'and I'm not saying it will, but if it did come to it, might I spend a night or so on your sofa? Would you mind?'

'A night or two?'

'Just that. Honestly, no more than that.'

'Lolly, what are you running away from? Or who?'

Lolly's eyes widened, as they tended to do when she felt cornered. 'Nobody. You know how it is, no fixed abode. Usually I am all right but there may just be the odd occasion . . .'

'You are welcome any time you like. So long as . . .' Violet checked herself. 'No, I don't want to lay down conditions. But it would make things so much easier if you opened up to people a bit more.'

Lolly nodded. The poor girl looked close to tears. For someone who was able to so directly tap into the life of a fictional character like Shakespeare's Viola, Lolly kept her own emotions under very tight wraps.

'Now go,' said Violet. 'Prue's waiting for you.' And she all but pushed her out the door.

18: Luncheon with Herbert

Aweek or so after Violet had first made his acquaintance the famous ginger head popped itself around her office doorway again, with an apology.

'I hadn't forgotten. I'm building another theatre, for my sins, right opposite the Haymarket, and it's taken up every waking minute. But I wondered if you were free to have lunch some day soon,' said Tree.

'Of course. Any day.'

'Any day? Splendid. Then how about this day?'

She would have liked more notice – why, she couldn't quite say. She would have liked to have taken more care over her appearance. But maybe it was best this way.

'I'll book a table at a little place nearby. They know me there, they will fit us in. I'll drop by in an hour, how's that?'

'Thank you, sir.'

'Not at all.' He turned to go and then paused. 'Herbert,' he said, with a little bow.

'Of course. Herbert.'

It was more like an hour and a half before he returned, by which time she had all but given up on him. The 'little place' turned out to be nothing less than the Café Royal, where Herbert was greeted with great warmth at the door; and when he explained – 'Sorry we're so late Pierre, I got held up' – the man named Pierre responded, with no hint of a French accent, 'Perfectly all right, sir', in a way that indicated this came as no surprise at all.

'This is a treat for me,' said Tree, as they sat down and leant back as the waiter, with a flourish, shook open the linen napkins and placed them on their respective laps – a ritual that, along with the practice of replenishing one's wine glass, amused Violet no end as it suggested the guest was too much of a child to do it for himself. 'I usually lunch on a boiled egg and a piece of buttered bread.' Tree tapped Violet's menu with a finger. 'Now you choose exactly what you like, don't stint.'

'It's certainly a treat for me, too,' said Violet.

Once they had settled, and ordered, and Tree had waved at friends across the room – he seemed to know most of them, and Violet could not help but notice that he, or maybe it was she, aroused a good deal of interest – he turned to her and said, 'Well now, tell me about yourself. What were you doing before you came to work for our humble establishment?'

It wasn't what Violet was expecting. 'Actually this is my first real job.'

'Indeed? Is that by choice or necessity, if you don't mind my asking?'

She felt slightly cornered, and defensive. 'I'm a widow,' she said. 'My husband, er, died.'

'I'm so sorry. Was it recent?'

'About a year ago. A riding accident.'

'A riding accident? So, was he a member of the cavalry, or . . .'

'Yes. No. He was a civil servant.'

'Ah, I see.'

His face was a picture of pained sympathy. He was obviously waiting for her to continue. 'So you see . . .' she stopped.

'And he left you unprovided for. Very harsh. But out of

hardship comes redemption, I always believe that.'

'Yes, I'm sure you're right.'

Her lies were as obvious and tangible as the wine glasses on the table before them, and they both knew it.

'A woman with secrets,' said Tree, with what may have been a wink. Then: 'And you never had an ambition to go on the stage?'

'Absolutely not. I would die of stage fright.'

'That's what people think. And nerves do play a part, I admit it. But you soon get used to it. And you have a very attractive appearance, if you were ever to change your mind.'

'I will let you know, thank you,' she said.

'Talented actresses are thin on the ground,' he said, as he tucked into his *pâté en terrine*. His fingers were, Violet couldn't help but notice, surprisingly feminine. As was his mouth. They were at odds with the rest of him, which was almost overpoweringly masculine. 'Especially younger ones, with little experience,' he went on. 'It's hard for any actor to gain experience, I warrant you that.'

'It's interesting you say that,' said Violet. 'Because I do know of one young actress who's very talented. I watched her perform just the other day. You must know of her. Lolly Mulligan?' She was buttering her toast, and when he didn't immediately reply she glanced up. He was busy eating and appeared not to have heard her, but she bumbled on. 'She gave a speech, Viola's speech from *Twelfth Night,* in my sitting room. Right there in front of us. It was' – she searched for the right word – 'extraordinary. In fact, it was Lolly who found me this job.'

'For which of course I'm sure we are all very grateful to her,' said Tree.

'You do know her?'

'Everyone knows Lolly Mulligan,' said Tree, as he broke off another small piece of toast. 'She is indeed very talented. But she is also, let's say, a problem. I'll leave it at that. And now, please tell me, what plays have you seen, and what sort of plays do you enjoy seeing?'

It was a polite but definite rebuff.

So they talked of plays, plays she had seen and plays she had read. 'You like to read plays, do you? How unusual. So, who is your favourite playwright? Do you like Shakespeare?'

'I love Shakespeare.'

'Any of his plays in particular?'

She thought for a moment. 'Perhaps *Measure for Measure.*'

Tree raised his almost-invisible eyebrows. 'The immaculate Imogen. Who would sacrifice her brother for her purity.'

'I didn't say I agreed with Imogen. I just like plays that question morality.'

'Do you know Ibsen?'

'Oh, I do. *Hedda Gabler*, and *The Doll's House*. I love Ibsen.'

'How splendid!' Tree raised his glass in salute. 'Here's to Henrik.' They touched glasses and both drank. 'I did *Enemy of the People* a couple of years ago, do you know that play?'

'Know it? I could almost recite it to you.' The wine was beginning to have an effect. Violet was feeling positively heady. 'I didn't see your production, I'm afraid. Though I did see *Trilby.*'

'*Trilby*. The fiendish Svengali.' Tree contorted his face so, before her eyes, he was transformed into Trilby's evil hypnotist. It was terrifying. 'The best part I ever played. And my most successful production. I am so glad you saw it. What did you think? Tell me honestly.'

'Honestly?' Violet took another sip of her wine. 'I thought it was rather silly.'

She looked at him in some alarm, but he just laughed. 'You're absolutely right. It was hogwash. But the audiences loved it. And I am not one to say the audiences don't know anything because they do, they know more than any of us. Too often there is no telling what will appeal and what won't. Which is one of the joys, and terrors, of theatre.'

'Ibsen on the other hand . . .'

'Ibsen, very much on the other hand.'

'I am so sorry I missed your *Enemy of the People*. I fell so in love with Dr Stockmann. I presume you played Dr Stockmann?'

'You fell in love with that rascal, did you?' Tree chuckled.

'Rascal?'

'He is a rascal. And a fool. A principled fool, but a fool nonetheless.'

'How can you say such a thing?' Violet was genuinely shocked.

'Such arrogance! He starts off as a decent, reasoned man of the people and the more obstruction he meets the more he goes completely off the rails.'

'But it's the people who drive him off the rails! One by one, all the people who agreed with him for exposing the poisoned baths, and the corruption of the local authorities, one by one they desert him! It's no wonder he goes off the rails. Oh dear, I really shouldn't drink so much. No, please . . .' It was too late, the ever-watchful waiter had already refilled her glass.

'I'm sorry,' said Violet, and took another sip.

'What for?' said Tree, doing likewise. 'Nonetheless, there were a dozen better ways he could have chosen to achieve his aim. Confrontation never accomplished anything. You will not change a person's mind by attacking him.'

'But he was driven to attack them, and *by* them! He was naïve perhaps, and obsessive maybe, but only in a way that truly good, passionate people are.'

'*That*,' said Tree, leaning across the table to her, 'is precisely what I love about this business.'

'What is?'

'Argument. And a writer who weighs the balance equally between his characters. Who gives his hero flaws and his villains virtues. Like Shakespeare.'

'Yes. Absolutely.' Violet was beginning to feel slightly indistinct. She was not used to drinking at lunchtime. She was not used to drinking much at all.

'Shall we order coffee?' Tree suggested.

'That would be a good idea.'

And so they drank coffee. And they went on to talk about other things, of Tree's new venture, the complete rebuilding of Her Majesty's Theatre, directly opposite the Haymarket, the biggest enterprise he had ever undertaken, and a dream come true. And how he thought he had found the perfect play to open it with, an American piece called *Seats of the Mighty* by Gilbert Parker, which admittedly had not gone down too well in its native land – 'But then the Americans are a very different kettle of fish'; and how whenever he was planning anything he thought first of the 'good folks in the gallery', what he called his core audience. 'Because they are there because they want to be there. They have saved up, and queued up, to watch rather than to be watched.' Unlike the more expensive audience members in the stalls who made a point of turning up late for a performance so they caused the maximum disruption, and thereby knew the eyes of the rest of the audience were on them and their hat, or their dress, or indeed their companion. 'But I wouldn't be without them,' said Tree, with a chuckle. 'To be precise, I *couldn't* be without them.'

Violet just sat and listened, and silently marvelled at his enthusiasm, his sense of fun, his passion. It was nearly four o'clock when he eventually stopped talking, looked around to see a near-empty restaurant and a line of waiters stifling yawns. 'Do you suppose we are keeping them up?' he whispered to Violet. 'Perhaps we'd better let them get to bed.'

And so they left. The fresh air came as a shock, and a necessary one. Tree took her arm as they crossed the road, and as they parted on the pavement outside the Haymarket Theatre he said, 'That was extremely pleasant. I can't remember when I last enjoyed such a stimulating conversation. Thank you, Violet.' He lifted her hand to his lips and kissed it. 'We must do it again.'

'A pleasure, Herbert. Thank you.'

He turned to go and then thought of something. 'Do you suppose Frank would allow me to borrow you from time to time?'

'Borrow me? In what sense?'

'There's a little task I need doing, and I think you would be the ideal person. I get all these plays sent to me, you see, from people I don't know. And I simply have no time to read them. So I wondered if you might consider taking some of them off my hands. Give them a quick glance. Most of them are not up to much, so it may be a bit of a chore for you. But if you think you could find the time . . .'

'I would be honoured.' Violet's eyes lit up.

'Oh, I wouldn't go that far. But it would be tremendously helpful to me, and who knows, you may just find the British Ibsen.'

'Of course, I would love it. I could take the plays home with me, read them in the evenings.'

'Splendid.' He looked at her for a long moment, as if there was something else. Then he lifted his hat and said,

'Well, goodbye, Mrs Graham. The mysterious Mrs Graham. I am so glad you are part of the team.'

'So am I,' she said. And she watched until he had disappeared through the doors of the Haymarket Theatre.

She continued to stand still for some time, there on the corner of Panton Street, thinking. Then she turned and made her way back to her office.

She sat down at her desk and addressed her typewriter. 'I must not,' she told it, 'on any account. I must not fall in love with Herbert Tree.'

The typewriter did not contradict her.

19: Confiding in Mr Kapps

On a whim, that evening as she arrived home, Violet climbed the extra flight of stairs and knocked on Mr Kapps' door. He took a while to answer it, but when he saw her he looked genuinely delighted.

'Mr Kapps,' she said quickly, 'I came to apologise for the other day. I was rude to you, I'm so sorry.'

'Not at all, Mrs – '

'Graham.' It slipped off the tongue so easily now.

'It was I who was being forward, I apprehend that.'

'You took me by surprise rather, and I am not used . . .'

'To being faced by a strange man on your doorstep. Who you thought was following you home.' He chuckled, and stroked his beard. 'Well, never mind. The offer is still available.'

The fact was that after this particularly exciting day, when Violet had come dangerously near to revealing everything about her background to a man she barely knew, and with whom she was, she privately admitted, mildly infatuated, she did not want to spend the evening alone. For the first time since she'd moved to Crighton Street she felt she could not cope with the solitude.

'Please, do come in,' said Mr Kapps, at last. And so she did. She noticed he did not completely close his door behind her, perhaps for her own feelings of safety.

'May I offer you a cup of tea?'

'You certainly may, thank you.'

'Please, sit.' He gestured her to a chair.

His room was not unlike hers – naturally, it was a replica, one floor higher. The furniture was similar, as were the curtains and the rugs. The difference was the walls, which were covered in pictures and photographs. As Mr Kapps made the tea Violet circumnavigated the room, peering closely at each photograph in turn. They were family photographs, adults and small children, mostly in formal pose and deadly serious, the younger ones included. Violet felt the slightest pang. She had come to find Anthony's family portraits and photographs oppressive; as if the house she lived in was part of them and she did not really exist. But these photos, stiff and solemn though they were, suggested a feeling of belonging, and context.

'Your family?' she asked him.

He came to stand by her and, pointing to each picture in turn, he explained: 'My auntie Dora, who brought me up. My cousins Katja, Lotte and Gunther. My father Jacob.' He stopped. He was staring hard at a skinny, stern-looking man dressed in a flannel jacket and loose trousers, scowling into the camera. 'He was a hard man. An unhappy man. Not a good father.'

Violet nodded. 'What happened to your mother?'

'She left,' said Mr Kapps. Then, 'Come, do sit down. Do you use sugar?'

'Take,' said Violet, as she sat. 'No, I don't, thank you.'

'*Take* sugar, thank you.' He turned to fetch the tea. 'It is the little things that catch us out.' He handed the teacup to Violet. 'Milk?'

'Thank you.'

At last Mr Kapps sat down and smiled at Violet. 'This is very pleasant.'

'It is.' She smiled back.

'So. How was your day?'

'As a matter of fact,' Violet replied, 'it was rather interesting.' She went on to describe her lunch, and her lunch companion, which led naturally on to a brief description of her job, and how she came by it.

'You are a working woman?' Mr Kapps raised his eyebrows slightly.

'Of necessity.'

It was really why she had knocked on Mr Kapps' door in the first place, because she felt the need to talk honestly to someone, someone she didn't know, someone who would not judge her, or laugh at her. But when it came to this moment she was tongue-tied.

'Tell me about your family,' she said instead. 'Why did you decide to come to England?'

Mr Kapps did not reply immediately. Then he said, 'It is a very long story. And one day I will tell it to you. But meanwhile, I sense there is something you need to as they say get off your breast.'

She couldn't help but burst out laughing.

'Ah,' said Mr Kapps. 'I've trod in it, again. Which was it this time?'

'Put your foot in it. And it's chest. To get something off your chest.'

'I believe sometimes people tell me these things on purpose.' Mr Kapps frowned in puzzlement. 'I have an assistant by the name of Danny. He is an urchin – is that the right word? A rapscallion.' He looked at Violet enquiringly and she nodded. 'A young rapscallion. He corrects my English all the time, not politely, as do you, but roughly, rudely. I believe he leads me up the garden track sometimes.' He paused. 'How am I doing?'

'You are doing very well,' said Violet. 'Though it's path, not track.'

'Up the garden path, thank you, I will try to remember.

And now.' He got to his feet and refilled her teacup. 'You were saying?'

'Was I?'

He sat himself down again and waited. 'I feel there was a reason for the knock on my door this evening,' he said. 'After all, it is some while since we first acquainted upon the doorstep. I have met recently some friends of yours, I believe, lively young women. It's good to have friends.' He finished, and drank his tea. 'So?'

Violet heaved a long sigh. 'My name is not Mrs Graham,' she said.

Mr Kapps nodded. 'I did doubt so.'

'Did you? Well then, you probably already know the story behind it.'

'I do not.'

So she told him. All of it, starting from her decision – at the suggestion of a friend – to change her name, and her identity, so that her estranged husband, should he decide to do so, would not be able to find her. Which naturally led on to the reasons why she had an estranged husband in the first place, and why – or whether – she had reason to be afraid of him.

Mr Kapps kept perfectly still throughout, nodding on occasion, and watching her, but never interrupting.

'And now,' she said, 'I am stuck with it. I am stuck with living a lie, pretending to be someone else. With a hazy background, which is false, about a husband who was killed in a riding accident, leaving me with nothing. Which is why I have to go out to work.'

'It is a very small lie,' he said.

'It is a total lie! I'm not a poor bereaved widow, I am a . . . I'm a selfish woman who left her husband for no good reason.' She stopped abruptly.

'I do not believe,' said Mr Kapps, after a moment, 'that any woman leaves her husband for no good reason, not in these days.'

'He was not unfaithful. He did not beat me. He did not humiliate me in public. He did not even really dislike me.'

'But you disliked him.'

'Yes actually, I did.'

'It is so much easier for a woman to leave a man who has been a beast. One can dwell on the past. One can beat oneself – is that correct? thank you – for one's past deeds, and for why? The deed is done. It was not so terrible. You were unhappy and you took an action. There are many unhappy people who do not have this kind of courage. It is always easier to stay still in the boat than to rock it.' He cocked his head. 'Am I speaking sense?'

'You are. You really are.'

Violet was half crying and half laughing.

'If I am making you laugh then I am certainly doing well.'

Violet brought out a handkerchief and dabbed at her eyes, 'I think,' she said, 'that perhaps you speak as you do deliberately, to make a person laugh. Am I right?'

Mr Kapps inclined his head ambiguously.

'But no matter. I don't mean to be unkind, Mr Kapps, your English is truly excellent.' She blew her nose. 'As is your company.' She replaced her handkerchief and smiled rather damply at him.

'That,' said Mr Kapps, beaming back at her, 'is the nicest thing someone has said to me for a long time.'

'Thank you very much. I have bent your ear, as they say, and you have told me nothing about yourself.'

'That is not true!' he cried. 'I have introduced you to my entire family!'

'In photographs, yes. But there is a story behind them, isn't there? A person does not leave his homeland without a good reason.'

'Perhaps,' said Mr Kapps.

'Well, one day, Mr Kapps,' Violet felt suddenly exhausted. She got to her feet. 'One day you will tell me everything. That's if you would like to.'

Mr Kapps inclined his head again and rose to his feet.

'Goodnight, Mrs Graham,' he said.

'Violet, please.'

'Zunker.'

'I beg your pardon?'

'Zunker. That, believe it or not, is my forename.'

'Zunker.' She stared at him for a moment. 'It doesn't suit you in the least. I think I'd have great trouble addressing you as Zunker.'

'Then you may call me Hans.'

'Why Hans?'

'Because all English people believe all German-speaking people are called Hans. And they believe all German-speaking people are German.'

'That may well be true.'

'The English are exceptionally islandish. I love them extremely, for their kindness, and their politeness, and of course for their humour. But if you believe you are, how shall we say, the most important nation in the world, this can also go together with an ignorance, or an uninterest, in the rest of the world. If you see what I mean.'

'I do.'

'I do not mean to offend, you understand.'

'You don't offend in the least. We are insular, and we are guilty of indifference to the rest of the world at times, I wouldn't deny it.'

Kapps gave a little bow. 'Nicely said, Violet.'

'My pleasure Hans. Zunker.'

'Goodnight, again.' He pushed the already open door wide. 'I am here, most evenings.'

'Thank you. Goodnight.' She gave him a warm smile, and she was gone.

20: The trouble with writers

Meanwhile, back at Panton Street things were changing.

Mrs Graham had toughened up. She was no longer someone a person went to with a minor complaint. An actor, no matter his or her standing, ran the risk of being given short shrift if she or he arrived at Violet's doorstep expecting her to resolve a dispute with a fellow actor. Mrs Graham had made it perfectly plain she was not there to solve problems of casting, or internecine squabbles, or any other playground complaint that adult professionals such as themselves could not work out perfectly well between them.

But just as she thought she had got the measure of actors along came another breed of visitor altogether: the writer.

The moment it became known that Violet Graham was the first port of call for a budding playwright and had the ear of the Great Tree himself – which wasn't strictly true – she was bombarded by them. They did not have the natural ease of manner and charm of their acting counterparts. They were mostly inarticulate, and scruffy, and marginally desperate. She sympathised with them, but she also found them exasperating; especially those who positioned themselves in front of her desk for minutes on end and described in great and often incomprehensible detail the plot of the script that lay before her and how it was written especially for the Great Tree himself; how he could play both the villain and the hero – as he so liked to do – with plenty of opportunity for clever disguises and outlandish accents. She felt for them, knowing they had spent months or even years on this one piece, which might or most likely might not even reach the eyes of the Chief, as she had been told strictly to weed them out, usually after reading just a page or two.

'You can tell immediately,' Tree had told her. 'If the first few pages don't grip you there's no point in reading further.' Invariably the first few pages were no more than preamble. 'One needs to plunge in,' Tree was fond of saying, 'in *media res* so to speak. I'm never quite sure what that means but I take it to mean *in the middle of something*. And if it's confusing so be it, the audience will find out what it's all about eventually. Grab their attention in any way you think fit, then explain yourself. Or not, as the case may be. Whatever you do, don't follow Shakespeare. Shakespeare is far too fond of the lengthy exposition – think of *A Comedy of Errors* – and we're not ready for it, we don't know who this person is and we don't care, so we're not listening.'

It was another endearing thing about Tree. He made out that he was semi-literate, that he never read books. He claimed to have very little time for intellectual matters and that the only way of learning was by doing. He rated instinct above technique – not always useful for an actor in a long run – and individuality above everything. And yet he read books all the time, and he knew more about Shakespeare, his verse and his meaning, than virtually anyone else in the country. His genius was partly in his constant search for what he called 'my truth; which is not the same as your truth, or the man in the street's truth; it's the holy grail, and you can only find it by searching,

searching, and not being distracted by other people telling you what it is.'

So Violet half dreaded these visits from hopeful playwrights. It pained her that she had to sit and listen to them all, knowing that for most of them it was probably a waste of time but that any of them just *might* turn out to be the next Ibsen. Among the submissions were endless variations on the theme of *Trilby*, Tree's great triumph; what Violet had dismissed as a bit of silly nonsense but which, she acknowledged, had made him enough money to buy the plot in the Haymarket and to build upon it, at great expense to himself and to many others, what would turn out to be the most dazzling temple to the dramatic arts the West End had ever seen. It was natural for any writer to want to cash in on a recent success, not always aware that such is the nature of theatre – where a new play will take up to a year to set up, to cast and to rehearse and finally to put on – that that particular bandwagon left the parade long ago.

There were exceptions, and there was one in particular. He strolled into Violet's office one morning, hatless, his hands in his pockets, and introduced himself as Haddon Chambers. He was tall, nattily dressed, disturbingly handsome, alarmingly over-friendly and Australian. And no, he wasn't trying to sell her a script, he'd already done that some years ago, with – he told her casually – some success.

He perched uninvited on the edge of Violet's desk and told her his story. How he had bumped into Tree, whom he'd met before briefly, in the street right outside these offices one day some years ago, and how Tree had suggested he write a play for him. Chambers was living above a shop in Bayswater at the time, scraping a living selling stories about England to Australian publications. He accepted the challenge, wrote the play, sent it to Tree and heard nothing more. So he hounded him and managed to secure a reading of the script the following day, but Tree went to a Turkish bath instead, so he followed him there and read the play to him in the steam room. Tree promised him a matinee, which led a while later to a full production starring Tree himself. It was Tree's first major success and established him as a force to be reckoned with on the West End theatre scene, Mr Chamber ended, modestly.

Violet listened attentively. She'd heard the story before, somewhere, and she knew it was true. It had been the talk of the company, that a play by an unknown writer from the colonies, with an absurd plot, had been responsible for putting Tree on the theatrical map. And here he was, this cocky young man, grinning down at her as if they'd known one another all their lives.

'What was the play about?' she asked.

He told her it was a fable about a Queensland bushranger called Captain Swift, who comes to England to escape his criminal past, and having saved the life of a toff whose horse was running amok in Piccadilly he is invited as a guest at the toff's grand house in London, where he falls in love with his host's niece. Things begin to fall apart when the butler recognises the newcomer as his estranged half-brother and the lady of the house realises he is her son, who she gave away for adoption as an infant. Then along comes a friendly Queensland squatter, who was once held up at gunpoint by Captain Swift, and an Australian detective who is scouring the country for him, and things don't look too good for the captain. Cornered finally, and realising his time has come and that a man cannot escape his past - "I'm a robber to the last, you see" – he does the decent thing and kills himself.

Violet gazed at him open-mouthed. 'And that play was a success?' she said.

'You bet,' said Chambers. 'Not back home it wasn't, they didn't believe a word of it,' he admitted cheerily. 'But Herbie loved it.' She had never heard anyone call Tree Herbie before. 'And so did the people. Herbie's the one, he knows what's what.'

Yes, thought Violet, the two men had a lot in common. She could well imagine it was Chambers' cheek that endeared him to Tree as much as the quality of his playwriting.

'I'm a colonial,' said Chambers, with a wink. 'Your class system is a goldmine.'

When he eventually invited Violet to dinner, which she was half expecting, she declined, which he was not expecting, on the grounds that she had too many scripts to read. He looked suitably crestfallen before he shrugged, grinned, removed his backside from the corner of her desk and stretched.

'Another time maybe,' he said, and sauntered off.

There was no other time. She never saw him again. The last she heard of Chambers he had taken up with the opera singer Nellie Melba and was teaching her to act. Among, so the rumours went, other things.

Later, she regretted declining the invitation, and not just because she had missed out on what she was sure would have been an entertaining evening. It hadn't really occurred to Violet until now that she had virtually no social life to speak of. Her evenings, and often weekends too, were spent reading scripts. She rarely saw her friends and she had totally lost touch with the suffragists. She had been so anxious to be wanted, to be of use to people – not just Tree – she had foresworn everything else. When Mr Kapps knocked at her door one evening, inviting her for another cup of tea, 'or something stronger perhaps?' she turned him away. If she was afraid, as she once had been, of solitude, she had only herself to blame.

But how typical of Tree, she thought later, to take on such an absurd play by an unknown writer, and a colonial to boot. From Shakespeare to Ibsen to nonsense like *Trilby* and *Captain Swift*. He certainly had a nose for a success. Nobody could accuse Herbert Beerbohm Tree of snobbery.

21: The loneliness of Mr Kapps

Mr Kapps, like his father before him and his father before that, owned a drapery shop. Unlike his father and his grandfather however the shop was not situated round the corner in a small town in Austria, but in a busy thoroughfare in a foreign city a long way from what had once been his home.

Kapps was fascinated by his adopted country. He spent a good deal of his day, when he was not working, walking the streets of London and observing people going about their business. He was intrigued by the way in which, amid the chaos and the racket of street hawkers, the cries of the costermongers and clatter of horses' hooves, one could detect a distinct order, a discipline, among people who knew their place and were comfortable in it.

This orderliness enthralled him. He understood that a person born to a certain class of society (he could write a thesis on the definition of that word 'class') almost invariably remained in that class. He was bemused by the fact that people were prepared to put up with lives that had been pre-designed for them, without protest. It meant for a well-organised world, and it was that organisation, and acceptance, that kept the wheels turning; that made England the calm, sensible, and largely peaceable country it was.

However in the midst of all this, even though he'd

lived in London for some years now and ran a successful business, with regular customers who greeted him by name, Mr Kapps still felt like an outsider. There was an ocean of difference between a customer and a friend, and the notion that he might invite one of them to tea in a café, or vice versa, was out of the question, he knew that. So he spent his evenings reading, mostly newspapers and contemporary novels by the likes of Dickens, Hardy and Trollope, all in an attempt to get to grips with the strange, friendly yet distant species called the Englishman.

Many of these novels featured people who had broken out of their pigeonholes: servants who became masters thanks to a surprise inheritance, or a marriage, or some less than legal shenanigans; masters, and mistresses, who fell from grace due to a gambling debt, or a family rift, or a misdemeanour to do with the opposite sex. The crime had to be serious enough to be unforgivable. The English were, thought Kapps, a particularly forgiving people, if only because they were anxious not to upset the *status quo*. If you were high-born and you wanted to remain so, you had to behave yourself. But those shifts in the merry-go-round of the English social hierarchy happened only in novels. Real life was something else, and it was real life that Kapps struggled with.

It was hard to make friends in London. Men didn't trust foreigners, and women were even more perplexing. He had not yet developed the knack of approaching a woman without sending her flying off in the opposite direction. Part of it he knew was to do with the natural English reserve, otherwise known as a suspicion of strangers. But mostly it was because he did not fit into an identifiable category, and that is what confused people. The typical Londoner 'did not know what to make of him'.

At home back in Austria he had lived a relatively comfortable, and pre-determined, existence in a small town near Vienna, where everyone knew one another and one another's business. His family had lived there since forever. They had a place. They 'fitted in'. His mother's disappearance was well-known but never talked about, within the house or without.

But as an émigré – of which there were quite a few in London – this was quite by the way. He might have made friends with fellow émigrés, in particular fellow Austrians, but he had not come all this way only to fraternise with people from the country he had just turned his back on.

He had escaped from a small town where everyone knew one another all too well to a vast metropolis where it was impossible to meet anyone. It was a conundrum.

Violet in particular interested him. She had done the rare thing of breaking with her past. But after their friendly meeting over tea some weeks ago he had barely seen her. He would watch her arrive home from work through his front window, clutching a large bag. He had once or twice stepped out onto the stairway as she was coming through the front door and called down to her. She always responded in a friendly enough manner, but lately she had sounded distracted, and hurried to her door before he had a chance to talk to her properly. He took that as a rebuff. And so he continued to be a lonely man.

Then one day he had the beginnings of a good idea. In all the time he had known her Kapps had never seen Mrs Graham – Violet – in the company of a man. And as a clever and beautiful young woman it was high time, in his view, she found someone to take her mind off whatever it was that was preoccupying her, which Kapps rightly assumed had to do with her work. He was not thinking of himself, gracious no, but rather someone of roughly her age, who was amusing, and cultured, and above all a gentleman. And how gratifying it would be if he, Zunker Kapps, might be the one to introduce her to such a man.

Surely then she would be his friend again.

It also struck him, though it seemed unlikely, that her aloofness had to do with her qualms about him. That as an unmarried man who was nearly twice her age he might have designs on her. A male companion would put paid to that. The question was: where would one find him?

He happened to be talking this over with Danny one morning – rather against his better judgement, as Danny, as has already been established, was not a trustworthy person. Yet it was one of those things that emerges out of idle conversation, and before he had time to move on to a safer topic Danny announced that he knew just the chap. He was a distant cousin – Danny had a lot of cousins – and he was single, and entertaining, and not a bad-looker, and above all he was a gentleman.

Ignoring the notion that this might be too good to be true, Kapps asked to meet this young man. 'What does he do?' he enquired.

'Oh,' said Danny. 'He dabbles.'

'In what?'

'Stocks and shares and stuff.'

'Ah. Is he a gambler?'

'If he is he's a successful one.'

'Then please, introduce him to me.'

A few days later as Kapps was about to shut up shop, a young man sauntered in through the front door, swinging a cane. He gave Kapps a sideways look, took off his hat and asked for Danny.

'Are you his cousin?' asked Kapps.

'More or less,' the young man replied.

'Then I am delighted to meet you.' Kapps extended his hand. 'Mr Kapps.'

The young man took Kapps' hand and grinned. 'Johnny Woodruff. Pleased to meet you too, I'm sure.'

Now, had Kapps been a bit more versed in the nuances

of English society he would have heard the alarm bells ringing at that point. For while the man's appearance was satisfying enough, and his voice showed a degree of breeding, no gentleman *ever* says when first introduced to a stranger, 'Pleased to meet you.'

This was, to say the least, unfortunate, as Kapps could and indeed should have nipped this little caper in the bud. As it was, he wasted an entire evening, and a good deal of money, on an expensive dinner in a restaurant in the Strand for both Johnny and Danny. It began well enough: Johnny was good company, and told amusing and only slightly *risqué* jokes. It wasn't until they had demolished a large dish of oysters each and were halfway through a side of beef and onto the second bottle of wine that Johnny's accent started to slip, and he and Danny began to vie with one another to tell the bawdiest, and loudest, joke; and soon they were clutching onto one another and crying with laughter, and other dinner guests were beginning to stare. At that point the waiter approached and whispered into Kapps' ear to the effect that if his guests could not keep their voices down he would regretfully have to ask them to leave. So Kapps, who had by now realised his mistake and that yet again - *yet again* – he had been made a fool of, raised his voice and told both men to get out. NOW.

This naturally was followed by a dense silence. All eyes were on Kapps. His guests were staring at him with their mouths open. Danny had never seen his boss lose his temper before. The young man who called himself Johnny got up, flung his napkin down and stalked off. Danny hesitated long enough to make a kind of apologetic gesture and followed. Kapps then paid the substantial bill, and with as much dignity as he could muster he left the restaurant and walked home and spent the rest of the evening crying with fury and frustration.

22: Redress

'So this is where you've been hiding!' said Prue.

'Hiding?' said Violet.

Prue walked straight past Violet into her sitting room. 'I thought you'd died. Or emigrated.' She removed her hat and cloak, dug into her bag and produced a bottle of champagne. 'Glasses?'

'Oh! What are we celebrating?' Violet rummaged in her cupboard and took out a couple of wine glasses. 'I'm afraid this is all I have.'

'We're celebrating you being alive, and still here.' Violet watched as Prue levered off the champagne cork with expertise and began pouring.

'To life!' said Prue, raising her glass.

'To life!' echoed Violet. But she didn't drink. Instead she said, 'The last time we did this . . .'

'Was the day you left your husband.'

'And we drank from proper champagne flutes.'

'So what? It tastes the same.' Prue plonked herself down in an armchair. 'Now, tell me what you've been up to.'

'There's nothing to tell. I haven't been up to anything except work.'

'Deserting your friends, cosseting yourself in your tiny little room . . .'

'It isn't tiny!'

'In your medium-sized room, doing goodness only knows what. You're not working now, are you?'

'I bring my work home,' said Violet. She sat down and explained the extra duties she'd taken on as Herbert Tree's unofficial script manager.

'Are they paying you for this?'

'Not strictly speaking, no. But it's good to keep in with Herbert – Mr Tree.'

'Herbert, eh?' Prue narrowed her eyes.

'And besides, I enjoy it.'

'Is he your lover, this Herbert?'

Violet laughed. 'Gracious me, no. He's a married man.'

'So? That never stopped a man before. Least of all your Herbert, from what I've heard.'

'And don't call him "my" Herbert.'

'So, what have you *really* been up to?'

'I realise the idea that work can take over a person's life makes no sense to you,' said Violet.

'The whole idea of work doesn't make a lot of sense to me,' said Prue.

'So there's no way I can convince you. But that pile over there,' Violet indicated a desk in the corner of the room, 'is my homework for the week.'

Prue grunted.

'But you can tell me what *you've* been up to,' said Violet. 'As I'm sure you're dying to.'

'I will,' said Prue.

So Prue related the story of how she had taken her friend Claudia – the one about to embark on the disastrous marriage – to the South of France in an attempt to get her to change her mind about the marriage and to introduce her to an eligible French alternative, both of which she failed to do. This adventure was followed soon after by the afore-mentioned wedding, which had so far survived the first few months, she said with some surprise.

She then went on to talk about her friend Sacha, a colourful character of novel sexuality who was also her brother-in-law and who, if Prue recollected correctly, was having an affair with Oscar Wilde.

'Having an affair with Oscar Wilde?' Violet exclaimed.

'I may have got that bit wrong,' Prue admitted. 'But he seemed pretty passionate about him.'

'Does it automatically mean a person is having an affair with another person just because he's passionate about him?'

'Usually.'

Violet laughed. 'Have you ever had a friendship with a man who wasn't your lover?'

'I am not a sex maniac, though you seem to think I am,' said Prue. 'Not like Lolly.' She took a sip of her drink.

'What makes you say that?'

'Well-known fact. It's why she's always in trouble, and homeless, or claiming to be.'

Violet remembered Tree's response when she'd mentioned Lolly. 'Poor girl,' she said.

'It's why she thinks she's being followed. She probably is. By a detective hired by the jealous wife of her latest paramour. Still, she makes up for the rest of us. For you, I should say.' Prue placed her glass down on the table and her hands in her lap. 'Unless there is something you are not telling me.'

Violet shook her head. 'Sorry to disappoint you.'

Prue waited for a moment. Then she sighed, got to her feet and said, 'Well, I suppose if you have work to do, and you have nothing whatsoever of interest to tell me, I may as well look for entertainment elsewhere.' She reached for her cloak.

'If,' said Violet, 'you could give me some warning next time I'll set aside a whole evening just for you. And I will cook for us. How's that?'

'As you like,' said Prue. She picked up the champagne bottle and peered into it. 'Still plenty left. I'll take it with me if you don't mind.'

'Not at all. Thank you for bringing it.'

'My pleasure,' said Prue. And she left.

It was difficult to concentrate after that. Violet could not keep her mind on the words on the page. There were occasions, too many of them, when she wondered if the writers of the scripts she had volunteered to read had ever actually sat in a theatre. Granted the Chief was known for the lavishness of his settings, but to place Act One in the formal gardens of a stately home, with peacocks, Act Two on a desert island, with live monkeys, and Act Three inside the reading room of the British Museum (fortunately with no wildlife), as per one example, was asking a lot. One script even featured a parrot that quoted from Sophocles. She set that one aside to show to the Chief as she thought it would amuse him.

She idly wondered if she might write a play herself one day, and if so, about what. Perhaps she could put herself on the stage, her own version of Ibsen's *Doll's House*. A tale about a young woman who left home because she felt stifled, only to plunge into and then out of a marriage because she felt stifled, and ended up on her own in a set of rooms in unfashionable Camden Town, where . . .

It was at that point that she heard a shriek from the room above. What was Mr Kapps up to?

It took her a moment – ten seconds at least – to realise what Mr Kapps was probably up to; or more to the point, the origin of the shriek. She got to her feet, fairly ran up the stairs and knocked on his door.

'Hello,' said Mr Kapps.

'Are you all right?' Violet asked. 'I heard noises.'

'I'm very all right, thank you Violet. Won't you come in?'

As Kapps stepped aside so Prue appeared, champagne glass in hand.

'We're onto our second bottle,' she giggled.

'Well, I might have guessed it. Mr Kapps – Zunker,' Violet looked genuinely concerned, 'is this woman bothering you?'

'Not at all,' Prue replied for him. 'And he's not assaulting me either. Nor am I assaulting him. We were just having a – a – what would you call it, Hans?'

Kapps ushered Violet into the room and closed the door behind her. 'A conversation?' he said.

'A confessional,' said Prue.

'Can I offer you a drink, Violet?' said Kapps. 'I believe there is a little left in the bottle.'

'No, thank you Zunker, I won't stay.'

'Zunker?'

'That is my name,' said Kapps. He gave a little bow. 'But I do not tell everyone.'

'Well!' said Prue. 'That puts me in my place.' She made unsteadily for an armchair and fell into it. 'We've been talking about you, as it happens.'

'Oh?'

'And do you know what Hans was telling me?'

'Please, Miss Brooks.'

'Don't worry Hans. Sit down, sit down, Vi.'

Violet, with a slight hesitation, did so. Kapps stood between the two women, all but wringing his hands.

'It was meant to be concerning just us,' he reminded Prue.

Prue waved away his objection as if it were a fly. 'He's been pimping for you,' she said.

'Pimping?'

'What is pimping, please?'

'What you've been doing Hans. It's called pimping. There are people who make a profession out of it. Men who procure women, or in this case, men who procure men for women.'

Kapps looked positively wretched. Prue reached out and patted his arm reassuringly. 'It's all right Hans, we're among friends.'

'I do not think . . .'

'Besides, it's time this woman,' Prue gestured at Violet with her glass, 'knew the lengths other people are going to, to make her happy.' She took a swig of her drink. 'Even if it didn't quite work out. Tell her, Hans.'

'No. You tell her, if you should.' Kapps sat down and looked miserably at the floor.

'This man,' Prue reached out once again and grabbed Kapps by the sleeve, nearly tipping out of her chair as she did so, 'was worried about you. He thought he'd offended you or something.'

'Offended him?'

'Because you were being unfriendly to him. And you seemed to be working too hard, or so he thought. As did I.' She shook Kapps' sleeve, which she was still hanging onto. 'Don't worry, *mein lieber*. So. He set out to – oh, and I forgot. He thought you needed a man.'

'That is not what I said,' Kapps muttered.

'I'll put it another way. He thought you might have been lonely, a single woman on her own. Am I telling it correctly, Hans?'

Kapps shrugged.

'So. He asked his assistant, Lenny . . .'

'Danny. And I did not precisely ask him.'

'He happened to mention it to Danny. And Danny said he knew just the person. So, two days later – was it two days, Hans?'

'Maybe.' Kapps glanced anxiously at Violet.

'There turned up on his doorstep a young man. Oh, and another thing – Hans thought perhaps that you were afraid of him in some way.'

'Afraid of him?' Violet turned to Kapps. 'Why would I be afraid of you?'

Kapps looked pained. 'It was a misunderstanding.'

'So, where was I? Young man, in his doorway. Nice-looking, charming manner, sleek black hair.'

'His hair was not black.'

'Never mind, it adds to the story. And so they go to dinner, Hans, Lenny and this – person. In an expensive restaurant. And they chat away, chit chat, chit chat. All very cosy. But then they've reached the third bottle of wine . . .'

'Second.'

'And the jokes are getting closer and closer to the knuckle until they are, you could say, bang on it. Bang!' Prue smacked her hands together and the remains of the champagne in her glass went flying. 'And they get thrown out. By the waiter of a smart, very smart, one of the smartest restaurants in Fleet Street.'

'The Strand.'

Violet looked from one to the other in confusion. 'I'm sorry but I don't understand,' she said.

'Forgive me, Violet.' Kapps' hands were clasped together between his knees. 'I just wanted – I had hoped – you seemed so lonely.'

'What made you think I was lonely?' She spoke more sharply than she intended.

'Steady on, Vi, he did it for you. He was trying to do you a favour. And he got done. Done over, as they say, by his lowlife of an assistant and his mate. Who was not a gentleman. Not by any stretch. So, our friend here,' she tugged on Kapps' sleeve again, 'was humiliated, in public, in one of the smartest restaurants in town. And all for you.'

'I don't know what to say,' said Violet.

'You could try saying thank you.'

Violet looked up. She was close to tears. 'Mr Kapps . . .
'

'Zunker, please.'

'Zunker. I am so sorry. I'm so sorry you went through this awful humiliation, and for me. I had no idea.'

'Of course not. And you would not have done except for your friend here.'

'I just thought she ought to know,' Prue said, firmly, 'what other people are going out of their way to do for her.'

There was a hiatus. Violet gazed into her lap. Kapps closed his eyes. Prue stared at her empty glass.

'So there we are,' said Prue. It was not clear if she was addressing the glass or the occupants of the room.

'Zunker, would you like to come and have dinner with me one day next week?' Violet asked. 'You too, Prue.'

'I accept,' said Prue, and hiccupped.

'I accept,' said Kapps, and bowed.

~

A couple of days later, at lunchtime, a young man appeared in Kapps' drapery shop in Drury Lane.

'I've come about the job,' he said. 'Is Mr Kapps here?'

'What job?' said the even younger man behind the counter, whose name was Danny.

'It's advertised in the newspaper. Here, I've got it somewhere.' The young man delved into his pocket and pulled out a tiny piece of crumpled newspaper and held it out.

Danny squinted at the paper. 'I can't read. What does it say?'

'It says,' said the stranger, "Assistant wanted at Kapps' drapery shop, Drury Lane, to fill unexpected vacancy. Start immediately. No experience necessary".'

He shoved the piece of paper back into his pocket and

grinned at Danny, who looked distinctly put out.

'But that's me. I'm his assistant. I . . .' Danny ran a hand through his hair.

'Are you? Oh. Whoops-a-daisy, have I gorn and put me foot in it?' The newcomer did a little tap dance and then he said, 'Sorry about that, mate. Is he in?'

'He didn't say nothing to me about an advertisement.'

'Well he wouldn't, would he, if you think about it. Tell you what, I'll come back when Mr Kapps is around.'

'Now look here, I don't know what all this is about.' Danny emerged from behind the counter. He was looking gratifyingly agitated.

'Just tell Mr Kapps I'll be back later.' The young man turned to leave and stopped in the doorway. 'And you can say to him Mrs Graham sent me. Mrs Violet Graham. Got that?'

And he left without waiting for an answer.

~

That evening Mr Kapps watched to see Violet arrive home and ran downstairs to knock on her door.

'Mrs Graham – Violet – you are the very devil!' he said, with a broad smile.

'Really, Zunker?' she replied. 'Why, whatever have I done?'

'I never saw him in my life work so hard. Running this way and that: "What would you like me to do next Mr Kapps? Can I help you with that Mr Kapps?" He even suggested to come in early and open up. I don't know what that young man said to him but it truly put the wind into him!'

'Didn't Danny tell you what he said?'

Kapps shook his head. 'Who was he?'

Violet smiled. 'He was one of the actors. His name's Jack. He's a great practical joker, he loves this kind of thing. I asked him if he would present himself at Mr

173

Kapps' drapery shop in Drury Lane at lunchtime, when I hoped you'd be out, saying he'd come about the advertisement for the position of assistant, to fill "an unexpected vacancy".' She cocked her head to one side. 'Did he do well?'

Kapps stared at Violet for a moment, then he laughed, long and loudly. 'Well I never, Violet. I . . . Oh my dear! I would never have supposed it of you.'

'I didn't quite suppose it of me either. It was all I could think to do. We can't let people like that get away with such rotten behaviour.' She stepped aside to usher him into the room. 'Won't you come in?'

'No, no,' Kapps waved a hand dismissively. 'Thank you, I don't wish to disturb . . . I just wanted to say thank you.'

'It's my pleasure entirely. Are we even now?'

'More than, more than.'

'Good. Then let's hope Danny has got the message once and for all.' She leaned towards her neighbour and kissed him on the cheek. 'Goodnight, my friend.'

'Goodnight, my little devil.'

23: The opening of Her Majesty's Theatre

On 28 April 1897, Queen Victoria's Jubilee Year, the doors of the brand new Her Majesty's Theatre were thrown open to the cream of London society, including, as guest of honour, Edward Prince of Wales, the heir to the throne. It was the event of the year.

Herbert Tree's new four-storey palace was decked out in the style of the seventeenth century French court at Versailles, all gilt, mirrors and mahogany, and portraits of the actor himself in costume and character everywhere you looked. The vast auditorium contained seating on four levels, with scarlet velvet upholstery for the stalls and wooden benches for the pit, tiered boxes flanked by Corinthian columns, a sixty-foot flat stage, and murals of semi-naked women in classical dress on every wall. All of it was lit by gilded electric lights and a vast chandelier suspended from the domed ceiling.

Violet had raided the Haymarket Theatre's costume department for the event and was decked out in a deep blue satin dress, with short puffed sleeves, a scooped neckline edged in pale blue lace and so tightly corseted she could only speak in short sentences. (She had had to seek assistance from the elderly lady in the costume department in order to hook herself up.) Her hair was dressed plainly, smoothed close to the head at the front and twirled into a bun at the nape of her neck, held in place by a diamante clasp. She had forgotten what sheer torture a society lady was expected to put herself through in order to appear presentable.

The competition among the ladies in the foyer was ferocious. She was aware of being scrutinised from head to toe, quite blatantly and through lorgnettes, by some of the more matronly patrons, with especial attention paid to the diamante clasp – no doubt to ascertain whether or not it was the real thing. She had invited Mr Kapps to accompany her, and he spent the entire evening gazing around him in amazement and pronouncing, 'Oh my dear,' at regular intervals.

The evening began with the recital on stage of a poem, written especially for the occasion and delivered rather nervously by Maud Tree attired as a lady of the court of King Louis the Fifteenth. This was followed by a lengthy rendition of the National Anthem, sung by the renowned soloist Clara Butt and the Queen's Hall Choral Society accompanied by a full orchestra, after which Edward, Prince of Wales, made his appearance in the royal box, to thunderous applause. Sandwiched amid all the pomp and ceremony was a rather forgettable American play called *The Seats of the Mighty*, featuring an oddly uncomfortable-looking Herbert Tree. The performance was followed by a heartfelt speech on stage from Tree, hanging onto the curtain for support, and ended up with a lavish party held above the theatre in the newly-created ballroom in what was known as the Dome.

Kapps did not accompany Violet to the after-show party. 'It has been the most splendid evening,' he said, as he bade her goodbye. 'I will never forget it. Now I will leave you to enjoy your friends.'

So there she was, in the grandeur of Tree's sumptuous ballroom, standing alone and drinking in every detail.

Violet was aware of being present at what posterity would no doubt consider a milestone in the history of London's theatre: the opening of the grandest, the most extravagant (ridiculously so if one came to think about it), the most outlandishly-designed building in the whole of London. She was here among the so-called cream of society, politics and art, many of whom were edging towards the tall figure of the King-in-waiting who in the company of Mr and Mrs Tree was circulating slowly around the room, nodding here, kissing hands there, smiling genially, what a handsome man. Aware suddenly of her conspicuous aloneness Violet sought the company of a familiar face and spotted Archie and his wife. She was introduced to Mrs Archie, a buxom soul 'with a mouth like a fishwife', as her husband described her, who found the whole event a hoot and was laughing loudest at the ladies with lorgnettes.

After a while the Chief appeared again, this time accompanied by a tall young man with fair hair and spectacles, whom he introduced to Violet as 'Algernon Lightly'. Mr Lightly smiled and bowed, while Tree whispered in Violet's ear, 'He's a critic, so please be *terribly nice* to him.' Then turning to Lightly he said, 'This is Mrs Graham, my clever and mysterious right-hand woman. She can tell you everything about anything.' Then he winked at Violet and left.

'So, Mr Lightly,' said Violet. 'What would you like to know?' And before he could reply she added, 'Is your name really Algernon Lightly?'

'Gracious no, it's just an affectation. I wear several hats, Mrs Graham. Lightly is my theatrical name, but you can call me Mr Robinson. Robbie for short.'

'I prefer Algernon Lightly. So tell me Mr Lightly, what did you think of the play?'

Lightly pinched his nose and made a strangled noise. 'To be honest,' he said, 'it was the least impressive part of a very impressive evening.'

'And shall you give it a bad review?'

'Not if I can help it. I will review the magnificent building, and the spectacular event, and the extraordinary achievements of Mr Tree and his company, and with a bit of luck there won't be much room left to talk about the play.'

'That's kind of you,' Violet said.

'I am a terrible critic,' he said. 'I don't like to cause offence, you see, like GBS. I prefer people to like me. And that's not the proper way of a critic.'

'GBS?'

'George Bernard Shaw. He is the scourge of actors, and actor managers in particular. They are terrified of him. That's what it means to be a proper critic, Mrs Graham, you say what you think, and the devil take the consequences. I see you have finished your drink. May I fetch you another?'

'Thank you,' said Violet, as she handed him her glass.

She watched as he weaved his way through the throng in search of a waiter. He moved lightly, in keeping with his name, like a dancer, two-stepping his way through the people and here and there swivelling sideways and lifting up onto his toes to squeeze between the voluminous skirts. It was quite a performance, and by the time he arrived back at her side holding two wine glasses aloft Violet was laughing.

'What is the joke, pray?' he enquired, handing her one of them.

'Were you ever a dancer?' she asked.

'No, I don't believe I was. It's one of the few occupations I have never tried. Why, do you think I'd make a good one?' He struck a pose on one leg and nearly overbalanced, spilling some of his drink.

'Perhaps not,' Violet laughed.

Lightly went on to ask Violet about herself and how she came to be working for 'the Great Tree'. She gave him a brief account of how she had 'fallen into' a job as assistant to the acting manager, despite her total lack of experience of work of any kind, and how she progressed from company dogsbody to company sergeant major. And latterly, as a result of a very pleasant lunch with the Great Tree during which they shared similar thoughts on plays and playwrights, she had been given the task of reading some of the unsolicited plays that arrived every day on his desk.

At this Lightly confessed he had himself submitted a play quite recently, under another name of course, and anonymously as far as Tree was concerned. He had received a delightful rejection letter from the Great Tree, explaining that while he enjoyed reading it immensely, he regretfully had to turn it down because of casting problems. 'It featured a parrot who quoted from Sophocles, you see,' said Lightly. To their joint delight, Violet then told him how she had read the play and had set it aside particularly for Tree to read, knowing it would appeal to him.

'And he has no idea you were the writer?' she asked.

'None at all. Nor will he. I may have another go another time,' said Lightly.

Lightly was, by his own description, a 'hack' who loved the theatre, which was why he became, among other things, a theatre reviewer. He worked for a newspaper called *The Weekly Chronicle*, covering a number of subjects under different by-lines. 'I am many people,' he said with a smile.

'As are we all,' Violet agreed, and laughed.

It was at this point, in mid-laugh, that Violet broke off suddenly and said: 'I'm so sorry, I have to go.'

'Oh. Why so soon?'

'Goodbye, Mr Lightly. It was a pleasure.'

And, like Cinderella, she was gone.

~

She arrived home in a state of high anxiety. All the wonderful memories of this historic evening had vanished before that glimpse across the room of the familiar figure of her estranged husband. She did not look twice. One glance was enough to send her into a near-frenzy. She felt quite sick.

She didn't think he'd noticed her, he seemed too engrossed in conversation, and the shock of seeing him put everything from her mind except escape. Now she kicked herself for not hanging on long enough to see who he was talking to. Yet why should she care? Why should she be interested in what her estranged husband was up to, and with whom?

Dammit.

And why did she feel so wrecked? It made no sense. Sometimes, she thought, there are things buried so deep inside us we don't realise they are there.

She remembered she'd been rude, excessively so. She'd been enjoying such stimulating conversation with . . . why, she was in such a state she could not even remember his name. Lightly. Algernon Lightly. What must he have thought of her?

With great difficulty, and without the aid of the helpful lady from costumes, she released herself from her dress and her corset and took her first full breath of the evening. 'Breathe,' she told herself. 'Just breathe. You are not dead.'

But she didn't sleep much that night.

The following morning at her desk she received delivery of a bouquet of wild flowers. Tucked into the middle of it was a tiny china shoe, and a note that read: 'I hope you didn't turn into a pumpkin. It was such a pleasure to meet you last night. I will be along in due course to see if the slipper fits. Your Prince trying-to-be-charming, Algie Lightly.'

It lifted her mood for a moment. But still she found it so hard to concentrate she told Frank she was feeling unwell and went home and straight to bed, where she slept for twelve hours.

24: Lolly Mulligan tells all

When a few days later Violet arrived home from work and discovered Lolly sprawled on her sofa she was only momentarily disconcerted.

She jumped to her feet as Violet entered. 'Your landlady let me in,' she said breathlessly. 'I told her you were expecting me. I'm sorry and you can throw me out right away if you want to.' She was barefoot, and barelegged, her skirt reaching only just below the knee. Shoeless and stockingless, she looked more like an urchin than ever.

Violet removed her hat and cape. 'You've come to stay the night, I presume. Or two,' she said.

Lolly nodded. 'I'll do anything you want me to. I'll clean and wash things. I'll do recitations if you like. Just don't ask me to cook.'

'I won't. And you don't need to do anything.'

Violet sat down and gestured for Lolly to do likewise.

'So, tell me.'

'Tell you what?'

'Why are you here? What does "no fixed abode" mean, precisely?'

'It means I don't have anywhere else to go,' said Lolly.

'I understand that. But why? You have parents, haven't you?'

Lolly nodded.

'So why aren't you living with them, like most normal people? Or do they live somewhere ridiculous, like Scotland, for instance?'

Lolly shook her head miserably. 'They live in London. But they don't always want me there.'

'Why not?'

'Because . . .' Lolly, curled up on the sofa with her legs beneath her, squirmed. 'I say, would you happen to have any alcohol in the place?'

'Alcohol? Yes, I do. I have a bottle of wine. It was a gift.' Violet got to her feet and fetched a bottle from a cupboard. She peered at the label. 'I think it's quite a good vintage, I'm not very knowledgeable about these things.'

'A gift from who?'

'Er, I don't remember.'

'Are you sure?' Lolly wrinkled her nose and Violet had to stop herself from laughing.

It was very hard to be angry with someone like Lolly, though a bit of Violet resented the fact that she got away with the little girl act. Nonetheless, if alcohol would loosen her tongue then so be it. She poured the wine and handed her a glass.

'You are now drinking some very expensive wine, which was a gift from Herbert,' said Violet, as she resumed her seat. 'There, I've told you. Now it's your turn.'

Lolly sat up on her knees. 'Did you have an affair with Herbert?' she asked eagerly.

'No, I did not. It was a thank you, for reading his scripts. And stop changing the subject. Did you?'

'Of course. I thought everyone had an affair with Herbert.'

'Don't be ridiculous. Why would they?'

Lolly settled down into the sofa again and took a swig of her drink. 'Did you know he has three illegitimate sons?

By another woman? And Maud knows all about it?'

'No, I did not.'

'Poor Herbert. He can't help himself.'

'Poor Maud,' said Violet.

'It's funny,' said Lolly. 'You sleep with a director so you can get a job and his wife finds out and won't let him give you the job.' She heaved a sigh. 'Sometimes you just can't win.'

'Go on.'

'That's it really.' Lolly took another drink and then she removed her legs from beneath her and stretched them out in front of her. Her toenails, Violet noticed, were painted bright orange.

'That's it? You had an affair with Herbert and that's it?'

'Yes. Well, yes and no.'

She was twirling her orange-painted feet in the air. Suddenly Violet stood up, snatched Lolly's glass from her hand and said, 'I think it's time you went home.'

'What?' Lolly was genuinely frightened. She lowered her feet to the floor and stood up slowly. 'All right,' she said, in a tiny voice. 'I'm sorry I get on your nerves, Vi. I don't mean to.'

'You don't have to tell me everything, Lolly. It isn't my business. But it's . . .' she struggled for the word. What she really wanted was to give Lolly a hug, and it took all her resistance not to. 'I'm honestly not trying to pry into your life. Well, maybe I am. Out of genuine concern for you. Do you get that?'

Lolly nodded. She was pouting, like a small child about to burst into tears.

'All right,' she said at last. 'Though I don't know why you want to know.'

She sat down again, on her hands this time. Violet placed Lolly's glass back down on the table beside her.

'I have affairs with men,' said Lolly. 'Married men. I

like them when they're married, they don't hang around afterwards, you know, bothering you and telling you what to do. The trouble is,' she removed one hand from beneath her and scratched her nose, 'not everyone sees it that way. Especially the wives.' She replaced her hand underneath her again and swung her legs up and down. 'And the point is, I'm not a threat,' she went on in a rush. 'Honestly not. I'm not a husband stealer, I just like to borrow them from time to time.' She took a sip of her drink. Violet smiled, despite herself.

'But why do you do it Lolly, when you know it upsets people?'

'Because,' she waved her glass in the air, 'it's better than doing stock in the provinces.'

'Doing what?'

'You don't know about the stock companies? They're hell on earth. They promise you the earth, and then they don't pay you. They're crooks. I've known actors who've nearly starved to death when the manager walks off with the takings.' Violet thought fleetingly of Shuffles. 'I didn't want to have to go through all that. And my parents hate me being an actress in the first place.'

'Why?'

'They think it's the same thing as whoring, which it isn't. But there's no telling them that.'

'So you decided to prove them right.'

'I thought, if you have to sleep with men to get an engagement it's better than starving in a gutter somewhere like Scunthorpe.' Lolly took another large mouthful of wine. 'Not that I've ever been to Scunthorpe.'

'Is it,' Violet began, 'and forgive me if I sound naïve, but is it really necessary to sleep with men to further your career?'

Lolly waved her head back and forth. 'It's what I was told. It was that or touring the provinces, and, well – what

185

would you do?'

'This isn't about me,' said Violet.

'You start out that way and then you get to enjoy it. It's how I got my first job. Then it gets to the point where the word gets around that you're "available". And they expect it.'

'They?'

'The ones who, you know, hold the power.' She took another mouthful of wine. 'It's not my fault, really it isn't. Just because society says this and says that, but men do it all the time! And the higher up they are the more they get away with it. Just look at the Prince of Wales!' She made a face, before adding, 'My parents don't see things my way.'

'I'm not surprised.'

'So they throw me out. Regularly. "Out you go, you little slut", they say.'

'They call you a slut?'

'More or less. "Out you go, and we never want to see you again." They don't mean it, of course. Well, they do at the time. They're hoping I will "see the error of my ways". Until the next time.'

A few moments passed. Lolly was still swinging her legs.

'At the risk of sounding like a prude,' Violet began.

'Which you are,' said Lolly.

Violet inclined her head in acknowledgment. 'I don't see why someone like you, who is genuinely talented, has to cheapen herself in such a way. I can't help thinking it's not doing your career any good. Can't you lay off for a bit?'

'I don't know that I can. I think,' said Lolly portentously, 'I cannot live without it.'

'You sound proud of it.'

'Herbert would never employ me.'

'There are others.'

'His wife hates me. And the funny thing is,' Lolly began to laugh, 'she can't act to save her life.'

'Who, Maud Tree?'

'They have the most dreadful rows, when he refuses to give her the parts she wants. He knows talent when he sees it.'

'That's a cruel thing to say.'

'It's a cruel thing to do. Not to cast your own wife in the lead part, just because she's your wife. But I admire him for it. There are not that many people with that sort of integrity.'

'You amaze me, Lolly,' said Violet, and she meant it. 'But thank you for telling me your story.'

'Once a slut, always a slut. And now . . .' Lolly turned to look directly at Violet, 'how about you? Come on, it's your turn.' She took her hands from under her and leant back in the sofa. 'Shoot.' She fired an imaginary pistol at Violet.

'Nothing to say,' said Violet.

Lolly leapt to her feet and in a horribly accurate impression of Violet she said: 'Now I won't have it! I will not have you shilly-shallying and avoiding my question. You don't have to tell me everything, Violet, it's none of my business, I am just concerned for you, that's all.'

Violet smiled. 'Point taken. The fact is, there hasn't been anyone since I left my husband.'

'I don't believe you.'

'Well, it's true. Except . . .'

'Except?' Lolly sat upright.

Violet didn't want to talk about Algernon Lightly. Why, there was nothing to say, not really. She hadn't seen him since the opening-night party and while, yes, he had been good company, and attractive in a way; and after sending her that charming bouquet he had apparently called round at the theatre a couple of times looking for

her; and it made no sense at all maybe, but thinking of him
reminded her of Anthony – just that glimpse of his head
across the room, and she couldn't help but connect the
two.

In the end she really only mentioned him to satisfy
Lolly.

'There was someone,' said Violet. 'We met at the
opening night party at Her Majesty's. He was fun to talk
to, and quite attractive in a way.'

'And?'

'I had to leave rather suddenly, and I think he was a bit
put out.'

'Why did you have to leave suddenly?'

'Because I spotted my estranged husband across the
room and I thought I was about to be sick.'

'Oh?' Lolly's eyes opened wide. 'And then what?'

'And then nothing. I haven't seen him since.'

'Well, we'll have to do something about that!' Lolly
jumped up again. 'What's his name, and where does he
live, and what does he do, and how do we track him
down?'

Violet laughed. 'No, Lolly,' she said. 'Please no.'

'You may as well tell me now, otherwise I will just
have to ask around and someone else will.' She was
dancing around the room now. She did a twirl, and then
came to a halt in front of Violet. 'Is he an actor?'

'No.'

'Writer? Director?'

'No, he's none of those things. He's a critic.'

'A critic.' Lolly clapped her hands together. 'The sperm
of the devil!'

'Lolly!'

'That's what Herbert calls them. Not in public, of
course. Well, that narrows the field. It isn't GBS himself, is
it?'

'Of course not.'

'Harry Walbrook?'

Violet shook her head. 'It's no use, you won't know him. And even if you did, he goes by different names.' Like herself, she thought.

'Different names?' Lolly ceased capering and stood with her hands on her hips. 'Hmm, the puzzle deepens.' She placed a finger on her lips. 'I will hunt him down, you watch me.'

A little later they ate a simple supper together of bread with cheese and cold meats, and Violet fetched some sheets and blankets and made up the sofa into a bed, into which Lolly snuggled, fully dressed, and was asleep in an instant. Lying there, dishevelled and snoring, she looked about ten years old. A ten-year-old slut, thought Violet fondly.

And yet in some ways this woman-child knew more of the world than Violet could possibly imagine. More precisely, she knew men, in the biblical sense, and she enjoyed them – that was what Violet found so hard to comprehend. Perhaps not every man was like Anthony.

There are more things in heaven and earth than I have ever dreamed of in my philosophy, was Violet's final thought before she too fell into a deep sleep.

25: The magic of theatre

With the opening of Her Majesty's Theatre Violet's office had moved from Panton Street into the theatre building itself. It was now only a few steps from her desk to the back of the gallery, so at quiet moments she would sneak into the auditorium to watch rehearsals.

One afternoon she was seated in the front row of the gallery during a rehearsal for *Julius Caesar* when the figure of Herbert Tree loomed out of the darkness and sat down next to her. He remained silent for several moments, staring at the stage, and then he began to mumble.

'I beg your pardon?' said Violet.

'I can't hear a word they're saying,' he muttered. 'Can you hear a word they're saying?'

'Not all of it, no.'

And then, so suddenly he almost had Violet leaping out of her seat, Tree stood up and bellowed, 'Speak up! We can't hear you up here!'

The actors on stage froze and stared out at the darkened auditorium.

'I didn't spend a king's ransom on the acoustics in this theatre so only half the audience could hear you!' he roared, and sat down again.

To Violet he said, 'If they can't be heard in the gallery there's no point in any of it.'

Then, as the actors resumed their scene, 'Louder!'

yelled Tree. 'Play to the gods, for God's sake!' He chortled at his witticism.

Rehearsals with Tree were highly entertaining, for the spectator if not for the actors. He was a tough task-master. He gave his actors free rein but if he didn't like what they were doing he would go over and over a scene until he was satisfied and they were almost on their knees. Yet it was all done, for the most part, in good humour. Tree's energy and enthusiasm was infectious. He gave one hundred per cent to everything he did and he expected everyone around him to do the same.

'Getting on all right, are you?' he muttered to Violet.

'What? Oh, yes, thank you.'

'I'm not overworking you, am I? Of course I am. But you can cope. You're a coper, aren't you, Mrs Graham? Violet?'

'I like to think I am, yes.'

He reached across and squeezed her hand. 'Very good to see you, dear girl,' he said, as he got to his feet. He tugged at his waistcoat. 'And now it's my turn.'

He had given himself the part of Mark Anthony, the 'actor's' part, as he described it. His delivery of Shakespeare's verse was idiosyncratic. Often jerky, rarely melodious, he would pause at unexpected moments in the middle of a speech. And it seemed to Violet as she watched him that he was far from the spontaneous performer he liked to pretend he was. He had obviously worked on scenes beforehand, he knew precisely where he intended to stand, where and when he would move and at what point he would turn to the audience and address them directly.

'Friends, Romans, countrymen! Lend me your ears.'

He had positioned himself upstage, on a rostrum (what later would become the plinth on which the statue of Caesar had once stood). With all the time in the world he stepped down from the rostrum and strolled to the front of the stage.

'I come to bury Caesar, not to praise him,' he began almost conversationally, his voice soft yet distinct, articulating every consonant. As he spoke his eyes roved across the rows of the imaginary audience, as if he were addressing each one of them personally. When it came to

> *'The noble Brutus*
> *Hath told you Caesar was ambitious:*
> *If it were so, it was a grievous fault,*
> *And grievously hath Caesar answer'd it'*

He strolled first to one side of the stage and then the other, still speaking as quietly as he dared allow himself. But as the speech progressed, so his voice, which in general conversation was light, even feminine, gradually crescendoed so by the time he was repeating the line for the fourth time he was effectively shouting:

> *'Yet Brutus says he was ambitious;*
> *And, sure, he is an honourable man.*
> *I speak not to disprove what Brutus spoke,*
> *But here I am to speak what I do know.'*

Here he paused, dramatically, still staring out over the auditorium. The end of the speech was directed firmly at the gallery:

> *'Bear with me;'* he roared, choking back the
> tears.
> *'My heart is in the coffin there with Caesar,*
> *And I must pause till it come back to me.'*

It was a bizarre display, thought Violet. Totally lacking in lyricism yet heavy on emotion, or what some people might describe as histrionics. And always utterly watchable.

"Not all good actors are watchable. Not all watchable actors are good." As some wise soul had once said.

It was quite wrong to say Tree was not a good actor. He

was. He knew exactly what he was doing. He understood Anthony through and through. He had the ability to get inside a character and make that character leap across the footlights to the audience. If what he did today he did not do tomorrow (he hated to repeat himself), and his interpretation in rehearsal differed from the first night, and every subsequent night, that was all part of his unpredictable, mercurial, altogether mischievous nature. His genius, you could say.

~

As Violet was passing through the wings of the theatre on her way home one evening she saw Tree standing stock still in the middle of the stage.

'Who's there?' he called, without turning his head.

'It's me, Violet Graham.'

'My dear Violet.' He strode over to her and held out a hand. 'Come here.' He drew her towards him and together they stood centre stage staring out at the auditorium.

'This,' he said, 'is what they call the point of command.' He was still holding her hand. 'Here is where you have the audience in your palm, all two thousand of them. How does it feel?'

'Terrifying,' said Violet.

'It's little wonder an actor loses his sense of proportion,' said Tree. 'Where else, other than the Coliseum of Rome, or an ancient Greek amphitheatre, does a mere mortal have two thousand pairs of eyes and ears trained only on him? Or her,' he added.

Violet nodded. If it terrified her to gaze out over an empty auditorium how must it feel when the place was full? It was unimaginable.

'Here,' said Tree, as he pulled her to the very edge of the stage, 'is where Hamlet delivers his soliloquies. Or here.' He dragged her to the other side. 'As close to the audience as he can, so he can get them on his side.

Shakespeare was not an actor for nothing. And right here,'
now he pulled her to the centre, 'is where during a
performance of King John, as I recall it,' he let go of her
hand and dropped to his knees, 'is where I knelt down
and addressed the fellow in the front row who was
reading a newspaper. "Who won the two thirty?" I asked
him. It brought the house down, as they say.' He chuckled,
stood up again and turned to look at her. 'You are
shocked.'

'I suppose I am. It seems so irreverent.' Violet wasn't
sure whether to be appalled or amused.

'I would say it is irreverent for a man to sit in the front
row of the stalls and read the newspaper,' said Tree. 'He
could have had the decency to position himself in the back
of the gallery if he wanted to catch up on the racing
results.' He looked out over the auditorium again. 'It is all
a game, you know. The audience understands that.
Sometimes,' he carried on without pausing for breath, 'I
like to take my fellow actors by surprise, for example . . .'
With sudden alacrity he bounded upstage, circled around
and appeared at Violet's shoulder, 'by appearing from a
direction they are not expecting, to catch them out.' He
chortled again.

'You play games on stage?' Violet tried and failed to
keep the outrage from her voice.

'Sometimes you can look at your fellow actor and he's
gone into a kind of trance. He's saying the words and
going through the motions but he isn't *there*. I like my
fellow performers to be flesh and blood, and present. If
they need a shock to bring them alive then I'll give them
one.' He looked at her and raised an eyebrow. 'You
disapprove, I can see.'

'I suppose you have to be an actor to understand,' said
Violet.

It was this strange mixture of illusion and reality that

Violet found hard to comprehend. That an actor could slip in and out of character at the drop of a hat without destroying the whole flow and atmosphere of the play, or the audience's concentration.

'It's trickery,' said Tree. 'The younger generation may not think so, but when one is young one takes everything very seriously. There are some actors who refuse to work with me.'

'I'm not surprised,' said Violet.

'The audience likes nothing better than to see something go wrong,' he ploughed on. It appeared he was not in the least put out by her remark. 'It reminds us we are all in this together and anything can happen and probably will.'

Violet was suddenly reminded of something Prue had told her. 'Like Mrs Pat's skirt, do you mean?'

Tree roared with laughter. 'A perfect example. Handled like a total professional! As Mrs Pat is of course, when she chooses to be.'

The little dig did not go unnoticed.

'You should try it, Violet,' said Tree.

'Try what?' said Violet, with alarm.

Tree made a wide gesture at the auditorium. 'Talk to them, see what it does. Go on. There's nobody there. Say something.' He gestured her to centre stage and stood back and watched her with his arms folded.

'Say anything,' he prompted.

After a moment she began to speak, quietly.

> *'All the world's a stage,*
> *And all the men and women merely players.*
> *They have their exits and their entrances,*
> *And one man in his time plays many parts.'*

She stopped.

'Not bad,' said Tree. 'Of course no one but the front row of the stalls would have any idea what you were talking about. But could you feel the power?'

'*One man in his time plays many parts,*' Violet thought to herself That's me, right there.

'With a bit of coaching we could make an Ellen Terry of you yet.'

'I doubt it.' Violet smiled. Shakespeare had it in a nutshell. You don't have to be an actor to play many parts.

She stayed where she was, still looking out over the vast expanse of emptiness, for some time. When at last she turned to look for Tree he was gone.

26: Dinner with Mr Kapps

M r Kapps was on expansive form. He was entertaining his guests with the story of the overnight transformation of his assistant from devious layabout to fledgling entrepreneur, and all thanks to the charade set up by none other than Violet herself.

'It was a bad shock for him,' he told her. 'His little joke got out of the hand I think. He was already ashamed. And then afterwards, when he thought he would lose his job, he was crying.'

'Oh dear, I never meant for that to happen.' said Violet.

'So I sat him down, and I gave to him a talk. I said he had a choice. He could find himself another position, or he could work hard and one day take over the business from me. He could be my pretended son.'

'That was quite an offer.'

'He was not persuaded by that. So then I told him how it is to own a business, how it is possible even for a person like himself, and then to pass to his son and so on. I told him how my father took the business from his father, and his father from his father, and so on.'

'Until it got to you,' said Violet.

Kapps took a sip of his drink and thought for a moment. 'There is a story,' he said.

'Do tell,' said Lolly.

And so, his halting way, Kapps related the history of

his childhood. How his mother left home when he was three years old and was never seen, or spoken of, again; nobody knew where she went and as far as he knew no one tried to find her. He and his father moved into his aunt's house and he spent his childhood there with her three children, his cousins. Over time his father changed from what his aunt told him had been a generous, genial and loving man into a surly tyrant, who never smiled, who only spoke when necessary, who worked a twelve-hour day, who beat his son regularly and showed no sign of humanity or kindness to anyone. He, Kapps, went along with it for the first forty years of his life until - 'Suddenly I woke up. Voom! As if out of a dream, or a nightmare. And I thought, this is the rest of your life, if you do nothing. You must go, get out, now! And so I did.'

He gazed into the middle distance for a moment before continuing.

'To England, I came. For no reason except it was not Austria, and it was far away. I did not say goodbye. I did not hear again from my father. My cousins tells me he does not mention me. Poor man. Twice in his life, first his wife, now his son, they walk away from him. Twice in his life he has lost his only close people.'

'By the sounds of it he asked for it,' said Lolly. Then: 'Didn't you ever want to get married, Hans?'

Kapps didn't reply for a moment.

'I am sorry, what did you say?'

'You must have had a lady friend, didn't you?' Lolly tilted her head. 'You know, a lover, an *amoureuse.*'

Kapps smiled. 'Yes, of course. But nobody could bear to stand my father. They were terrified. He had a big temper.'

'So you could say,' Lolly went on, 'your father had a lot to answer for. A man who beats his son, and is cruel to everyone, and then drives all his son's lady friends away.'

She pouted. 'How can you say you're sorry for him?'

'Of course. A father is always a father. I will always have guilt.' Kapps shifted in his chair. 'So this I tell to Danny, more or less, not the detail. I tell him how a family business goes from father to son. And as I do not have a son, then . . .' he shrugged. 'If he played his cards, he could make much money, more than me, because he has a spark and I do not. He has a good future ahead, if he wants it. And all this,' he turned to Violet, 'I owe to you.'

Violet was quite taken aback. 'I'm delighted to hear it Zunker, though I can't pretend to be responsible. I just wanted to teach that cocky little upstart a lesson.'

'But what about since you arrived here, Hans?' Lolly wasn't going to let this one go. 'There must have been lady friends, haven't there?'

Kapps shook his head.

'I mean, you are not a bad-looking cove, I could quite go for you myself if you were twenty years younger.'

Kapps laughed. 'And if I were twenty years younger I would not know which one of you to make love to first,' he said. Then he added, nervously, 'There, you see, I say the wrong thing. Again. Now I have offended you. What is the word? Appropriate. I can never find the appropriate word to say.' He turned to gaze glumly into the fireplace.

'Hans,' Lolly stood up and went to give him a hug. 'I love you, Hans. I truly do. I love you for your inappropriateness. And for the funny words you come out with.' Then, to Violet she said, 'We should set him up with someone.' She resumed her seat and then jumped up again. 'How about Dorothy?'

There was a stunned silence, and then Lolly, and to a lesser extent Violet, burst into laughter.

The invitation to dinner had been relayed to Violet earlier that evening by Lolly, who had clearly arranged the whole thing herself. There was a twinkle in her eye that suggested mischief, which may or may not have had something to do with Kapps, or something else.

Kapps took out his watch. 'We will eat soon. Are you hungry?'

'We'll give it a few more minutes, shall we?' said Lolly.

Violet looked from one to the other. 'What's going on?' she said.

'Nothing,' said Lolly.

'You will see,' said Kapps. He was drumming his fingers on the arm of his chair. Then he collected himself and to Violet he said, politely, 'So how is the world of the theatre, and the great Mr Tree?'

'Well, as it happens . . .' Violet began.

There came a sudden knock on the door. Lolly jumped up to open it and there, with a 'Sorry I'm late', was Algernon Lightly.

'Robbie, at last.' Lolly gave him a hug. 'Come in! We were just about to talk about you.'

'Oh, good,' said Robbie. 'I do love to be talked about. Good evening, Mrs Graham.' He bowed to her and smiled.

'You know each other, I think,' said Lolly, with a coy cock of the head.

'Good evening, er, Mr Lightly.'

'This is Mr Kapps, our host,' Lolly explained. 'He has several names as well. I call him Hans, Vi calls him Zinker. You can call him what you like.'

'I answer to all names,' agreed Kapps, getting to his feet and shaking Robbie's hand.

'I am the only one in the room who is one person,' said Lolly.

'Oh?' Algie looked from Lolly to Violet and Violet flushed. 'Of course, Mrs Graham is also Cinderella.' He beamed at her. 'And the prince has had a right old time tracking her down.'

Violet cleared her throat. 'It's good to see you again, Mr

Lightly.'

'You too, Mrs Graham.'

There was a slight pause.

'Let's eat, Hans. I am starving.' Lolly grabbed hold of Kapps' hand and gave him a push towards the kitchen cubicle. Then she pulled out a side table and began to arrange four chairs around it.

Algie looked at Violet and Violet studied the carpet.

'Was it something I said?' he asked, *sotto voce.*

She looked up and gave him her gentlest smile. 'No,' she said. 'It was nothing to do with you.'

And that, it appeared, was all she had to say on the matter. For the time being.

~

It was a very convivial evening. Kapps told amusing stories about his customers while privately worrying whether or not he'd put too much salt in the dumplings. Lolly related, or rather enacted, her latest (unsuccessful) attempt to seduce a producer - 'Lordy Lordy, I did everything except expose my breasts to him!' – before she realised he played for the other side, as she put it. 'I can usually spot 'em a mile off, but now and again . . .' she shook her head sorrowfully. Violet described how Herbert Tree had stood her on stage at Her Majesty's Theatre and made her address an imaginary audience, which she found both terrifying and thrilling. Lightly/Robbie described his day reporting the goings-on in Parliament – with his serious hat on, as he described it – which included a debate on the female suffrage movement. This led to a heated discussion around the table of the pros and cons of the movement, which had now fragmented into so many different groups, all with different names and with different aims, that it was hard to keep tabs on who was who or what was what.

'What's your view, Robbie?' Lolly demanded, with her

mouth full.

'On women's suffrage? I am a journalist,' said Robbie, 'I don't have views.'

Lolly gave him a sharp slap on the arm. 'Come on now, you're a flesh and blood person too. Aren't you?' She pinched his arm and he jumped.

'The arguments against it are getting increasingly desperate, you could say,' he said.

'That's not answering the question.'

'Isn't it more important to know what our politicians are saying than the paltry opinion of a jobbing reporter?'

'Not in this case, no.'

'Well then.' Robbie toyed with his wine glass. 'I can see no argument against it. Unfortunately.'

'Unfortunately?'

'I am afraid that giving women the vote will expose the manifold weaknesses of what is supposed to be the stronger sex.'

'That's very Oscar Wilde of you,' said Violet.

'It's like allowing women into a gentleman's club. The reason they are exclusively gentlemen's clubs in the first place is because they permit the so-called stronger sex to behave like the children we really are. If we let the women in the secret would be out.'

'Do you really think we are that ignorant?' Violet raised an eyebrow.

'No, quite the opposite. Personally speaking if I were a woman I wouldn't want to go anywhere near a gentleman's club. You are better off without them, just as you could say you are better off without the vote.'

There was a heady silence.

'You should be very careful what you say here, Robbie.'

'I know. But you're the one who asked the question, Lolly.' Algie/Robbie lifted his glass. 'Here's to women's franchise,' he said. 'It's only a matter of time.'

And so the conversation moved on to more everyday matters. Violet asked Algie if he'd ever seen Lolly perform on stage (he hadn't) and did he know how talented she was (he didn't). And what a shame she wasn't constantly working alongside the greats, like Ellen Terry or even Maud Tree (Lolly snorted loudly at this). Then between them Algie and Violet concocted a wild idea that Robbie the writer would write a play with Lolly in the central role, playing any kind of character she liked – 'Nell Gwynn!' she said immediately – Violet would produce it and Kapps would provide the costumes. They would hire a theatre and invite everybody who was anybody to the first night, including and especially Herbert Tree (but not Maud, said Lolly). Algie under his critic's name would give it a glowing review, and Lolly would be the toast of the town and would never have to seduce a producer again.

'I might just miss that.' Lolly stuck out her lower lip.

As the evening progressed, behind the scenes as it were Kapps, having been reassured about the salt level in his dumplings, was able to sit back and observe his guests and to marvel that such beautiful, lively and intelligent young people should have chosen to adorn his makeshift dining table; and to ponder on which of the two lovely young women had the eye of the young man and to come to no particular conclusion. Lolly meanwhile deliberated to herself whether or not Florence Nightingale, or even Elizabeth Garrett Anderson, might make a better heroine-figure in her new play, if only they were a little prettier. Violet secretly speculated on how Lolly had managed to track Algernon Lightly down, and whether or not the familiarity between them meant they had had an affair, and why she should care one way or another. And Algie spent many happy moments, when Violet was not looking directly at him, contemplating the near-perfect outline of her cheek in profile and wondering what, and how long, it would take before he was allowed to caress it.

The party broke up after midnight, and not before Algie managed to extract a promise from Violet to accompany him to the theatre the following week. And Lolly had flung her arms around an astonished Kapps, given him a smacking kiss on the cheek and said, 'Hans, you are the best, you truly are. If you weren't so old I would propose to you on the spot!'

~

And then it was just Lolly and Violet, together in Violet's living room.

Lolly yawned. 'What a wonderful evening! He is so in love with you Vi.'

'Who?'

'Don't be ridiculous. Robbie. He could not take his eyes off you all evening. Are you blind?'

'I suppose I am.' Violet sank into an armchair. The whole evening had been rather overwhelming.

'I've never seen him like it before. Robbie's always been one of those . . .' Lolly hesitated, 'enigmas. Is that the right word?' She began to undress. 'Such a handsome man, yet he never seemed to really . . .'

'To really what?'

'Don't mind me,' she said, as she stripped down to her undergarments. She wore no corset, Violet couldn't help but notice, but then there was so little of her.

Lolly unpinned her hair. 'I don't know what I'm trying to say. But he was on good form tonight, and all because of you. He can be quite melancholic, can Robbie. And before you ask,' she shrugged off a petticoat, 'no, we have not slept together. He's not married, remember?'

'I never gave it a thought,' Violet lied. 'But you've obviously met before, you seemed very chummy.'

'Oh, you know what the theatre biz is like – everyone knows everyone.' Lolly was down to a simple chemise now, in which it appeared she intended to spend the night. She paused in her undress to look directly at Violet. 'You will be kind to him, won't you?' she said, appealingly. 'He is a sensitive type, more than he lets on.'

'I will be kind to him,' said Violet. But she wondered if that was true.

27: Mrs Warren's Profession

As theatre outings go it was both less and considerably more exciting than Violet was expecting. In anticipation of a premium seat in a smart theatre – being as she was in the company of A Critic – she had dressed accordingly. But then Algie led her down a small alleyway near Leicester Square and up a narrow flight of stairs to what was really little more than a room, in which there was a makeshift stage with odd bits of furniture on it, and arranged around it fifty or so wooden chairs for the audience.

They were there by private invitation from none other than George Bernard Shaw himself, who was hosting the evening's events. He greeted Algie like a close chum, then shook Violet's hand and gazed into her eyes with disconcerting directness – not, she realised, so much for her own sake as out of curiosity about Algie's companion.

Once the audience – most of whom Algie appeared to know, consisting as it did almost entirely of theatre people – was settled, GBS took to the stage to introduce the evening. He was a striking-looking man, with vivid red hair and a ginger beard, and when he spoke he glared at each member of the assembly in turn.

'Ladies, gentlemen and others,' he began, in his strong Irish brogue. 'Thank you for attending what I can safely say will turn out to be an auspicious evening, one none of us is likely to forget, and which will provide you with enough dinner-table chitchat to last a lifetime.'

He paused, to allow his comments to sink in.

'The play you are about to see has, I am unsurprised to say, been forbidden a licence for public performance by His Eminence the Lord Chamberlain; not, I hasten to add, due to its subject matter but because the writer, who is myself, does not condemn the subject-matter.'

He then went on at some length to explain that while the duty of the censor was to uphold the *status quo* it was equally the duty of the playwright to challenge it; that rather than following in the footsteps of some of his contemporaries (unnamed), who reached a delicate hand into the darker reaches of society before quickly withdrawing it in order not to upset the delicate sensibilities of an audience, his entire *raison d'etre* was to do exactly that. He regarded the theatre as a medium for social change, he told them, the most powerful medium of all, and while the play they were about to witness was not taken directly from real life it could be regarded as a true story, told with neither decoration nor a happy ending, on a subject well enough known in polite society *but never spoken of.* And that although it dealt with sex it was not designed to titillate; that any reference to titillation was entirely in the mind of the censor, and an audience expecting anything of the kind would be much disappointed.

Finally, amidst much coughing and shuffling of feet from the addressees, he wound up his dissertation and with a flourish he announced: 'Ladies and gentlemen, I present to you *Mrs Warren's Profession.'*

~

After it was over they made their goodbyes quickly before, whispered Algie into Violet's ear, GBS had a chance to launch into another lengthy monologue. As they bade him goodbye the great man said to Algie, 'I don't want to know what you think,' before turning to Violet and adding, 'he never has a bad word to say about anything. Whereas you, young lady, now I would be more than happy to hear your views.'

'Of course,' said Violet.

'Another time, GBS. Goodbye.' Algie took hold of Violet's arm and steered her towards the door.

When they reached the street he said, 'I have taken the liberty of booking a table at a little place around the corner for a spot of supper. Are you hungry?'

'Famished,' said Violet.

'Excellent.'

He took her arm again, and as they wended their way through the alleyways behind Charing Cross Road to the tiny restaurant in another alleyway off St Martin's Lane, Algie gave Violet a running commentary on his colleague and chum, who was, he asserted, one of the most brutally honest and courageous men he had ever met.

'Unique,' he said. 'And not a romantic bone in his body.'

'I could see that,' said Violet.

As a critic he had been feared by everyone, Algie explained, so it was exceptionally foolhardy of him to expose his own work to the business end of the firing squad, so to speak.

They were in the restaurant now. It was dimly lit, with deep scarlet walls and matching tasselled lampshades. A venue for *trysts*, Violet imagined, and not the sort of establishment where the waiter placed your napkin on your lap.

'What kind of a critic are you?' she asked.

He told her he was a terrible critic – neither as cutthroat as GBS nor as clever as William Archer. Too much of an enthusiast to be sufficiently detached, and too much of a coward to upset people, especially actors.

'Or you could put it another way,' Lightly continued. 'Anyone who can stand exposed on a stage in front of thousands of people has more daring than most of us could possibly imagine.'

Violet thought back to her moment on the stage of Her Majesty's Theatre. 'That is true.'

'And who am I to criticise them?'

'Isn't that your job?' she said.

'Not as I see it,' said Lightly. Then, 'She reminded me of you,' he said.

'Who did?'

'Vivie.'

'No!'

'Spirited, clever, independent, quite the new woman.'

'And heartless.'

'Pragmatic maybe, there is a difference.'

'But what a way to treat your mother! She accepts the fact her mother made her fortune running . . .' she hesitated.

'Brothels.'

'Thank you. And then a complete change of heart, when she realises she's continuing to do so. It makes no sense!'

'I'm surprised to hear you say that.'

'Why?'

'It's clear Mrs Warren loves her work, she loves being a businesswoman and making a lot of money. I would have thought you would have understood that.'

'That's my point. *I* understand it, but Vivie, who seems to live for her work, seems not to.'

'Well, it's her upbringing that's turned her into a young lady with high standards.'

'Turned her into a little prig.'

Algie laughed.

'Does she offer to pay her mother back? If she is so offended that all her privileges have come from immoral earnings? No! She takes, she judges, she rejects her mother, the only relative she has. And she turns on the boy who loves her.' Violet shook her head. 'I really cannot think of one good thing to say about her.'

'And yet . . .'

'And not an iota of compromise. Really Mr Lightly, if you think that Vivie and I have the slightest thing in common then I am truly disappointed in you.'

'She is a genuine GBS heroine.'

'You call her a heroine?'

'Oh yes. She's just the sort of girl he has the highest regard for.'

'Well.' Violet threw her hands in the air, and gave a little laugh.

'Don't forget to eat,' said Algie.

'Yes, I'm sorry.' Violet picked up her knife and fork. The food was so-so, but then Violet's mind was not on the food particularly.

'Am I really heartless?' she said, eventually. 'Do you think I'm heartless, Mr Lightly?'

'Algie. I believe you live for your work.'

'Is that the same thing?'

'You are not what I would call a romantic.'

Violet frowned. 'I don't know why you should say such a thing. You know nothing about me.'

'No, I don't. You made it very hard for me to do so.'

She bent her head in acquiescence. 'Perhaps,' she began, and he waited. 'We do have things in common, Vivie and I. I am not a good daughter.'

'Did your mother run brothels?'

She laughed. 'No. On the contrary, she's a vicar's wife. Had she run brothels I might have taken more interest. And perhaps, without realising it, I have neglected . . .

other things in favour of my work.'

Once again he waited for her to continue.

'I owe you an apology,' she said.

'You certainly do! What for?'

'The reason I ran away, that time . . .' She stopped.

'Yes?'

'I saw my husband on the far side of the room.'

'Ah.'

'And it gave me quite a shock.'

'It would do. You thought he was dead. *I* thought he was dead.'

'I have let it be known he was dead, yes. It seemed simpler.' She was staring blankly at the tablecloth, lost in thought.

Algie called for the bill and paid it.

'Let's walk you home, shall we?'

And so they did, up Charing Cross Road and along Tottenham Court Road towards Euston. It was a mild evening, the air was soft, and there were still a few people about. Violet linked her arm in Algie's. She felt surprisingly safe, surprisingly at peace.

'It was a wonderful evening,' she said. 'What do you suppose will happen with GBS's play?'

'It will get on eventually. When the time is right. In our lifetimes maybe. Or maybe not.'

'Where would we be without hypocrisy?' She sighed. 'Playwrights would have nothing to write about.'

'From Shakespeare on. And, I suspect, forever more.'

They walked in silence for a while.

'You never really told me what you thought of the play,' said Violet.

'Well, I could safely say GBS thinks better of women than he does of men.'

'That's true.'

'And he possesses a genuine wish to bring about social

change.'

Violet nodded. 'Very worthy.'

'There is no question his heart is in the right place.'

'Does it usually take this long to get an opinion out of you?' She gave him a sideways look.

'When you have a reputation, as I do, of never saying a bad word about anything – which by the way is not strictly true . . .'

'No?'

'Sometimes it can be quite tricky. As a treatise on the plight of women I cannot fault it. As a play . . .'

He didn't finish his sentence and Violet wondered if he'd lost the thread.

'As a play?' she prompted.

'It is mould-breaking, for sure. One could pick holes: it strikes me as odd that a woman of such strict conscience such as Vivie would not have demanded to know how her mother made her fortune long ago. Then there's the question of who brought Vivie up, and where was her mother when she was most needed? And is one to feel sorry for Mrs Warren, for her self-sacrifice which is no such thing? And did neither of them consider compromise?'

'You're criticising the characters, but as a piece of performance?'

They had arrived by now at the house in Crighton Street, where Violet relinquished Algie's arm and turned to face him.

'It is thought-provoking, and didactic,' he said. 'And ahead of its time. Exactly the sort of play one would expect from GBS.'

'So, you can live up to your reputation.'

They smiled at one another.

'Thank you for inviting me,' said Violet. 'GBS was right, it was an evening I will never forget.'

'Thank you,' said Algie. Then: 'And by the way, I forgot to tell you.'

'Yes?'

'You are looking astonishingly beautiful tonight.'

'Why, thank you sir.' She found herself inadvertently mimicking Lolly.

He took hold of her hand and kissed it, and held onto it for a long moment.

'Goodnight,' he said at last. He let go of her hand and waited while she ascended the steps and unlocked her front door. As she opened it she turned to see him tip his hat, wave a goodbye and walk off down the road until he was a silhouette against the light from the street lamps, and then he was gone.

When she reached her room, which to her relief she found was empty, Violet slumped onto the sofa without taking off her things. There was something bothering her about the evening. She feared she had missed out on something that might not come around again. She would have liked to have called Algie back and said . . . And said what, exactly?

That she was not like Vivie, not in the least. She had made that very plain. But did he believe her?

Maybe he was right, and she was, after all, right down to her priggishness.

She sighed, rose from her seat and made her weary way to bed.

Meanwhile Mr Kapps, closing his window against the night air, witnessed the little scene taking place on the pavement outside, lit by street lamps. He sighed with pleasure. At last, he thought. Violet and Algie.

He also saw something the young couple did not. As Algie walked away down the road, a shadow detached itself from a dark doorway across the street and wandered off in the opposite direction.

28: New century, new woman

It wasn't easy being a new woman at the turn of the century. A woman in business had to work twice as hard as a man and be twice as businesslike, Violet had discovered. She could have taken a leaf out of Mrs Warren's book and used her femininity to advance herself; but Mrs Warren had the benefit of harsh necessity. Born and brought up in poverty, for her it was the factory or slaving behind the bar of a public house or skivvying in domestic service, all of which meant toiling until your feet dropped off, and for a pittance. Who would not want to do anything to escape that?

But Violet had the disadvantage of her middle-class respectability. She had neither the urgency that desperation breeds nor the unflinching focus of the destitute. She was too well-bred to be ruthless. But a new woman does not make an easy wife. It would take a special kind of man – a 'new man' you could say – to understand that the new woman works because she wants to, because it stimulates her, it validates her, and above all because it's a good deal more interesting than lounging in drawing rooms sipping tea with duchesses.

Whether or not Mr Lightly – Algie – was a new man Violet couldn't say, not yet. It disturbed her to learn that he saw her as a Vivie, immersed so completely in her work at the expense of everything else; partly because, yes, she cared what he thought, and partly because she feared it might be true.

Of course she had put all her energies into her work; from the outset she had strived to make herself useful. Listening to people's grumblings, solving everyone's problems – Prue was quite right, it was not a dream job. But Violet had needed to prove herself, and even when she knew she had done so, she had made herself indispensable, still she felt she had to keep striving, always to do better, forever justifying her existence.

Dammit, isn't that what a man does? Why should it be so different for a woman?

~

In her mission to prove to herself that she was not Vivie, Violet decided to visit her parents. It had been some time since she'd done so. True to form, they had largely lost interest in her ever since she left to get married. She assumed it was not so much indifference as the lack of a frame of reference. Her marriage had taken Violet into a world so removed from theirs they no longer knew how to talk to her, or she to them. So it was not so surprising she had not yet got around to telling them her marriage was over. It had seemed simpler not to rock the boat.

However, Violet did not want to be Vivie and reject her mother outright. And so one day she made a day trip to Newbridgeworth, expressly to bring her parents up to date with the happenings in her life.

The house seemed even smaller and darker and more oppressive than she remembered. And her parents seemed to have shrunk as well. They were old now, and showing it, her father in particular. He walked stiffly, and it took him some time to get up out of his chair.

They congregated together in the front parlour of the tiny house, which faced due south but where the windows were so small the sun barely seemed to penetrate.

'I thought I ought to tell you,' Violet began. 'I have left my husband.'

'You have *what*?' exclaimed her father.

'I left him. He was brutal.'

'Did he beat you?' Her mother sat bolt upright in her chair.

'No. But he taunted me. He was beginning to hate me. He hated that I was involved with the suffragists, that I didn't . . .'

'Suffragists?' Her father's eyebrows shot to the top of his head. 'You never told us about that.'

'Actually father, I believe I did. Maybe you weren't listening.'

'Uh,' said the Reverend, as his eyebrows settled back down.

'He didn't want me to do anything other than shop and entertain, or be entertained. I felt stifled.'

'What do you mean, stifled?' Her mother looked quizzical.

'So I left him.'

There was a long pause.

'And what then?' asked her father. 'He's supporting you, I presume.'

'No, he cut me off without a penny.'

'Oh!' Her mother looked at her father in alarm. Now they were in truly foreign territory.

'So how are you managing to live?'

She told them about her job. She explained about Herbert Tree, how he was what was known as an actor-manager, which is to say an actor who also manages a theatre company. She tried to describe her fellow actors, whom she loved because they were funny, and open, and they lived off their wits, and on the edge of survival, which made them sharp and emotional and often needy, which is where she came in. She tried to describe how she spent her day solving other people's problems, and the scripts she read for Mr Tree, most of which were poor if well-meant attempts, but now and again there was a jewel. The more she talked, the more she lost them. She could see from their expressions how little they were following what she was saying, yet still she burbled on.

'It sounds exciting,' said her mother finally, without much conviction.

'Yes, it is.'

'Is it a secure position?' asked her father.

'I believe so.'

Both parents were staring at her – not with disapproval, or even particular disappointment. It seemed they didn't really know what to say.

'You're not getting divorced, are you?' asked her father.

Violet smiled. 'No. There's no point.'

'Good.'

'Oh.' Her mother looked at her father. 'Then you cannot marry again, Violet.'

'No.' Violet agreed. 'I have no intention of doing so.'

'Oh dear,' said her mother. 'That's a shame.'

'You really have no need to worry about me, mother. I am perfectly happy. I enjoy my work and I get well paid for it, enough to keep me in some comfort.'

'Where are you living?'

'I have rooms off Hampstead Road. Quite near to town.'

'Hmm,' said her father, and scowled into the fireplace.

Violet felt a sudden affection for her parents, for not condemning her, or even casting any kind of judgement on her. So what if they didn't care much either way; it left her free to do as she wished and to tell them just so much and no more than she wanted to.

But then she saw her mother had tears in her eyes.

'What's the matter?' she asked.

'Nothing dear. I just wondered . . .'

And that was it.

Until later that day, when the Reverend was out visiting parishioners and the two women were left together. They were drinking tea, in polite silence.

'There's something up mother, please tell me what it is.'

Mrs Frogg shrugged and stared into her lap. Then she turned to her daughter and said, rather wistfully. 'Nothing really, dear. I was just wondering what it was like, to be a modern woman, going out to work.'

'It's challenging. But very freeing. And above all you feel – *I* feel – I am contributing something to the world. Even if it is only in the make-believe of theatre.'

Her mother nodded. 'And you don't feel lonely?'

'No. Well, yes and no. We all feel lonely at times. I have never felt as lonely as I did when I was married.'

There was a heavy silence. Mrs Frogg brought out a handkerchief, and to Violet's dismay she began to cry.

'Oh, mother!'

Now what? Should she put her arms around her? Such intimacy was unheard of in the Frogg household, so Violet held back. 'What is it? Please tell me.'

'Nothing,' sniffed her mother. 'Nothing at all. There.' She gave her nose a final swipe and replaced her handkerchief in her pocket. 'All done. All over.'

And it was. There was no getting anything more out of her mother, not then, and probably not ever.

Violet left that same evening. The crying episode was not referred to again; it was as if it had never happened.

'Thank you for coming to see us, dear,' said her mother. She gave her daughter a peck on the cheek.

'Why don't you come and visit me one day?' said Violet.

'Oh no dear, I couldn't do that.' Mrs Frogg shook her head vigorously.

'Whyever not? It's only an hour away.'

'*No.*' It was as if Violet had invited her mother to visit her in hell.

'Well, if you ever change your mind.'

'Yes dear. Thank you. I won't.'

Violet looked at her mother for some time. What a family of secrets we are, she thought.

'Goodbye papa.' She leant to kiss her father on the cheek.

'Goodbye Violet.' Reverend Frogg shoved his hands in his pockets. 'Thank you for visiting.'

And that was it.

As she walked to the station and on the train back to London Violet pondered on her mother's obvious unhappiness. It wasn't always a good idea, she concluded, to bring the outside world into other people's lives. Being a vicar's wife is all very well, and bearable, if it is all you know. But if you hear of other possibilities, perhaps your dull old life doesn't seem so bearable after all. Perhaps that is why her mother was so adamantly opposed to visiting her. She was afraid she would glimpse a world she might, under other circumstances, have known, and enjoyed.

As her one-time maid Amy would say: 'If you want a straightforward life, know your place and be content in it.'

But that was something Violet simply could not do.

She had done her duty, and no matter what feelings she had for her mother she had a strong suspicion she might not see her again, or not for some time. Maybe she was more like Vivie than she cared to admit.

29: A Sharp exit

One day Frank summoned Violet to his office to tell her he was retiring. He'd been trying to retire for years, he told her, but the Chief wouldn't hear of it. He'd had enough of actors and he was getting on and there were a lot of racehorses out there demanding his undivided attention.

'I'm sorry to hear that, Frank,' said Violet. 'Who will be your replacement?'

'That's the point,' he replied, 'I'm not telling anyone until he's appointed and the deal is struck, otherwise the Chief will only get me to change my mind again.'

'Until "he" is appointed?'

'Yes.' He looked at her blearily. Curmudgeon he might be, but she would miss him.

'Well, if you are looking for someone,' she said, 'how about me?'

'You?'

'Yes. I know the job already. I do the job already, or a good deal of it. So?'

'Out of the question,' said Frank.

'Why?'

'For a start, you have to negotiate, with actors, and their agents. That means haggling, and drawing up contracts, and all manner of tedious business.'

'I can do all that.'

He stared at her. It seemed he couldn't quite grasp what she was saying.

'But you're a woman.'

'So?'

'Organise tours, theatres, transport, accommodation – yes, you probably could handle that. But negotiating?' He shook his head. 'No one would take a woman seriously. Especially you.'

'What do you mean?'

'Well, let's say if you were an old witch of forty, who behaved like a man, and looked like a man, you might just get away with it. But . . .' He gestured towards her. 'No, my dear. You are clever and competent, but there's no escaping the fact that you are female.'

That appeared to be that, in his mind.

'There are women doing those sorts of jobs all over the place. What about Genevieve Ward? Or Sarah Bernhardt?'

He laughed loudly at that. 'Have you met either of them?'

'No. But they're both women. And they've both produced plays, and acted in them. They're forces to be reckoned with.'

'Yes, well, if you were already a performer, and you commanded a wide audience, and you had the friends and the contacts, and you were the toast of all the major cities in Europe, and America, then it might just be possible.' He ran his hands through his hair. 'I don't really think you are in their league, Vi.'

'I'm not asking to be in their league!' Violet was more outraged than she expected to be. 'I am just saying I could do your job, Frank, you know I could.'

'I'm not sure about that, Violet. Anyway it's a question of perception. The world isn't ready for it.'

'Then it's time it was.' Violet got to her feet and strode to the wall and back again. 'Really Frank, I am disappointed in you.'

Frank blinked. 'I can see that. You have to understand –
oh sit down, for God's sake.' After a sulky pause Violet
resumed her seat. 'I'm getting on, Vi. I've been in this
business too long. Changes don't happen overnight. Not
even in the theatre.'

Violet said nothing. Frank regarded her steadily.
'You're a good worker. You do the business, you never
complain – not to my face anyway. The actors love you.'
He stopped, and chortled before he continued. 'And that is
precisely the problem.'

'What do you mean?'

'But *this* – this job that I do is on a different level
altogether. You cannot negotiate with actors and be their
friend at the same time. It doesn't work that way.'

He tilted his chair back and studied her. 'Could you tell
an actor with a wife and six children that he has no talent
and his services are no longer required?'

She didn't answer this.

'Or inform the fellow who's been with the company all
his working life that he's been drunk once too often on
stage and this time he has to go. Hmm?'

'I'd hope to find a solution to that.'

'A solution? What solution?'

'To his drinking. I'd talk to him first.'

'You see?' Frank threw his hands in the air. 'That's
what I mean. Typical woman's reaction. What does talking
do?'

'What do you think I've been doing for the last
however long?'

'That's emollient, maybe. But someone has to wield the
axe in the end and that person is not you Vi, you know it
as well as I do.' He brought his chair forward again and it
landed with a thump. 'It takes a man of steel and a heart of
ice. Who doesn't waste his time making chums with the

people he works with. Someone like me. The Chief may laugh and wonder why I want to work with people I don't understand, such as actors, and I tell him it's not a contradiction, it's a necessity. He wouldn't understand it. He couldn't fire someone if his life depended on it. He gets other people to do it for him. Like me. And you may think I've passed all the most unpleasant tasks in this business on to you but I haven't.'

He clasped his hands together on the desk in front of him and said, 'I am sorry Vi.'

'So am I.'

'In any case, I have someone in mind for the job. He's young, he's clever, he has a good head for business. You will get along, I'm sure.'

She didn't reply.

'Please don't sulk, Violet. I'd hate to leave the job knowing you hate my guts.'

She smiled. 'I could never hate your guts, Frank,' she said. 'I just hate your point of view about what women can and can't do.'

He inclined his head in semi-acknowledgement of this. 'I'm of the old generation. I'm a Victorian man. You are a twentieth century woman. I have no doubt you are right, or you will be right one day soon. But not yet.'

He unclasped his hands and rubbed them together.

'If I were you,' he said, 'I would find myself a good husband and retire from this whole business altogether.'

Violet stared at him.

'No need to look so horrified. You're a widow, aren't you? And – ' he gestured vaguely at her, 'presentable. Very presentable even. If you don't, you might well end up like some of those old maids who throw their lives away for the sake of – of what, I couldn't tell you. Like Winnie Walters.'

'Who?'

'In costumes. The theatre business is a monster. It can swallow you up and spit you out without a care in its head – raise you up one day, stamp on you the next. There are plenty of Winnie Walters, lurking in shadowy corners. They give their whole lives to the business and it gives them nothing in return. The older they become the more invisible they get.'

Winnie Walters. The name rang a bell but she struggled to remember her. She made a mental note to seek her out.

'Just don't marry an actor.' Frank pushed his chair back from his desk.

'I'll try not to.' But she did try to smile.

'Or a critic.'

'Why did you say that?' Violet looked at him in alarm.

Frank shrugged. 'No particular reason. So.' He stood up, and hitched up his trousers. 'Once I've spoken to Mr Dunkett and we've arranged a deal I'll tell the Chief and then . . . it's goodbye and good luck.'

Goodbye and good luck indeed.

Violet was probably, with the Chief, one of the few people who was genuinely sorry to see Frank leave. True to his convictions he had made no attempt to endear himself to the company as a whole. And if his theory was correct, that you cannot negotiate with actors and be their friend at the same time – which Violet disputed – it was a price he was presumably happy to pay.

~

One day in late June Frank's replacement marched into Violet's office, shook her hand heartily and said in a very loud voice: 'Mrs Graham, my name is Theodore Dunkett. I've heard all about you, I am delighted to be working together, I am sure we will get along famously.'

He was tall and plump and good-looking in an off-puttingly wholesome kind of a way, with ruddy cheeks and little button eyes and a moustache. He was also younger than Violet, which was mostly, though not entirely, why she took an instant dislike to him. She was predisposed to despise Frank's replacement anyway, sour grapes notwithstanding, but this creature, with his overconfident manner and his *youth*, was beyond the pale. He can't have been out of school for more than five years. And he had a moustache.

She did her best to give him the benefit of the doubt. It worked for a while, but it didn't take long before she realised how impossible he was to work with. He was twice as demanding as Frank and was constantly standing far too close to her looking over her shoulder and checking to see what she was up to. He would stride into her office without invitation or reason. He had her writing lengthy, overblown letters to everyone he could think of in the theatre business, by way of introducing himself and drawing their attention to the supreme (and exaggerated) importance of his position. He had a way of leering at her that reminded her of a schoolboy playing puerile games with a schoolgirl. Everything she had loved about her work – the fact she was left alone to do whatever she decided needed doing, in whatever way she thought it should be done – was undermined by his intimidating, unwanted presence. What Frank could possibly have seen in this rambunctious, overgrown boy was a mystery.

She remonstrated with him, politely, and perhaps just a bit patronisingly. She told him she'd been working for the company for however many years and that she knew what she was doing, thank you very much. He listened to her pityingly, with a sly smile on his face. And when she was done he stood up, placed a hand on her shoulder, leant down so his face was so close to hers she could feel his breath, and said, 'Thank you Mrs Graham, for putting me in my place. And now perhaps you will get on with whatever work it is you say you do so well.'

She thought about complaining to someone, but who? Certainly not the Chief himself. There was nothing for it but to keep quiet and get on with things in the hope that in time he'd forget all about her, just as Frank had done.

Talking of whom, she composed a long letter in her head telling her departed boss exactly what she thought of his *protégé*, and hoping all his horses would fall at the first fence.

Vivie would never have put up with it.

30: Winnie Walters' predicament

In the event Violet didn't have to go looking for Winnie Walters, as Winnie Walters came looking for her.

Violet remembered her the moment she saw her. It was Miss Walters who had helped her dress on the night of the great opening of Her Majesty's Theatre. (To which, it occurred to Violet now, though not before, Miss Walters had not been invited.) She was a slight woman, with a pale face and greying hair and an apologetic manner. She walked stiffly, with a stoop, and she looked considerably older than Vi recalled, which was probably due to the stoop. She appeared at Violet's door one afternoon and asked, in her soft and musical voice, if she could have a word.

'Of course,' said Violet. 'Sit down, please.'

'My name is Winnie Walters. We met once, I believe, some time ago.' She edged herself onto a chair.

'Yes, we did.'

'I work in the costume department, I've been here for some time.'

'You helped me with that wretched corset. I remember you very well.'

'Ah,' said the older lady. 'And what a picture you were.' She tilted her chin and squinted through her spectacles at Violet like an elderly and over-indulgent aunt.

'You've been here for longer than almost anyone I believe,' said Violet.

'Well . . .' Winnie bowed self-deprecatingly, and coughed discreetly into her hand.

'The word is you were around when Tree was just a slender branch.' It was Violet's feeble attempt to put the other woman at ease. They both laughed, just enough. 'I would have loved to have seen him when he was younger.'

'He was no different, no different at all,' said Winnie. 'Always eager, always pleased to see you. Optimistic, and happy all the time.' She spoke with wonder at this, as a woman who, Vi surmised, was very far from happy all the time. 'I always knew he would be a success. People like that usually are, aren't they?'

'People like what?'

'People who know they will be successful, they usually are. It's their belief that gets them there. Life is so simple for people like that. They don't see the problems, and if you don't see the problems up ahead, they aren't there. Are they?'

Violet was not at all sure about that, but said nothing.

Winnie looked at her lap for a moment. Her fingers, Violet noticed, were calloused and swollen with arthritis. And she a woman who worked with her hands.

'He always had such energy, even when he was a stripling. And on stage you can't take your eyes off him! That's not something you can learn. You either have it or you don't.'

'That is true. Although I'm not sure his judgement always matches his personality.'

'What do you mean?' Winnie looked quite taken aback at this unexpected slight.

'Some of the plays he produces, and some of the parts he gives himself – you can't help but wonder if, just occasionally, he could do with someone to advise him. And yes, I know, he pretends to consult with all sorts of people but in the end he takes very little notice of what anyone else says. I'm not sure if that's the best way to manage a company.'

'But no one knows more about theatre than he does!' Winnie's eyes were almost popping out of her head with outrage.

'I'm not disputing that. I'm just saying that sometimes a person with his optimism, as you put it, and his experience, may not always see the wood for the trees. And I apologise for the pun.' She smiled at the other woman. 'Every king needs his court jester.'

Winnie's expression softened. 'Oh you do know him so well, I'm sure you do. Me – I can't see anything other than a shining star. Dazzling!' She shrugged exaggeratedly, and for a moment she looked like an infatuated child. 'You are very wise,' she added.

Violet laughed. But oddly enough, faced with this bedazzled woman-child she did feel quite wise, and quite old as well.

Winnie was gazing at Violet with a mildly vacant smile, as if her mind were elsewhere. It was taking some time to get to the point, if there was a point in the first place.

'So,' said Violet, as gently as she could. 'How can I help you?'

Winnie drew herself up straight, wincing as she did so. She fingered a strand of hair that had strayed across her face and then she said, 'I have to have an operation.'

'Oh dear. I'm sorry to hear that.'

'On my back.' Winnie twisted in her chair and grimaced again. 'It's rather painful. And it means I will be away from work for some time.'

'Of course. How long, do you know?'

'No. But maybe a month. Or two, or three.' She looked at Violet appealingly. 'And the point is . . .'

'Yes?'

'Will I – is it possible I might be paid while I'm away? I know it's a lot to ask, but I haven't taken any time off, more or less, ever since I came to work here.'

'Of course.'

'Really?' Winnie smiled with relief. 'And when I come back – that is to say, shall I still be able to come back? You see,' she was off like a steam train now, 'I am not married, I have never been, except to my work.' She tittered. 'And I have no family support. And this operation is costly, even though they have offered me a special price. It will cost me more than I can afford, but it has to be done. I have always worked my hardest for Mr Tree, my work is my life, and I wouldn't have it any other way.'

Violet opened her mouth to say something, but Winnie was off again.

'It isn't easy for us spinsters, as they call us.'

'I'm sure it's . . .'

'You would understand that, Mrs Graham, being a woman, and a widow. Without support. I knew I would find a sympathetic ear in you. Because otherwise, what else is there for me?'

'Well . . .'

'The workhouse!' Winnie shrieked with laughter, and then she calmed down. 'I'm getting hysterical,' she said, needlessly.

Violet was quite shocked, and dismayed.

'Listen, Miss Walters. First of all I am very sorry to hear you need to have an operation, you must be in a lot of pain.'

Winnie nodded.

'The point is, it is not my decision to make, whether or not your position remains open to you.'

'Oh!'

'However,' Violet continued quickly, 'I think if we keep this between ourselves, no one else need know, do they? Except your immediate colleagues, of course.'

Winnie nodded slowly, and uncertainly. 'I could find a replacement, a temporary seamstress.'

'Perhaps. But I suggest we keep this as simple as possible. You take your time off, as much as you need, and we tell no one. And you continue to be paid. And when you feel ready, you come back and carry on as if nothing has happened.'

Winnie nodded again, this time with more enthusiasm.

'It will mean your colleagues will have to work that much harder, but if I talk to them I'm sure they will understand. And I might manage a slight increase in their wages, to keep them – you know.'

Violet knew she was making promises she was in no position to make. She could feel her heart racing. But it was the right thing to do, of that she had no doubt at all.

Winnie's eyes were filling with tears. 'You are very kind. And understanding. As I knew you would be.'

'I am a woman too,' said Violet. She thought of Frank, and what he'd have to say if he'd been listening in to the conversation. She tried to shut him right out of her mind. Likewise Mr Dunkett, even more so.

Once Winnie had gone, backing out of the door with repeated and profuse thanks, Violet sat completely still in her chair for several minutes.

'What have I done?' she asked herself. And then she forgot all about it.

~

'You did the right thing,' said Kapps.

'You think so? As a man, and a businessman?'

It was the evening of that same day and they were sharing a bottle of Schnapps. Violet had taken a distinct liking to the stuff, almost too much so, she sometimes told herself.

'As a human being. What is three months, after all? The woman probably never took a rest, she deserves it. As a businessman . . .' He drew in his breath. 'Again, yes, you did the right thing. Because from now on if you did not have it before you have her complete loyalty. That is how we treat our underlings – is that the right word?'

'No it isn't, but I know what you mean.'

'The other side is, you may be exploited, they may be advantaging you, and that is a chance you take. However,' he raised a finger to forestall her interruption, 'from the point of view of you, maybe it was not such a good thing.'

'How do you mean?'

'You have the authority to say this to her?'

'No, I don't.'

'And if it is discovered?'

Violet hesitated. 'I have no idea.' She had told him a little about Theodore Dunkett, just enough. 'And honestly I don't care. I care less and less each day.'

Kapps looked alarmed, but he did not interrupt her.

'Since Mr Dunkett, I no longer look forward to going to work, and that's the truth.' She hadn't realised it fully until she'd spoken it out loud. 'He's a nightmare, and if he does find out, and if he does sack me, frankly I don't care.'

She was feeling distinctly light-headed. She was downing the Schnapps as if it were water.

'I've got as far as I can get in this business,' she went on. 'Frank made that perfectly clear. There's nowhere else for me to go. A woman cannot do his job, nor any job with any real responsibility. So what do I do? I stay put and end up like Winnie Walters? Who has to come grovelling to someone thirty years younger than her, and her inferior in every sense, to ask to keep her job because otherwise it's the workhouse?'

'You get married.'

'Not you too!' Violet exploded, with unexpected violence. She stood up and began to pace the room. 'Sorry Zunker, but really! Is that the only choice for a woman? Work as an underling – your word by the way, in its proper sense – for someone you despise, knowing that that is your lot for the foreseeable future? Or get married for the sake of it? Heavens above.' She placed one hand on her hip and the other melodramatically on her forehead, as she'd seen in pictures of Sarah Bernhardt. 'What sort of a world is this?'

'What else do you suggest?'

Violet shrugged. 'I have no idea.'

'Why do you have such a big obstacle to marriage?' Kapps asked mildly. He was, though he tried not to show it, very much amused.

'I am still married, you may remember. And I do not have a good experience of it. I don't believe I am cut out for it.'

'"Cut out for it?" This means what, exactly?'

'I'm – I'm – ' Violet gestured wildly. 'I am too used to my independence now. Doing what I want to do.'

'But you just said you are no longer doing what you want to do.'

'Don't deliberately misunderstand me!' She was almost shouting. 'There is no man in the world who wants to marry a woman who wants to work. That is a fact. I don't have the wherewithal to sit at home all day sewing, or playing the piano, or reading. It would drive me demented.' She picked up her glass and drank from it greedily.

'Why do you say no man wants to marry a woman who works? This is not true.'

'Well, no one I know of anyway.'

'Mr Lightly?' He spoke the name tentatively.

'Algie? Phhh!' It was a strange noise, but there was no mistaking the contempt.

'Why do you go – "Phhh"?'

Violet had to laugh at this. 'I don't know, Zunker, he's vanished off the face of the earth. And it's probably just as well.'

'Why do you say that?'

'I don't know, as I said. I don't know anything any more.' She sat down and went to take another drink, then changed her mind.

'Have you tried to see him?'

'Why should I do that?'

'You are afraid, perhaps. Or are you waiting for him to communicate with you?'

She thought about this for a second. 'I suppose I am, yes.'

'You call yourself a modern woman? And you wait for the man to do the – the doing?'

'"Do the doing?"' Violet repeated tipsily. 'Yes, I do. Is that wrong?'

'Not wrong, not right. But . . .' Kapps shrugged. 'A woman wants to work, and she does not want a man but she wants a man to pursue her. She wants change and she does not want change. It is a puzzle. For a man. I open the door I do not open the door. I call on the lady, I wait for the lady to call on me. Which to do? Right or left? Right or wrong?'

Violet loudly, and hiccupped.

'I think I've drunk too much, Zunker.' She studied her near-empty glass. 'This stuff is lethal.'

'Have some more. It suits you.'

'It makes me indiscreet.'

'As I said, it suits you.' He smiled, and she smiled also, and there was a brief and comfortable silence.

'Anyway,' said Violet eventually, 'I wouldn't know

where to find him.'

'His work perhaps?'

'Hmm?'

'The newspaper, where he works.'

'Oh, yes,' she said, blearily.

'You could write to him there.'

'Yes, I suppose I could.' She rubbed the palm of her hand along the arm of her chair. 'Yet I still think – chide me if you want to – I still think if a man were interested in a woman he would let it be known.'

'I believe he did let it be known. The evening he was here, there was no doubting it.'

'Hmm,' said Violet again. Then she got to her feet, stumbling a little. 'Whoops!' she said, as Kapps stood up to steady her. 'Got up too fast. Thank you, Zunker.'

'My pleasure, Vi.'

'So you think . . .' she began.

'Yes?'

'What do you think I should do? Tell me Zunker, because I don't know anything any more.'

'Write to Mr Lightly, at his work. Tell him you love him.'

'Tell him I *what*?' She lurched again, and he tightened his grip on her to keep her upright.

'Or that you do not love him. But he would be surprised to receive a letter to say, "Dear Mr Lightly, Algie, I am writing to tell you I do not love you".'

'Heavens above!' Violet steadied herself. 'Well, we shall see.'

Kapps guided her slowly towards the door. 'Will you be safe on the stairs? I would not like to see you kill yourself with a stumble.'

'Thank you Zunker, I will be very careful.'

In the doorway he said, 'Oh, by the way, I was meaning to tell you. There has been a man following you, I think.'

Violet turned abruptly. 'What?'

'I saw him the first time, after Mr Lightly was leaving. Then again, another time, as you were coming back from work.'

'I don't understand.'

'He stayed until you were in the door and then he left. I don't mean to alarm you,' he added, quickly. 'I just thought you should know.' He looked at her anxiously. 'I think it is probably nothing. Or if not, we tell the police.'

Violet frowned. Then she turned, slowly, and walked with great care step by step down the stairs. Kapps watched her as she went, and waited until she had entered her room and closed the door behind her.

31: Violet's stalkers

He was a master of disguise. One minute he wore long, straggly hair and a beard, the next he was close-cropped and clean-shaven. His top hat became a cap, his shabby raincoat a Savile Row suit. He was tall one minute and squat the next. He was the spitting image of the baker's assistant and the next time she looked he was the postman. There was only one constant: he was everywhere.

He was leaning up against the wall outside her office when she arrived in the morning, and when she stopped dead he sauntered off soundlessly along the corridor. He was waiting for her outside the stage door as she left the theatre and he followed her up Haymarket towards Piccadilly Circus, but when she turned to look at him he was gone, like in a ghostly form of Grandmother's Footsteps. He was eyeing up the cabbages in the greengrocers when she went for her daily shop, and sniffing suspiciously at the pork chops in the butchers. When she caught his eye he smiled and tipped his hat like any polite stranger. As he followed her to her door she turned to confront him and he vanished, right there in front of her. She thought she was going mad. She was going mad.

She woke in a cold sweat.

Paranoia is a dangerous beast. Once it has you in its

grip it is hard to escape. Now every man who looked at Violet in the street – and there were plenty of them, there always had been – was a spy, a stalker, or a private detective. She even looked twice at familiar neighbours, and shopkeepers. Every gesture, every word, had a double meaning. Mr Badham the butcher's smile was broader than usual, why? Even Mrs King in the pharmacy looked strange, even concerned, when she dropped by for some lavender water. She knew it was irrational but it made no difference. Just because you are paranoid does not mean people are not talking about you. Distraction didn't help. Inertia was worse. Sleep offered no escape. The waking world had become a continuous nightmare.

And then one morning she woke up and the familiar ceiling gazed back at her indifferently. On her way to work the omnibus was as busy as it had ever been, the passengers – many of them familiar by now – smiled blandly at her and then forgot her. She was not being followed. She was not the centre of the universe. The world that had tipped dangerously on its axis had righted itself, without her participation. She was relieved, and she was a little disappointed too. She was no more nor less than an ordinary woman, just like millions of others.

Algie.

She was not supposing for a moment that Algie was responsible. He had no reason, nor was he the type, as far as she knew. But then she did not know him that well. He had told her nothing at all about his background, but she assumed it was the usual: upper-middle class, professional family, boarding school, Oxford or maybe Cambridge. She had never pretended with him, other than keeping him in the dark as to her marital status; he had no reason for jealousy, or whatever it was that forced people to hire people to spy on people.

It was a true puzzle. Next time she saw the man she

would ask him outright, and politely: 'Excuse me, but may I enquire why you are following me?'

But now she was on the lookout for him he was no longer there.

> 'Yesterday, upon the stair
> I met a man who wasn't there
> He wasn't there again today
> I wish, I wish he'd go away.'

She had to find something to distract her.

One evening she sat down to write to Algie.

> 'Dear Algie, I expect you are surprised to hear from me . . .
> Dear Algie, I hope you don't mind my writing to you like this, but the point is . . .
> Dear Mr Lightly, where the hell are you?'

It was no good. She hadn't the faintest idea what to say to him in a letter. So instead she did some looking up and located the offices of *The Weekend Chronicle* in a small street off Gray's Inn Road. When she called round the staff gazed at her with some curiosity before explaining that Robbie Robinson had taken leave of absence 'to attend to family matters'.

'Oh,' said Violet. 'Do you know where he might be? I mean, where his family live?'

They looked at one another vaguely. Someone said they thought it was somewhere in Oxfordshire. Another thought it might be Surrey, or Wiltshire. They smiled apologetically and offered her a cup of tea, which she refused. They offered to pass on a message, which she also refused. So after a series of embarrassed pauses, on all sides, she nodded a goodbye and left.

32: The family of Robbie Robinson

Robbie's family was not as Violet had imagined it. It was not as anyone might imagine any family. It was based in a small village called Kern, in Essex. Robbie's father, now dead, had been a carpenter by trade but a gambler by nature, with fluctuating luck and fortune. One minute there was so much food the dining table legs complained of the weight. The next the family was living off nettles and potatoes. One day there were so many servants around the place you'd be tripping over them, the next day they'd be gone. Some were sons and daughters of local people, some had been 'borrowed' from other more consistently well-to-do employers. They all lived out, as the house could not accommodate any extra people. They did not expect to be there long, but while they were there they enjoyed generous wages and a happy atmosphere. They came for 'the lark'. Robbie's father was generous to a fault when he was flush so when he was not the locals made sure his wife and five children did not starve.

It made for an unpredictable life, to state the obvious. Schooling was very much a hit and miss affair. In good times a tutor appeared, threw a few facts in the direction of the children and left, leaving them in suspense, not knowing What Happened Next. For Robbie, if he wanted to know what occurred after Guy Fawkes was caught red-handed, or why the hedgehog hibernates in the winter, he had to find out. Thus he grew up with a well-honed sense of curiosity and a facility for knowing where to discover the answer to any question. It was not surprising he became a journalist.

Mr Robinson senior was unrepentant. He claimed his temporary riches gave his children opportunities they would never have otherwise had, and their transient nature made them all the more precious. Mrs Robinson meanwhile took everything in her stride and never attempted to curb her husband's habit. She knew about his gambling before she married him, and when things were good she made the most of it. She splashed out on dresses, and jewellery, and fancy trinkets and treats, for herself and for her daughters. She indulged her love of music and theatre, and as often as she could she took the train to London to enjoy the latest offering at the Gaiety or Wilton's Music Hall. On the way home on the train she would sing all the songs, with gusto, to the amusement of her fellow passengers and the squirming embarrassment of whatever children happened to be with her.

Robbie's first experience of the stage was *Robinson Crusoe* at the Drury Lane Theatre; a pantomime where, traditionally, if rather confusingly for a young child, the men played women and the women men. It starred Arthur Roberts, of music hall fame, the most celebrated – and the naughtiest, according to Robbie's mother – actor in the world, plus a chorus of hundreds, live animals, and scenery and costumes the like of which Robbie could never have imagined possible on a stage. It was raucous, fast-moving and colourful, and a lot of it went right over his head. But he was hooked. And while the prospect of having to sit through a pantomime now, now he was a sophisticated theatregoer, was unthinkable, that first experience stayed with him and lit a flame in the young Robbie that had burned brightly ever since.

But now his mother was dead too, and he mourned her. He also mourned the fact that as the younger of the two brothers, and the unmarried one – though why that should be relevant was not explained – it was left to him to sort out the chaos. For years, since his father's death, he had been supporting his mother and his one remaining unmarried sister, while helping to pay off his father's debts. Now that sister was, happily, about to marry, and with his mother gone there was a house and its contents to be sold. It was the end of an era.

Robbie sat alone in the family house and listened to the ghostly echoes of his mother's voice trilling upstairs – she did not confine her singing to railway carriages – and the yells and yelps of his siblings and his father's bellowing overpowering them all. It had been a happy childhood, but he felt alienated from it now as he had become estranged from his siblings, who accused him of being a 'toff', fetching up in London and giving himself fancy names. They had all stayed local, as was expected of a family such as theirs in those days, among people who knew them and loved them, and of whom many were Mr Robinson senior's creditors.

And now there was endless paperwork, and those local people who had helped support the family over the decades had to be paid back. It was a question of whether the proceeds from the house would raise enough to pay off those debts so that, for the first time in his life, Robbie could be in the black.

It took a long time, and it was wearisome, and Robbie missed Algie and his London life. He thought from time to time of Violet, and her lovely, glowing face. Once or twice he sat down to write to her:

> 'My dear Violet, I am writing to tell you that I
> am away, at the family home in Essex. My
> mother has died and . . .

My dear Violet, You may be wondering where
I am and why I haven't called to see you.
My dear Violet, I miss you more than I can say.
I am away at present but I hope to be back in
London in . . .'
In what?

He gave up, and got back to the paperwork.

After what seemed like weeks, if not months, it was done. Two plus two equals four. Two minus four equals minus two. It did not quite tally. It was going to be several years before he could declare himself solvent.

On the final day, as the men arrived to remove the furniture Robbie discovered an envelope inserted into the webbing on the underside of the sofa. There was another glued to the bottom of an armchair. And yet another beneath a side table. The envelopes contained money, in pound notes. Added up, they came to just under one hundred pounds.

One hundred pounds! Not a fortune, though it would have kept a labourer alive for a couple of years. It had been his mother's security, typical of her, hidden away in good times for what she would have called 'a rainy day'. She'd probably been hiding it away all her life. She hadn't been as profligate with her treats and trinkets as she'd led people to believe. And either she had forgotten all about it or, which was more likely, she was still waiting for that proverbial rainy day.

> *'Annual income twenty pounds, annual*
> *expenditure nineteen nineteen and six, result*
> *happiness. Annual income twenty pounds, annual*
> *expenditure twenty pounds nought and six, result*
> *misery.'*

So said Charles Dickens' Mr Micawber – a character he based, it was said, on his own father.

Miraculously, there was enough to pay off the debts

and leave Robbie with a bit over. Strictly speaking he should have consulted with his siblings, but strictly speaking he regarded the extra as rightfully his anyway, not just because he had been keeping his mother and sister afloat ever since his father died, but as payment for all his hard work sorting out the family chaos. Besides, he knew exactly what he would spend it on.

He could see nothing but happiness ahead.

33: The disappearance of Violet Graham

Robbie wrote to Violet before he returned to London, and this time he did not tear the letter up. He told her of the sad death of his mother and the selling off of the assets. He did not mention the secret treasure he had discovered strapped to the furniture but he did tell her that for the first time in his adult life he was not in debt, and would she like to celebrate with him one day soon?

He received no reply.

When he returned to work there was much catching up to do. His colleagues had decided between them, justifiably or otherwise, that since he had taken so much time off it was only fair he be given extra duties, especially the more mundane ones: the daily debates in Parliament; an alleged scandal involving a government minister (that, true to say, was quite interesting); an interminably boring fraud case at the Old Bailey; a series of minor thefts in the East End and so on and so on. He had no time to visit the theatre, nor to think much about anything other than what he was expected to cover from day to day, and inevitably he found himself writing up copy until late at night. It was exciting in a sense – no journalist wants to sit at his desk kicking his heels – but it was tiresome too.

So it was some time before he could find a moment to call on Violet at her work.

He was already concerned. He had written to her three

times, in increasing anxiety. The last letter had said, 'If I am a nuisance you only have to say.' And now he was wondering whether something terrible had happened to her. Or even, God forbid, that she'd gone and got married again while his back was turned. Not likely, surely, but you can never be sure. He hardly knew her, after all. There was her estranged husband, the one she told him was dead, and then was not dead, whom she spotted at the opening of Tree's theatre all those years ago. What was the story there? She was in many ways a closed book. And yet in others, so open, so engaged, so engaging. She was a puzzle. A fascinating, tantalising, infuriating puzzle.

He tapped on the door of her office and an unfamiliar voice called, 'Come in!'

He did so. Behind the desk sat a small grey-haired woman with spectacles.

'Hello,' said Robbie, halfway through the doorway. 'I'm looking for Violet. Mrs Graham.'

'She left,' said the woman, without a smile.

'Oh.' Robbie stood there for a moment, slightly stupefied. 'Why? Do you know?'

The woman shrugged, and carried on with her work.

'Can you tell me exactly when she left?'

'The week before I arrived.'

'And that would have been?'

The woman looked up, irritably. 'I don't count the days. I am here temporarily. I move around all the time.' She picked up a sheaf of papers and rather aggressively banged them on her desk to straighten them. 'You'll have to ask Mr Dunkett.'

'Mr Dunkett? Who's he?'

'I am he,' said a voice behind Robbie. It made him jump. He turned to see a large man with eyes like pebbles and a moustache, standing rather too close to him and smiling. 'May I help you?'

'I was looking for Mrs Graham. Where's Mr Sharp?'

'Mr Sharp left, I am his replacement. And if you are looking for Mrs Graham she is no longer with us.'

'What do you mean?' cried Robbie, in alarm.

'She left.' The tiny pebble eyes were no longer smiling. 'Suddenly.'

'Oh.' Robbie thrust his hands in his pockets and stared at the floor for a moment. Then: 'Can you tell me why?'

'I could. I could give you a number of reasons. First, she undermined my authority. Second, she ignored my instructions. Third, and most serious, she made important decisions without consulting me. And one in particular.' Dunkett thrust out his chin, like a recalcitrant child. Robbie had to stifle a laugh. So young, so pompous.

'My word,' he said. 'So, you gave her the sack?'

'No. She took it herself.' He was staring at Robbie, chin rampant, like a schoolboy spoiling for a fight.

Robbie took a step back from him. 'Well,' he said, pleasantly. 'Thank you for the information. Goodbye.' And he left.

That evening, in lieu of writing up a piece for the newspaper, he made his way as soon as he could to Crighton Street.

Mrs Sargent let him into the house and told him immediately that Violet was not there.

'Oh, that's a shame. Perhaps I can leave a message for her,' he said, reaching into his pocket for his notebook. (A journalist always carries a notebook.)

'No,' said Mrs Sargent. 'I mean she's left. Gone.'

'Gone? You mean – left? For good?'

She nodded.

'Gracious. Did she . . . do you know why?'

Mrs S shook her head.

'Or where?'

'No. She said she would send someone to collect her

mail, if there was any.'

'Well I never!' He was momentarily poleaxed.

Mrs Sargent looked at the visitor anxiously and the visitor frowned and stared into the middle distance. He was thinking, but nothing was coming into his head. Nothing that made sense.

It was at that point that the head of Mr Kapps appeared over the banisters.

'Mr Lightly,' he said. 'You are looking for Violet?'

'Yes,' said Robbie. 'Where is she, do you know?'

'Come on up,' said Kapps.

With a nod to Mrs Sargent and a muttered, 'Thank you,' Robbie ascended the stairs to Mr Kapps' room.

'Sit down,' said Kapps, as he closed the door. He looked grave.

'So,' said Robbie. 'This is a turn up.' He looked at Kapps' expression. 'Is it bad news?'

'It is, for she is gone.'

'But gone where?'

'Nobody knows,' said Kapps.

Robbie breathed a slight sigh of relief. 'So she's alive at least?'

Kapps shrugged. 'Assumably. I have not heard from her since she left. She went very suddenly, one day, without saying goodbye.'

'How extraordinary! Have you any idea why?'

'I have theories, but no more.'

'Tell me, please.'

'First, she had a bad row at her work. With her boss, her new boss. You knew about her new boss?'

'I met him earlier today, as it happens.'

'He took the job some months ago, and she disliked him very much.'

'I'm not surprised. What happened to Frank?'

'He retired.'

'Ah.'

'So this new man, she disliked him as I said. For many numbers of reasons. Then there came a lady to ask her permission to take absent time for a back operation, and Vi said yes, and yes again, she would be paid and could return.'

'What lady was this?'

'Winnie something. Working in costumes, I believe. Vi was very strong about her, she said she had worked all her life there and never had time away, she was – how do you say it – on her side?'

Robbie nodded.

'Very fierce.' Kapps said proudly. 'She is very fierce to defend people. But then her boss found out, and he didn't like it. He said it was not her business to allow the permission, and she knew that, and she was playing above her station and he would not stand it.'

Robbie found himself smiling, partly because of Kapps' use of language, but also because he was picturing the scene: Violet the fighter, standing up for the underdog against an overgrown schoolboy. For that moment he loved her completely.

'I would have liked to have been a fly on the wall,' he said.

'There ensued what Vi called a storm to conquer all storms.' Kapps frowned. 'Or something like it. And out she went.'

'She left. Just like that.'

'Just like that. It was 'on the cards' she said, from the moment he came in her life.'

So, Robbie mused, all this was going on while he was away, sorting through paperwork, engrossed in family and the past. He felt bereft.

'That is a very sad story,' he said gruffly. 'She loved that job.'

Kapps nodded. 'It is a sad story.' He cleared his throat. 'And there is more.'

'Ah.' Robbie felt a stab of something approaching panic.

'I told her she was being followed. I had seen – once, more – a person behind her as she came home from work. I think I frightened her. It was not my meaning to, I just thought she should know. And we could go to the police. But then I did not see him and I think he was gone.'

Robbie frowned in confusion. 'What sort of man?'

'An ordinary man. With a cap.'

'And you didn't report him?'

Kapps shook his head. He looked upset.

'I'm sorry Zunker, it's not your responsibility, I don't mean to be . . .' Robbie drew a deep breath and turned to look towards the window. He imagined Kapps there, of an evening, with nothing much else to do but gaze out at the street and see things. Things that were or maybe were not there.

'She did not say goodbye.' Kapps was close to tears. 'One day she tells me she has left her job, and then it is a week later and she goes and does not come back. And I hear from Mrs Sargent that she has gone. Truly gone.' He produced a handkerchief and wiped his eyes. 'No word, nothing. And she was my friend. We were good friends. And no address. Nowhere to write to her a letter.'

Robbie stood up, thrust his hands in his pockets and strolled to the window. He stood there for some time, gazing out. It was a quiet residential street, with no shops, and few passers-by. If someone had been following Violet he would have been noticeable to anyone who spent their time staring out of the window.

After a while he turned and asked: 'Did you talk to any of her friends about this? Did you talk to Lolly?'

'Lolly called round one day, she didn't know, she had

no idea.'

'My word.' Robbie walked to the fireplace and absently, yet gently, began kicking the fender. 'Well Zunker, there's not a lot we can do, is there?'

'No. But if you write to her she will send a person to collect the letter.'

'All very clandestine. Like a bad novel.' Robbie was annoyed. He'd been worried, and now he was annoyed. Annoyed that she'd run off without even a goodbye to her closest friends, or a forwarding address. She owed it to them, and to him, not to treat them with such contempt.

'Well I must say,' he said, turning back to Kapps. He still had his hands in his pockets. 'I would never have thought it of her. I imagined we were her friends.'

'I thought perhaps she had run to you,' said Kapps.

'To *me*?'

'It was all I could think. But why not to tell me? I have no answer.'

'Well,' said Robbie, with something approaching decisiveness, 'I intend to write her a letter and tell her what I think.'

'Do not be harsh on her,' Kapps pleaded.

'I won't be harsh on her,' said Robbie. 'Or perhaps I will, just a bit. She owes us an explanation, don't you agree?'

'A person's life is a person's life.' Kapps was hardly in a position to censure someone who had run away from home without leaving a forwarding address.

'All the same, she has upset us. She has upset you, and I've no doubt her other friends who have helped her. She has no right to run off like that.'

Kapps said nothing.

'I will write her a letter and drop it round here. And when whoever it is comes to collect it I want you to make sure you apprehend that person and ask where she is.'

'Me?' Kapps looked surprised.

'You are my only hope, Zunker.'

'I will do my best,' said the poor man. But neither of them believed he would.

On his way out Robbie paused in the hallway long enough to notice a small pile of letters on the hallstand. He riffled through them quickly. And yes, his letters were still there, all of them. He picked them up and stuffed them into his jacket pocket.

~

He wrote to her again. It took him several attempts until he was able to summon the clarity of mind to tell her what he thought of her. The final result, which he hesitated over but sent anyway, went like this:

> 'Dear Violet,
>
> Where are you? You have run away from your friends and we are alarmed. I came back from the country where I was trying to make sense of my family's affairs after my mother died, and there you are, gone! I do not chide you for myself, but for your friends, and in particular for poor Mr Kapps, who is beside himself with worry.
>
> I had such good news to tell you. There is no point in telling it now. It did concern you, but now you are gone without a word there is no point.
>
> Perhaps you have been kidnapped? Do you know what anxiety you have caused by running off like that? Should we get the police to hunt for you? Why could you not at least explain yourself? Do you not owe that to Mr Kapps, who has all the time looked out for you, cared about you, listened to you? Do you not see how astonishingly selfish you have

been? He is distraught! If it is not our business, and clearly it is not, then tell us so. Tell us you are well, at least. That you have disappeared for a positive reason, that you are not running away but running to something. Then we can rest easy in our beds.

I miss you. And I love you. I wanted to tell you that to your face, but you make it impossible.'

On reflection he omitted the final paragraph. He did not want any displays of affection or tenderness to intrude on his anger. Because he was, to his surprise, fiercely, overwhelmingly angry.

LIFE FOUR

1902-1903

Mrs Humphreys

34: Enter Mrs Humphreys

'Where did you learn to knit like that, Mrs Humphreys?' asked Lady Armstrong's daughter.

Violet hesitated mid-stitch. Truth be told she'd picked it up from pictures she had seen in magazines, and quite recently.

'Why?' she asked. 'Am I doing something wrong?'

Olivia wrinkled her nose. 'It's just a bit odd, that's all. I've never seen anyone knit that way before.'

'Well, show me how it's done then.' Violet gathered up the garment – a scarf, knit one row, pearl the next, it was about all she could manage – and handed it to the sixteen-year-old girl who sat with her.

Olivia took the needles and placed each one into the crook between the thumb and forefinger of either hand. It looked altogether daintier. 'So,' she said, scrutinising the garment and hooking the wool over her little finger. 'Where are we? Pearl row.' And she demonstrated.

It was impressive. Her hands barely seemed to move as they danced their way swiftly along the row, flick flack, flick flack, to the end, and with a twirl of her wrist she flipped the garment around and made her way back along the knit row before she handed it back to its owner.

'Well!' said Violet. 'That was remarkable. I was never taught, you see. I just sort of picked it up. I'm not sure I could do what you did, but I'll give it a try. So . . .'

Olivia went to stand behind Violet and guided the needles into the correct position in her hands, entwining the wool in and out of her fingers. 'I hate knitting,' she said, as she did so. 'I hate anything to do with needlework. It's boring.'

'I find it quite soothing,' said Violet, as Olivia resumed her seat. 'I never used to as a child, but now that I'm older, I suppose things are different.' She dropped a stitch, swore under her breath, lost control of the wool between her fingers and laboriously tried to weave her needle through the coils of stitches to retrieve the escapee. 'On the other hand,' she muttered, 'maybe I'm too old to learn how to suck eggs.'

'How old are you?' asked Olivia. She was making twisting patterns in the air with her hands, like a conjuror.

'My dear girl, that is not a question you should ever ask of a lady. Or a woman, come to that.'

Olivia sighed. She got up and sashayed around the room absently. 'Are you a lady?' she asked.

Violet looked up, startled. 'Exactly what do you mean?'

'Nothing,' said Olivia.

Olivia was a pretty girl who pouted a lot. She had very dark hair which she wore short, despite her mother's objections. She was slim and moved gracefully, like a dancer. She had learned ballet in her younger years and in idle moments such as this one she did little balletic movements, flicking out a leg with a perfectly pointed toe, and lifting her arms above her head in that elegantly languid manner ballerinas have.

She was enormously, and profoundly, bored, and she wanted the world to know it.

Violet felt sorry for her. Born of aristocracy, and traditionalist aristocracy at that, her future was entirely mapped out for her, and she knew it. Marriage to a man with a title, and property. Servants, balls, expensive holidays, shopping excursions, trips to Town for a play or a concert. Children. Sitting back while her husband steadily climbed whatever ladder he had chosen to climb, engaging in trivial conversation with friends chosen for their social standing rather than their entertainment value or their compatibility. A gilded prison, for which Olivia was not cut out.

What she was cut out for was not yet clear. She was not particularly bright, but she had a spark and a rebellious streak. Her world was very small and there was a lot in it she took for granted: someone to cook and clean for her, make her bed, dress her, buy her clothes for her, and plenty of people to talk down to even if they were almost twice her age, such as Violet. She would not want to relinquish any of that easily.

Yet Violet was fond of Olivia, and vice versa. She was really the only person the young girl felt she could say anything to.

But when she asked Violet, out of the blue and with studied indifference, while examining her nails: 'What did you do before you came here, Vi?' Violet was on immediate alert. She sensed Olivia had been put up to it, so her instinct told her to stall for time.

'What did you say?' she asked.

'I asked you,' Olivia said, with emphasis, as if to the deaf, 'what you did before you came to work here.'

'All sorts of things,' said Violet.

'"All sorts of things." Such as what, exactly?'

Violet placed her needles together and rolled the scarf-in-progress around them. She had been expecting this question for some time, ever since she'd come to work for Lord and Lady Armstrong, yet she'd never quite decided how she would respond.

'Well.' She held her knitting on her lap and said, 'I worked in the theatre, as a matter of fact.'

'The theatre?' Olivia made a grand gesture. '*Fantastique!* As an actress?'

'No no. I worked behind the scenes.'

She described her job, in broad terms, how she got to be there, and working for Herbert Tree and so on.

'Herbert TREE!' Olivia leapt to her feet and struck a pose. She was so like Lolly in many ways, thought Violet, though a lot less worldly, of course. 'I have heard of Herbert Tree. How *magnifique!* What is he like?'

'He's delightful,' said Violet. 'He treats everyone just the same, whether they're a famous actor or a minion like me.'

'You were a "minion"!' She pronounced it *mignonne.*

'In the larger scheme of things, yes. I read scripts for him.'

'Hah!' said Olivia. She continued to twirl and sashay for a moment, before declaring: 'It must have been a bit of a coming-down then, to find yourself here. Have you ever been a housekeeper before?'

That was the question Violet didn't want to answer. 'A long time ago, yes,' she said. She cleared her throat, as if to cleanse herself of the lie.

'I do not believe you,' said Olivia, again with emphasis. 'I believe you are a Countess down on her luck.'

Violet laughed heartily. 'Dear me, what makes you say that?'

'You are far too *classée* for a housekeeper. At least that's what mama said.'

'Your mama? Said that?'

'She was curious.'

'I see,' said Violet.

'And how, pray, did it so happen that you left the theatre and arrived at our humble abode?'

'It's a long story.'

'So?' Olivia sat down at last, placed her elbow on the

arm of her chair and her chin on her hand, gazed at Violet and blinked dramatically. 'And where is Mr Humphreys?'

'All these questions!'

'*Is* there a Mr Humphreys?'

It was getting all too complicated for words.

'You are right, I am asking too many questions,' said Olivia. 'You don't have to answer them. But if you do not, I will be compelled to ask you again, another time. And yet again. So you may as well save yourself the trouble and answer them now.'

She was beginning to get on Violet's nerves. 'You are being extremely intrusive, Olivia, and rather rude.'

'Ooh!' Olivia made a silly gesture with her hands and wobbled her head. 'I don't think the housekeeper is supposed to talk to the daughter of the house like that.'

'I don't suppose she is. But she does expect to be treated with some respect, nonetheless.'

Olivia continued to make mocking gestures. 'Well, thank you for putting me in my place, I'm sure.'

That expression. Violet closed her eyes and thought of the dreaded Theodore Dunkett. Suddenly she laughed.

'What's so funny?' Olivia more or less snapped.

'I was just reminded of a man I worked for.'

'Was he your lover?'

'No, far from it. But you reminded me of him. He spoke to me rather as you did, with the same kind of patronising sarcasm.' She looked at Olivia for a moment. She was such a child. 'I apologise if I was sharp, Olivia, but the point is . . . I may be your inferior, or you certainly seem to consider me so. And I would not dispute that. But the one thing a lady should have is a sense of manners.'

'Manners? Don't speak to me of manners! Mama talks of nothing else.'

'There is nothing wrong with manners. It's just another word for respect. For treating everyone as a human being whether they are your servant or your mother or – the King, if it comes to that. It will stand you in good stead in life, I promise you.'

Olivia slumped in her chair. 'Now you sound like *Trudie*.' She pronounced the name with a French accent. Trudie was Olivia's governess, a middle-aged Frenchwoman whose English was just this side of incomprehensible. 'Indeed, come to think of it, why aren't you a governess rather than a housekeeper?'

'Because I don't enjoy teaching, I never did. I enjoy being a housekeeper.'

'Really?'

'Yes, as a matter of fact, it suits me.' It was true, it did, more than Violet had anticipated. She enjoyed being in charge, and having people under her. It was a happy household. Her Ladyship, while conservative, even reactionary in outlook, was a kind and generous person to work for. Unlike her daughter, Lady Armstrong respected Violet's opinions and left her alone to run the household as she thought fit, with minimal interference. The servants were friendly, and biddable, and well enough paid as these things go. Violet made sure they were never overworked, she even gave them one day off a week, which was unheard of. She had time for everyone, from the lowliest scullery maid to the chief cook, and if there was a problem she wanted to hear about it. In that respect it was not unlike her last job, only this time there was nobody to boss her around. The house was grand yet comfortable, and her quarters were considerably superior to the shabby rooms in Crighton Street. Outside there were umpteen acres of beautiful country, with formal gardens, a well-kept lawn rolling down to a lake, and an ancient wood. And all that hearty, healthy, fresh country air. Yes, she was comfortable here, and happy. For how long she didn't know. But for now, it did her very nicely.

~

Back at His Majesty's Theatre things had happened very fast.

She had arrived at work one morning to find Theo – Mr Dunkett, as he insisted – sitting behind her own desk, with a face like thunder. She didn't need to ask what the matter was and he didn't seem to need to explain. He launched right in.

'Do you take me for a fool?' he raged. 'Did you think I wouldn't find out? Did you imagine you could take the law into your own hands, without consulting me, and get away with it?' Violet opened her mouth to speak but he carried right on. 'Can I not trust you to do your own job and leave me to do mine? Hmm? Is there some confusion there? Did I not explain things to you properly?'

He stopped. She waited for him to continue, and he did.

'Was there ever a time when a member of the company was allowed leave, for whatever reason, and still be paid? And to know that when she returned her position would be kept open for her? Has that ever happened before? Was there a precedent? What if everyone decided they wanted a few weeks off, would you still tell them they could take as long as they wanted and come back whenever they felt like it, would you?'

'No one else has ever asked to do that,' said Violet.

'Did you assume you could give the woman permission to come and go and keep it a secret? Was that what went through your mind? Well, what do you have to say?'

Violet felt surprisingly calm. He had given her plenty of time to get over the shock of finding someone else sitting behind *her* desk. The shock of her secret being discovered was, oddly, not so startling.

'I did not consult you because I knew you would have

said no,' she said.

Dunkett shot back in his chair. Her chair.

'She has been with the company for longer than any of us,' Violet continued. 'Working her hands to the bone, quietly and conscientiously. She is a valuable member of the company and her work means the world to her. If she could not be paid while she was having an operation on her back – an expensive operation, by the way – and know she had a position to return to when she was better, she would have been destitute. She would have had no money, no prospects. Nothing.' She paused. The longer Dunkett stared at her the smaller his tiny button eyes became. 'I did not think that was either fair or moral.'

She shifted her weight onto one foot and regarded him steadily.

'Is it your business to make moral judgments?' he demanded.

'It is my business to be humane. It is everybody's business to be humane.'

Dunkett nodded slowly. 'You think so.'

She continued to meet his gaze, calmly and confidently, even as she watched her job floating out of the window.

'Well, that is NOT how other people see things!' He banged his fists onto the table. His face had gone extremely red. 'And it is NOT your business to make such decisions. Who do you think you are?'

Violet shifted her weight onto her other foot. 'A decent human being,' she said, with a slight smile. 'Who understands people and believes in treating them properly.'

Dunkett kicked his chair violently as he stood up. 'I do not appreciate your tone, Mrs Graham. It seems to me in the time we have been working together that you have become more and more insubordinate. I cannot have it.'

He placed his hands on the desk and leaned across it. 'I

demand an apology. And an assurance that in future you consult with me on – every – single – decision – you – make.' With each word he banged a fist on the desk. 'Is that understood?'

Violet continued to look at him coolly for a moment, before she said: 'I cannot agree to that, to either of those demands. I do not regret what I did. And if you need someone who has to consult with you on every tiny little thing then you had better find yourself another assistant.'

She walked around the desk. 'And if you'll excuse me,' she went on, 'I will pack up my things and be out of your sight.'

Dunkett stepped back. 'What?'

She gave him a look that said 'You heard me,' and began opening drawers and removing her personal items.

'You can't just leave, like that, without notice.'

'As a matter of fact I can. I do not have a contract, I never did. Frank didn't either.' Violet bent down to reach the bottom drawer of the desk. 'It's what they call a gentleman's agreement. Between gentlemen. And ladies, of course. It works well, among people one can trust. When the trust breaks down, then . . .'

She pulled out a bag from the drawer and, taking her time, she placed her few personal bits and pieces into it. She was very aware of him standing there, motionless, breathing heavily, which is why she was in no hurry. Then, quite unnecessarily, she went through the drawers of her desk one more time, as if checking there was anything she had missed. She was so enjoying the moment she didn't want it to end.

But finally she stepped away from the desk. 'Goodbye, Mr Dunkett,' she said. 'I wish I could say it's been a pleasure but you know I would be lying.'

Then she turned to the door, which was still open, exited, and closed it behind her very, very quietly.

35: The reunion with Amy

Afterwards Violet walked home, slowly, dawdling almost, gazing into shop windows, stopping to watch an altercation between a hackney cab driver and a boy with a cart full of oranges who pulled out in front of him at the junction of Haymarket and Jermyn Street. It was a warm, balmy day, the air felt fresh and she took deep breaths.

At Saskia's in Cranbourn Street she was seriously tempted by a dress in the window display, but common sense stepped in just in time. The days of spontaneous consumption were over, for now at least. She was not panicking; she had known the moment Theodore Dunkett appeared on the scene she would be disappearing out of it. Now it was done she felt almost a sense of relief. The end of another chapter in her life.

Strolling up Charing Cross Road she paused to look into the window of a bookshop. She became aware of a man standing next to her, his hat tilted so she could not see his face. Was she being followed, again? She laughed at her paranoia, and continued straight on up the road across St Giles Circus and on to Hampstead Road. As she turned into Crighton Street she heard them, footsteps, following her to her doorstep. Yes, it was the man at the bookshop. She turned at her front door and said to him, 'What are you doing?'

The man lifted his head so she could see his face. He was not familiar.

'Is your name Mrs Anthony Turnip?' he asked.

'Who are you?'

'I am nobody,' the man replied. 'Are you Mrs Anthony Turnip?' he repeated.

'Who wants to know?'

She bit her tongue as she said it. Was that tantamount to an admission? The man appeared to think so, as, unsmiling, he tipped his hat to her and sauntered off down the street in the direction in which he had come.

Now she was panicking. This was not a paranoid dream, or nightmare. That was the real thing. There was only one person who would have set that man on her, and the mere thought of him made her heart beat so hard she thought it would burst out of its socket.

In the refuge of her room she sat down until her pulse had returned to normal. She remained perfectly still, thinking, and then trying not to think. Images swam into her mind – Frank, with his permanently harried expression; Tree, who always looked so delighted to see one; Sebastian, Jack and Peter, actors; the haughty Merry and Gaye; Lolly; and Archie, kind, unflappable Archie, who looked at the world as if it were one grand comedy, peopled by comedians, and tragedians – in Archie's eyes there was little difference. Archie, perhaps the most contented man she had ever met.

Then another face drifted into her mind, of another contented soul: Amy, her one-time personal maid.

She had kept in touch with Amy, on and off, through the post. She had not seen her since they said goodbye on the doorstep at Humphreys Street. Amy was no longer there of course, and yet . . . servants talk to one another. Servants know more about what goes on in their households than anyone. Amy had been close friends with

Clara, the cook in Humphreys Street. She might just know what had been going on in the Turnip house.

Violet pulled out a sheet of paper from her desk and began to write.

That evening she spoke to Kapps. She told him about the row, and how she had walked out without saying goodbye to anyone. Kapps listened without speaking, nodding every so often, his brow wrinkled in anxiety.

'You walked out without saying goodbye?'

Violet nodded. 'I just needed to get right away. I've never been good at goodbyes, I don't see the point in them.'

'And now what?' asked Kapps.

'I have no idea.'

'No idea at all?' Kapps' brow was so deeply furrowed he was almost scowling.

'You don't happen to have a vacancy for an assistant, do you?' she joked.

'No. But I could ask for you. Ask around, is that how you say it? For a fine and stylish young woman as yourself, there should be something. There should be many opportunities.'

Violet shook her head. 'I don't think so, thank you Zunker. I think I need to get right away, out of London.' She wondered about telling Kapps about the man on the doorstep, and decided not. He would only make a fuss.

'How is – what's his name, your assistant?' she asked.

'Danny? Danny is . . .' Kapps paused, and touched his beard. 'At heart he is a rapscallion – is that the word?' He chuckled to himself. 'However, he is also a natural showman, not like me. When he tries he can charm the tusks off an elephant.'

Violet laughed. 'Where did you get that expression, Zunker?'

'From Danny himself. He is not a modest person. But if

he tries, he does very well. He has more natural skill than me. He can charm a lady with his talk, which I can never do, as you know, although . . .' He stopped, and mumbled something into his beard.

'Are you blushing, Zunker?' asked Violet.

'Oh yes, probably.' He looked up, smiled shyly, and looked down again.

'You have met someone.'

'Yes. I have.'

'Oh, please, tell me.' Violet reached out to touch him on the arm. 'Who is she? What is her name? Where is she from? How did you meet? What does she look like?'

Kapps waved Violet's hand away, saying, 'In turn. Her name is Constance, she is from Romania, she is an *emigrée*, like me, she came to the shop. She knows no one. Like me when I first came to London.' He paused. 'Oh, and she is tall, and very elegant, like you, and her nose is – very distinguished.' He came to a halt.

'And that's it? She has a distinguished nose? Has she anything else?'

'Yes. She has a sense of humour. She laughs at herself, and the world. Not like me.'

'She sounds quite delightful Zunker, I can't wait to meet her.'

'I would love for you to meet her. But you are going away.'

'Am I? Oh. Yes, so I am. What a shame. Still,' she beamed broadly at Kapps. 'I am truly delighted for you, Zunker. It's high time.'

~

They met in a café in Charlotte Street. It was as close to the West End as Violet was prepared to go.

She was surprisingly nervous. She had not seen Amy for four years. Amy was part of her old life, the life she had gone to such lengths to get away from. Four years is not a long time, in one sense, but for Violet it was another world.

'How are you?' she began.

Amy smiled. 'I am very well, madam, and how are you?' She looked quite unchanged.

'Please don't call me madam. Call me Violet, however hard you find it.' Violet smiled back, uncertainly. 'I'm all right, really. How are your Chelsea people?'

'Mr and Mrs Richardson? They are very well, thank you.'

'I mean how is it, being in their employ?' Amy could be quite hard work.

'It's very good. Yes, they are kind people, and very rich.' She giggled. That's more like it, thought Violet. 'They have their own carriage. And stables for the horses. And footmen for the carriage.' She arched her eyebrows. 'And a very large staff.'

'That's good.'

'And how about you, madam?' asked Amy politely. 'How is the theatre?'

'Violet, Amy, please. The theatre is all right.' She didn't want to go into all that. 'The point is, I need to know something.' She cleared her throat. 'Do you ever hear of Mr Turnip?'

Amy paused with her teacup halfway to her lips. She replaced it slowly and carefully before she replied. 'Sometimes, yes, I do.'

'And?'

'And what, ma – Violet? What is it you wish to know?'

'Do you still talk to Clara?'

'Oh yes, we are still good friends.' Amy lifted her cup again and drank from it.

'I am going to ask you to be indiscreet, Amy. I know it pains you, but I need to know what's going on in – with Mr Turnip.'

'You mean, how he is?'

'No, I need to know more than that. I need to know . . .' How on earth could she put this? 'Is he still living on his own?'

Amy didn't answer this for a moment. Then, 'How do you mean, on his own?'

'I mean does he have another woman living with him?'

Amy frowned, and stared at her plate.

'All right Amy, I may as well tell you,' said Violet. 'There has been a man following me.'

'What?' Amy looked up in alarm.

'And I have reason to believe it has something to do with Mr Turnip. So I need to know why he is having me followed. I know you hate to be indiscreet, Amy, but . . .' she hesitated. 'I'm frightened.'

Amy was frowning still, and conflicted.

'It need go no further,' Violet added, by way of encouragement. Amy would make a magnificent spy, she couldn't help thinking. 'I can't begin to tell you how terrifying it is to have someone following you, and speaking to you.'

'Speaking to you? What did he say?'

'He asked me if I was Mrs Anthony Turnip.'

'Oh.'

'Your tea is getting cold.'

'Oh, yes.' But she made no attempt to drink it. 'I think,' Amy began, uncertainly, 'he may be looking for a divorce.'

'Go on,' said Violet, encouragingly.

'There is another woman, yes. I have heard. Though whether or not they are living under the same roof . . .' She hurried on. 'Clara said he talks about her constantly, and how he intends to make her his wife.'

'Thank you, Amy.'

'And I believe he mentioned something about . . .' she coughed discreetly into her hand, 'adultery.'

'Adultery? Whose adultery? His or mine?'

'Yours.' Amy looked at Violet directly. 'This is what Clara said. She heard it from Billy, at table one evening. Mr Turnip was talking to his lady friend, something to do with hoping to catch you out with another . . . ' she pursed her lips.

And then quite suddenly, and together, they burst out laughing.

'Oh my goodness!' Violet pulled out a handkerchief and dabbed at her eyes. 'So he thought if he could catch me out with another man, he could divorce me for adultery.'

'I believe that is what he had in mind, yes.'

'Well, well, what do you know? The bastard! Sorry, Amy.' She touched the younger woman's arm briefly. 'So, the man who was following me – how disappointed he must be.'

But her mind was racing, back to when she arrived at her doorstep with Algie, all that time ago.

'I have given up my job, Amy, and I don't know what to do next.'

'Oh. I am sorry.'

'I do not want his money. I do not want to hear from him again. I do not want to hear *of* him again. Now that you've put me in the picture. I am so grateful to you, Amy. Would you like some more tea?'

'Why, yes, thank you.'

Violet beckoned for a waitress and ordered a fresh pot of tea. 'I want to get right away from here,' she went on. 'Away from my work, my friends, away from Anthony. Goodness only knows where. Oh, thank you.' This last to the waitress, who removed their empty teapot and replaced it with another.

'I do know of a position going as a housekeeper,' said Amy. 'For Lord and Lady Armstrong. They are desperate,

I hear, their last housekeeper left quite suddenly.'

'Oh? Why?'

'I believe she was very ill. There was no disagreement. Lord and Lady Armstrong are delightful people, so I've heard. Not that you would think of becoming a housekeeper!' She giggled, and poured the tea.

Violet turned to look out of the window. A small child was playing tug of war with its nanny. The child won.

'I might,' said Violet, turning back.

'Never!' cried Amy.

'I might well.'

'But you're a – how can you think it, madam?'

'I'm not madam any more Amy, I haven't been for some time. I'm just plain Mrs . . . Mrs . . .' Heavens above, she had quite forgotten who she was for a moment. 'I rather fancy the idea of a complete change, away from London, with accommodation thrown in. Tell me more.'

Amy was staring at Violet with her mouth open.

'Well?'

'They have a beautiful house, so I'm told, right in the Sussex countryside. With acres and acres of land, and a lake and everything.'

'It sounds very appealing.' Violet drank her tea. She felt so much better, now she knew exactly what was going on. 'Would they consider someone with no experience?'

'If you are serious, madam – Violet. They would not need to know that. Necessarily.' Amy looked at Violet over her teacup.

'How do you mean?'

'I am very good at writing letters of application,' said Amy, replacing her cup. 'I have done it for many people. I'm known for it, in fact.' She smiled. 'I could help you, if you really mean this.'

And that is how it happened. Right there and then, borrowing a sheet of paper from the manager of the café,

Violet, prompted by Amy, who giggled throughout, wrote a letter to Lady Armstrong applying for the position of housekeeper, ready to start immediately, available for interview at a moment's notice. References to follow.

'And how shall you sign it, madam?'

'How do you mean?'

'With what name?'

'Oh, gracious, I hadn't thought about that.' But she did think about that now. Could she possibly give herself yet another name? Yes, she could, and should. 'Mrs Humphreys,' she said, and she signed accordingly. 'And not a word of this to anyone Amy, not even Clara. Especially not to Clara.'

'My lips are sealed like a widow's tomb,' said Amy.

The references never did follow. Violet was invited down to Sussex the day after she sent the letter and enjoyed a delightful chat with the charming Lady Armstrong, who in the course of half an hour of conversation never once asked to see a reference, or questioned her about her housekeeping experience, and who hired Violet on the spot.

36: Downstairs

So Mrs Graham assumed yet another new name, and as Mrs Humphreys she decided in the few days before she departed for the countryside to gen up on the responsibilities of the housekeeper according to the authority of all authorities, Mrs Beeton. She read that it was the duty of that lady to be honest and hard-working. That she should set an example to the rest of the staff of cleanliness, punctuality and order. It was also necessary – and here Violet baulked slightly – for the housekeeper to 'thoroughly understand accounts'. This was the only area in which she had no expertise whatsoever. There should be different account books for different kinds of expenditure, Mrs B went on, and evenings were the best time for the tallying of the day's finances and the righting of any discrepancies. She should always rise early; and last, but by no means least, like "Caesar's wife" her sobriety and vigilance should be absolute.

There was nothing there that Violet did not already know of course, though seeing it written down gave it that extra *gravitas*. And there was nothing there she couldn't handle perfectly well, apart from the accounts. And in that regard she would just have to hope for the best.

It tickled her, the idea that she, Mrs Anthony Turnip, née Frogg, aka Mrs Graham aka Mrs Humphreys was about to embark on a new life 'downstairs'. That at a time when most people's aspirations headed upwards she should deliberately set off in the opposite direction. It was an opportunity not many people came by.

~

Kenley Manor was an unintimidating early nineteenth century edifice, set in acres of glorious Sussex countryside and beautifully and lovingly maintained by generations of Armstrongs. The current incumbents were affable and undemanding, and downstairs was a friendly, well-organised place where the daily routine ran like clockwork. The tone was set by the butler, a plump, jolly gentleman by the appropriate name of Mr Gross. He welcomed Violet warmly, shook her hand until it nearly dropped off, introduced her to everyone, sat her down in the steward's room and told her everything she needed to know about everything and everyone, including his wife, Mrs Gross, who was the head cook and was as jolly as her husband, if a good deal quieter. They were a grand couple, who laughed and joked with one another constantly and reminded Violet of characters from a Dickens novel. Before he ventured upstairs Mr Gross's jacket had to be inspected for signs of flour on the back that indicated he'd been canoodling with the cook, yet again. As romantic attachments go, it was the warmest, the easiest and the most equable Violet had ever witnessed, and it made her sigh with pleasure, and yearning, and a number of emotions she could not readily identify.

She was given a uniform. A plain navy blue dress, as worn by housekeepers throughout the country, throughout the world. She didn't mind in the least, it made the business of deciding what to wear every morning so much easier. It even gave her a kind of authority, more than she felt she'd ended up with in her last position. And unlike last time she felt ready. Her baptism by fire in Tree's company had toughened her, taught her how to prepare for anything. How to stand up for herself, and bluff where necessary.

For an upstairs household of four – Lord and Lady Armstrong, their son Rupert, who was away for most of the year at university, and their daughter Olivia – downstairs was generously staffed, and the servants were rarely overworked. Their Lord- and Ladyships entertained quite rarely and were often absent, visiting friends or spending time in London. The only stipulation they made was that no one was to feed their dogs other than themselves, except of course while they were away. The atmosphere below stairs was relaxed, and merry, and surprisingly unhierarchical. On quiet evenings they would gather around a piano, played with more enthusiasm than expertise by the under-cook, Bridie, and enjoy a sing-song. Best of all, Mr Gross was a wizard with numbers and was only too happy to explain the accounting system to Violet and to help out whenever it got too much for her. She had, you could say, fallen on her feet.

Nobody showed much interest in her background, or her experience. That she and Lady Armstrong got on so well was enough to keep the household upstairs running smoothly and life below stairs happy.

They gossiped, as servants do. They made running jokes about Lord Armstrong's eyebrows and Lady Armstrong's habit of sticking pencils into her hair and forgetting about them. They had little time for Olivia, whom they regarded as a spoiled brat. Young Rupert, son and heir, whom Violet had yet to meet, was, as they described him, 'fortunately absent' for a good part of the year.

There was no doubt Olivia was rude to the servants, and yes, one could call her a spoiled brat, though that depends on how one defined 'spoiled'. Of course she had had everything a child could want by way of food, and comfort, and beautiful surroundings and so on. But what she had never had was the sort of attention and love that can only come from a parent. She had been brought up, like all upper-class children around the country, by a series of nannies and nurses and governesses. She rarely saw her parents when she was small and as a result they knew little about her and understood even less. It was only fairly recently that she'd been allowed to share the dining table with them, and then the conversation was desultory and commonplace. As parents Lord and Lady Armstrong showed very little interest in the thoughts and the desires – and the fears – of a young girl approaching womanhood. In that respect Violet felt she and Olivia had one thing in common.

So that is how the friendship sprang up between Olivia and the housekeeper, who was not only far nearer to her own age than her governess, but to whom she felt she was able to say pretty well anything and know that it would go no further. Violet never criticised Olivia for anything other than her rudeness, which was deeply rooted and quite prodigious.

One day a couple of letters arrived for Violet, forwarded on by Amy. Reminders of the world she had left behind so suddenly. One was a formal notice, from a solicitor, of her estranged husband's desire to divorce her, details to follow. The other was from Algie.

It was not a nice letter, not at all. It was hard, and cold, and full of reproach for what he described as her astonishingly selfish behaviour – running away suddenly without saying goodbye to anyone or telling anyone where she had gone. Did she not realise how much anxiety she had caused?

She huffed and puffed, swore quietly, tore the letter into tiny pieces and threw it into the fire. Two minutes later she regretted it. What was it he had said about good news? Too late. She would never know now.

As for divorce, so what? She was perfectly happy to concur without the need for anyone to prove adultery, if such a thing were legally possible. It made no difference to her either way. She had become used to living the life of a single woman, albeit with a married name. It was not as if she had plans to marry again, not now, and probably not ever.

~

Winter was hard. Working hours were longer in the winter, with all the fires to be lit, and the grates cleaned, the coal fetched and the fenders polished till you could see your face in them. And there was all that darkness. Early on Violet took the unprecedented step of undertaking, herself, all the various tasks that were normally done by the housemaids, the chambermaids, the scullery maids and even the footmen. She scrubbed the grates, she cleaned the bedrooms, she made the beds, she chopped the onions, she even laundered the bedding. In a moment of spontaneous excitement at the novelty of her new position she declared she could not ask anyone to do anything she would not be prepared to do herself; and that until she had tried her hand at the scrubbing and the washing and the chopping and even on one occasion – to the bemusement of their Lord- and Ladyships – the waiting at table, she could not fully appreciate what was expected of the various members of the downstairs community to keep the house running smoothly. After some initial bewilderment, and suspicion, since no housekeeper had ever dreamed of doing such a thing before in anyone's experience, the servants looked at Violet with new respect.

It was a long day – from five thirty in the morning until ten o'clock at night, on average, with no days off for herself – and the work was unremitting. Overlooking 'all that goes on in the house,' and seeing 'that every department is thoroughly attended to' was a full-time business. Above all it kept her mind busy. There was no time for contemplation or reflection or, most importantly, thinking about the future.

So the conversations with Olivia were really the nearest Violet came to relaxation and she looked forward to them.

She tried to explain to Olivia the ludicrousness of a world in which an accident of birth dictated that one person should own a property with twenty bedrooms and a sizeable chunk of East Sussex, and lord it over a gaggle of servants who worked a seventeen-hour day for a relative pittance. But Olivia didn't get it, or didn't want to get it. To her it was as natural as daylight. Such a glimpse into the rarefied realm of entitlement was, to Violet, both fascinating and alarming.

But then Kenley Manor was a world in itself, a claustrophobic world; some of the servants had been there for upwards of five or even ten years and knew very little of life outside. Nor for the most part did they seem to care. Lord and Lady Armstrong could up sticks and take themselves on a holiday to the Riviera, or the Italian lakes, without a second thought. The notion of overseas travel to the folk downstairs on the other hand was as foreign as the countries they would never have a chance to visit. It was absurd, but it was.

The closer they became the more Olivia and Violet confided in one another. Olivia let her guard down more with Violet than anyone else. She even forgot, on occasion, to talk down to her. In fact one might even say that she was beginning to look *up* to Violet as a Woman of the World, who had been places and done things. She even envied her. She wanted to know everything about her. There were of course secrets Violet was not prepared to divulge, so for the time being, as far as Olivia was concerned, Violet had divorced Mr Humphreys when she was quite young and, needing to make a living, had found a position working behind the scenes in the theatre and then, as a result of a 'difference of opinion', she had quit that job and come to work as a housekeeper at Kenley Manor. And yes, she had had servants when she was married. She had employed a housekeeper, so it was a bit of a turnaround you could say, but she was none the worse for it. In between times she had become briefly involved with the suffragists, which was partly the cause of the breakdown of her marriage.

Now Olivia was on full alert. 'Tell me all!' she demanded. 'Didn't Mr Humphreys approve? Why not? Was that why he divorced you? Or did you divorce him? How does it work, this divorce thing?'

'It works in the man's favour,' said Violet. 'Which is partly why there is such a strong need for women to be given the vote.'

'Do you mean women don't have the vote?' asked Olivia.

Violet did her best to hide her astonishment. 'No, they don't.'

'Why not?'

'That is exactly the point. Nobody has a proper answer to that. It is men who run this country, and while only men are allowed to vote, that is how it will stay. Indefinitely. Unless someone does something about it.'

'So who is going to do something about it?'

'People like you,' said Violet.

Olivia's mind was struggling to absorb all this fresh information. 'What can someone like me do?'

'You could get involved. They are eager to recruit people like you, young people.'

'But aren't they all awfully common?'

Violet laughed. 'What do you mean?'

'You know. Common people. Cockneys and so forth.'

'As a matter of fact they are far from "common", as you call it. Most of them are highly educated and extremely well bred, frighteningly so in some cases.' Violet thought back to the haughty Lady Dalloway. 'There are doctors, and nurses, and lawyers and actresses. You'd feel very much at home among them, I'm sure.'

Olivia was straining forwards in her chair now. 'Tell me about them.'

And so Violet gave Olivia a brief rundown of the history of the women's suffrage movement: of Mrs Millicent Fawcett and her sister, Elizabeth Garrett Anderson; of how for years, in the century just gone, they lobbied Parliament, leafleted, held meetings, and did everything within the law to bring the topic of women's suffrage to the centre of public awareness. How a lady named Mrs Emmeline Pankhurst had recently appeared on the scene and was threatening to raise the stakes. There was talk of acts of civil disobedience if the suffragettes – as they were now called – continued to be ignored.

'So, there we are. And after all these years we are not much closer to being given the vote than we were fifty years ago,' Violet concluded.

Olivia had sat perfectly still and silent throughout Violet's oration. Now she said, 'Can I join? How can I join? Could you introduce me?'

Violet laughed gently. 'Why do you want to join the movement, Olivia?' She had a good idea, but she wanted to hear it from the horse's mouth.

'Because it would be brave, and adventurous!' Olivia threw both hands in the air dramatically. 'And worthwhile, of course.'

'You don't become a suffragette for fun. It is hard work. Hard and relentless. And the way things are going you could find yourself in deep trouble.'

'Deep trouble, yes!' cried Olivia. She stood up and did a twirl.

'It is not a game, Olivia. If you really, really believe in women's rights, then . . .'

'What are women's rights?'

Heavens above. 'The right for a woman to do everything a man does.' That would have to do for the time being. 'If you believe in equality for women, because that is what the movement is all about, that carries a responsibility.'

'I do believe in equality for women. But you try persuading ma and pa!' Olivia stood, hands on hips, her legs spread wide.

Violet smiled in acquiescence. 'One step at a time. Perhaps,' she continued after a small thought, 'you could find it in yourself to turn your parents' ideas around. Now *that* would be an important achievement.'

37: Suffragist to suffragette

Violet sat in her room and gazed out over the lawn at the back of Kenley Manor. Winter was coming to an end but the trees were still starkly bare, and on a clear day you could see right across the Downs almost as far as the coast. Unusually, the housekeeper's room was not located downstairs in the basement but, along with Mr and Mrs Gross's quarters, on the ground floor, as was the kitchen. Again, this was Mr Gross' innovation. Nobody, in his view, should be made to live and work without daylight.

Violet had received her latest bundle of forwarded letters. Among them was one from Mr Kapps, telling her he had proposed to his Constance and been accepted, and how happy they were and he so much hoped Violet would attend the wedding. He did not ask her about herself, and unlike Algie – whom he did not mention – he did not tell her off for disappearing without saying goodbye. His letter was so full of quiet joy it brought tears to Violet's eyes.

She stood up and went to look out of the window. There was a crow perched on a wall outside. He was looking right at her. She stared right back at him, and as he began to hop sideways along the wall, so she did the same, until they were hidden from one another by the window frame. After a short pause he hopped back into view, hop hop hop hop, and she mirrored him hop by hop as if in some surreal ballet. This went on for a considerable time before she remembered the task in hand.

She began writing:

> 'Dearest Zunker. Congratulations. I am
> delighted for you. You deserve all the joy in
> the world. I look forward to meeting your
> Constance . . .'

When? Where?

> 'I look forward to meeting your Constance one
> day. I am doing well.'

There. He did not need to know any more about where she was or what she was doing. In the ecstasy of his happiness he probably didn't care.

There was nothing from Algie. He had clearly given up, and she could hardly blame him. It was years since they'd stood outside her house, he holding onto her hand for too long, arguing about *Mrs Warren*, comparing her to Vivie and telling her how beautiful she looked. Was that really the last time she'd seen him? And then there was that angry letter he'd written, not so long ago, which she'd thrown into the fire and to which she had not responded. All water under the bridge now.

No doubt he had found himself another lady friend and she wished him all the happiness in the world, and please do NOT invite me to your wedding, whenever that may be.

She pondered on the sort of woman Algie might marry. Someone high up the social ladder, no doubt – beautiful, and clever, but only moderately so. No man wants to marry a woman who is cleverer than he is. She would bear him children, something she, Violet, was apparently not able to do, and they would live comfortably in a pleasant house in somewhere like South Kensington, or maybe Knightsbridge, overlooking the park. As the years went by however Mrs Robinson would become crabby, and fat, and spiteful, and would begin having affairs. She would mock Algie for making light of her insults, especially since she had put so much effort into them. The more she made his life hell the more time he spent at work, and after several years of working a twelve-hour day he became the editor of *The Weekly Chronicle*. Meanwhile in his spare time he continued writing plays that nobody wanted to produce.

Violet stopped short. Where did that little outburst come from? She apologised to her imaginary version of Algie before turning her attention back to the crow, who was straining forwards as if trying to regain her attention. She waved at him. He did not wave back. He stared at her a moment longer and, seeing that she was no longer interesting or entertaining, he flew off.

Where was she?

Dorothy. There was a letter from Miss Dorothy Moss, proud and passionate suffragist. Now that *was* a surprise.

'Where are you and what are you up to?'

She hadn't changed, clearly.

'I called round the other day and you weren't there and no one knew where you'd gone. We haven't seen you at meetings recently. No doubt you've given up, like so many others.'

Violet closed her eyes for a moment. Dorothy's voice rang in her ears.

'The Victoria & Albert goes from strength to strength. It is so popular they've built an underground station solely to serve the museum.'

She went on to describe, with extended enthusiasm, some of their latest acquisitions, including 'the smallest imaginable glass weights from Ancient Egypt for measuring coins' and a bed belonging to the actor David Garrick. She also sounded off about the idiots running the

country and how it was high time they were voted out.
And she concluded with:

> 'I don't suppose you are interested but Mrs
> Pankhurst is addressing a meeting at Caxton
> Hall a week next Tuesday the 24th, at 2
> o'clock. "Deeds not words!" That is our new
> slogan. There are exhilarating times ahead.'

It seemed, the suffragists – or suffragettes as they now appeared to be known as – had been galvanised, at long last, mostly by the formidable Mrs Pankhurst, about whom Violet was highly curious.

She could take Olivia, thought Violet. She could introduce her, and who knows, maybe the girl would take a genuine interest. It would give her life some purpose and take her out of her environment. Moreover, Lord and Lady Armstrong were about to go away for their annual early spring sojourn in Switzerland, so there was really nothing to stop her and Olivia making a day's excursion to London.

Yes, it looked highly possible. And a day out would do both of them the power of good.

> 'Dear Dorothy. I am delighted. . .' No. 'I am
> very pleased to hear from you. I am well and
> living in East Sussex. However I will do my
> best to come to the meeting on the 24th, and
> look forward to seeing you then. Yours
> sincerely, Violet.'

'Yours sincerely, Violet.' It seemed so formal. And to someone whom she had known so intimately. Violet shivered with excitement. She found she was almost looking forward to seeing Dorothy again. She would talk to Olivia immediately.

Olivia took no persuading at all. Trudie was not quite so straightforward. There was much gesticulating and exclamations in a mixture of French and English before she finally shrugged, tutted and said, '*D'accord.*'

~

As they travelled to London on the train Violet described some of the more colourful women she had come into contact with in the suffrage movement, including Dorothy Moss and Lolly Mulligan, and of course Prudence Brooks, who had tried unsuccessfully to storm Parliament. She was aware Olivia was taking not the slightest notice of anything she was saying but was gazing vacantly out of the carriage window at the passing countryside.

Violet was apprehensive now at the prospect of seeing her old suffragist acquaintances again. The movement, and her temporary involvement in it, was too much tied up with a past life she was trying to forget, and she did not want to have to explain to the likes of Lady Dalloway why she had apparently abandoned the cause completely. And yet. Here they were.

It was a short walk from the station to Caxton Hall, but Olivia strung it out as much as she could, peering, at length, into every shop window. She was like a puppy, released into the world for the first time and eager to take everything in. And why not?

'I love London,' she said, approximately five minutes after arriving there.

The Hall was packed, as it had been all those years before. But they were a very different crowd. To begin with they were all women, and mostly young, and there was an atmosphere, an excitement that had not been so obviously present in the earlier days. Violet recognised one or two of the attendees, who nodded at her and went on their way. Of Lolly or Prue, or of Lady Dalloway, there was no sign.

Then she felt a tug on her arm and there was Dorothy.

'You came. Bravo! Come and sit with me.'

She asked Violet no questions at all. She took rather

more interest in Olivia – 'Young blood, excellent. Your first time?' – and as she steered the two of them towards a row near the front she gave Olivia a potted biography of the distinguished speaker they were about to see. Mrs Pankhurst was a remarkable woman, down in London from her home in Manchester with her daughter Christobel, another remarkable woman, from an altogether remarkable family. Despite being the widow of Dr Pankhurst, the failed parliamentarian, who died leaving his wife penniless and forced to go out to work to feed her four children, Emmeline Pankhurst's passion for women's suffrage was unassuaged. Olivia listened, or appeared to listen, without saying a word.

At last the Hall hushed, as the lady herself appeared, with her eldest daughter by her side. She was smaller than Violet had expected, a slim, almost frail figure with a pale, handsome face framed by neatly-coiffed black hair.

She stood perfectly still, head bowed, as she was introduced, to a round of applause. After a moment she looked up and there was immediate silence.

'Ladies,' she smiled. 'How gratifying to see so many of you here today.'

Her voice was light and thin, like the rest of her. She spoke quietly, yet clearly, as if she were addressing friends in her drawing room.

'There have been a number of arguments put forward over the past fifty years or as to why women should not be given the vote. Let me iterate some of them for you.'

She produced a lorgnette and consulted her notes.

'"It is against the will of the Almighty".' She looked up briefly, and continued.

'"You must not have the vote because there are so many of you."

"It will lead to domestic discord and the neglect of home life."

"You wouldn't use the vote if you had it."

"This is an experiment so large and bold that it ought to be tried by some other country first".'

She removed her lorgnette and waited for the laughter to die down.

'Let me deal with those arguments one by one.

'Firstly – "It is against the will of the Almighty." God, in other words, does not approve. It is just possible that those who make such claims have a direct line to the Divine Will on the subject; but where in the Bible, I ask them, does it say to women "Thou shalt not vote"?

'Secondly: "There are too many of you." Yes! Indeed there are. There are many of us, and there are many men too. Does that mean our very weight of numbers is the reason we should not be given a voice? What comes next?'

She glanced at her notes again.

'"It must lead to domestic discord and the neglect of home life." Why? How long does it take a woman to cast a vote? As long as it takes to walk to the shops and back. As for domestic discord, can a marriage not withstand a bit of healthy argument within its doors?

'Next – "Let the colonies try it out first. They'll soon see what a mistake it was."'

She paused.

'Last year, New Zealand and South Australia introduced votes for women. Before that, the Isle of Man, and several of the United States of America did the same. Where are the revolutions? Where are all those evils that are supposed to be raining down on those poor nations? In New Zealand, women voted in the same proportion as men, infantile death has been reduced by half, a minimum wage now applies to women as well as to men, and moreover men for the first time are beginning to take an interest in women's affairs. All thanks to women's suffrage.

'However, according to the anti-suffrage press, if you say nothing about something it is as if that something never happened. So the world at large remains ignorant of the proven advantages and progress created by women's right to vote.'

She described her experiences visiting workhouses in Manchester and watching heavily-pregnant women forced to scrub floors. She told of little girls of thirteen who came into her office to register the birth of their babies – 'illegitimate, of course' – and in many cases it was the child's own father, or another close relative, who was responsible. The workhouses were full of educated, law-abiding women, widows of artisans or men who had served their country in the forces, who had been left destitute when their husband's income and pension died with him. Many of the women were there because of abuse, or neglect, by men. But while women were denied the vote these issues would continue to be ignored.

She spoke dispassionately, yet eloquently, of the conditions inside these workhouses. Of the darkness, the drabness of these women's lives, the prevailing atmosphere of apathy and despair. Images of Winnie Walters floated into Violet's mind and she felt the prick of tears. Half the Hall was dabbing at their eyes by now.

She glanced at Olivia from time to time. The girl's mouth was hanging open, as it tended to do when her attention was so absorbed she forgot herself. Maybe it was those thirteen-year-olds impregnated by their fathers, or the young servant girls whose masters treated them as fair game and then discarded them; or maybe it was her realisation of a world outside her own that she knew nothing about. Violet reached over and gave her hand a reassuring squeeze.

As Mrs Pankhurst sat down, to thunderous applause, her daughter Christobel got to her feet and introduced the assembly to the newly-formed Women's Social and Political Society, open to women only, whose slogan was 'Deeds not words'. Christobel, though very young – not too much older than Olivia – and occasionally tripping over her words, nonetheless spoke firmly, and ardently, acknowledging the groundwork laid by Mrs Fawcett and others but hinting at more direct action to come. 'They are calling us suffragettes now.' she announced. 'And we are proud to be so!'

Then Mrs Pankhurst stood again and talked of the impending general election. 'We are placing our support with the Liberal Party but only, and I stress this, only if they support our cause. If they continue as the current incumbents in government have been doing, debating for hours on end the pros and cons of whether or not a cart should carry lights in front as well as behind, laughing and joking as they do so, with not a care for anything except for making sure there is no time left over for a discussion of women's suffrage, then we withdraw our support immediately.'

It was at that point that Olivia began to scowl, and to idly kick the chair in front of her, causing its occupant to swivel and hiss, 'Please!' in a stage whisper. The remainder of the row also turned to see who was causing the fuss. Violet thought she saw Olivia stick her tongue out at them, which was her cue to whisper to Dorothy, 'We have to go,' and then, to the annoyance of the ladies in their row, to squeeze their way past all those pairs of knees to the exit of the Hall and out into the street.

38: Mrs Morphett's Macaroons

She was silent all the way along Victoria Street. She walked with her head down, lower lip jutting, looking neither to right nor left. When Violet suggested they stop for a cup of tea Olivia just shook her head and kept on walking. Either the meeting had had such a profound effect on her she'd been rendered speechless, or she'd been so utterly bored she could not be bothered to communicate. There was no way of knowing with Olivia.

At the station they paused by the indicator board while Violet looked for the platform to Renwick. Olivia stood beside her, head still bowed. Anyone watching them might wonder if she was a prisoner on day release, submissively following in the footsteps of her guardian. Then as they made their way towards the platform Violet's eye was caught by a poster on a wall. She stopped dead, and stared, while Olivia marched on. After a whole minute Violet followed her, quickening her pace to catch up.

They were both completely silent on the return journey to Sussex. Olivia gazed out of the window, thoughts unknown. Violet, sitting opposite, thought about the poster. It was advertising a special Saturday matinee of a play called *Mrs Morphett's Macaroons*, written by Robbie Robinson and featuring Lolly Mulligan as Annie Addeley, to be held at the Comedy Theatre on Saturday 4th April.

Just under two weeks away.

Olivia vanished to her bedroom on arrival. She had still not spoken one word since they had left Caxton Hall. Violet suppressed her annoyance and made her way downstairs in the hope of finding someone more congenial to talk to.

She lay in bed that night and thought how the crazy notion they'd cooked up all those years ago over dinner with Zunker Kapps – she, Lolly and Algie – had actually come to fruition, and without her. She didn't know whether to laugh or cry. She either had to see it, or she had not to. If she really and truly had expected to put her past life behind her then she should not have seen the poster. Or having seen it, she should have just averted her eyes and passed on by. It should not be keeping her awake the entire night. *Mrs Morphett's Macaroons* indeed. She hoped that was not a cheap way of drawing attention to itself. But then what else is theatre about other than drawing attention to itself? *Mrs Morphett's Macaroons*. It would be a farce, or more likely a satire, with that title and that author. A satire aimed at Mrs Fawcett? Surely not. And who was Annie Addeley?

Of course she wouldn't go. It would be altogether too painful to meet up with all her old friends again, and have to answer so many questions. Not to mention having to be civil to the dreaded Mrs Lightly, or Mrs Robinson as she would be rightly known. But then she wondered if Kapps might be there, with his Constance. And how interesting it would be to catch up with him and his wife-to-be. It was all too much to think about.

It was a couple of days before Olivia at last deigned to pay Violet a visit in her room one evening after dinner. Her first question was unexpected.

'What were you looking at, that time in the station?'

'I beg your pardon?'

The girl had plonked herself in an armchair where she sat, or rather slouched, her legs spread before her, feet twitching.

'You stopped to look at something. I was walking along minding my own business and all of a sudden you weren't there.'

Violet did not reply.

'Well?' Olivia hauled herself up in her seat and looked at Violet. She was chewing her lips.

'Gracious, what a surprising question to ask me, Olivia.'

'Why?'

'You haven't said a word since the meeting. You walk around gazing at your feet, ignoring everything, not answering my questions. And now you come out with this?'

Olivia harrumphed, and, characteristically, examined her feet, which were still twitching.

'There are a million questions I have been wanting to ask of you, but I could see there was little point.' Violet placed her knitting on her lap. She had no idea why she continued such a practice; she didn't enjoy it, she was always dropped stitches, and she now had at least four pointless scarves completed and sitting ownerless in a drawer.

'Such as?' drawled Olivia.

'Such as – what did you think of Mrs Pankhurst? And the suffragette ladies? I assume from your behaviour that you found the whole thing too tedious for words.'

Olivia did not reply.

'I apologise for forcing it on you.'

Olivia muttered something.

'I beg your pardon?'

'You didn't force anything on me.' Olivia spoke with sudden fierceness.

'If you keep chewing your lips like that you'll have nothing left.'

Suddenly Olivia started to weep. Her pert little mouth turned downwards, like a small child's, but the tears were real enough.

'Oh my dear child, what now?'

Olivia shook her head. She went on shaking her head for some considerable time. Violet scrabbled around in a pocket and produced a handkerchief, which she refused.

They sat in silence for a while.

'Were you crying for those poor girls in the workhouse?' It was a shot in the dark, but it appeared to hit the spot. Olivia shook her head, and then nodded, and wiped her eyes roughly with the back of a hand.

'I did wonder,' said Violet gently. 'It's a shocking world out there, and I am sorry it upset you so much.'

Olivia continued shaking her head, with more ferocity.

'But that is how the world is,' Violet went on. 'It is deeply unfair. And it's thanks to the likes of Mrs Pankhurst that there are people, good people, who are prepared to go to such lengths to do something about it. Because left to its own devices this wretched world of ours won't change. There are too many people with vested interests in the status quo. Men, that is. Not that I have anything against men as a whole. Unlike Dorothy.'

Olivia looked at Violet for the first time. 'Who's Dorothy?'

'Dorothy Moss. You met her at the meeting. She cannot resist any opportunity to take a swipe at the male of the species.'

Olivia smiled, surprisingly. Violet sat and waited for her to say something. She rather wished she had taken up her knitting again, but at this stage it might send out the wrong signal.

'I don't hate men,' said Olivia eventually.

Violet nodded. 'I'm glad to hear it.'

'Do you?'

Violet raised her eyebrows. 'Of course I don't.'

'Then why aren't you married?'

'I'm . . .' She stopped. For the life of her she could not remember what she had told Olivia and what she hadn't. 'We are rather getting off the subject, Olivia. I want to hear more about you. I don't want you worrying about the poor girls in the workhouse. I just thought it would be a good idea to let you see what's going on in the world outside. If you decide to join the suffragist ladies, that's up to you. If not, well, at least you know something about them.'

'What was on the poster?' Olivia asked.

Violet was tempted to say something along the lines of, 'Why should I tell you my secrets if you don't tell me yours?' but that seemed too petty for words. So she plumped for the truth.

'It was for a special matinee performance of a play written by a friend of mine, and featuring an actress who is also a friend of mine.'

'Oh my!' said Olivia, suddenly alert. 'Shall you go?'

Violet shrugged. 'Probably not.'

'Why not?'

'Because it's part of my past. And the past is behind me.'

'Pasts are usually behind one,' said Olivia. It was, thought Violet, one of her wittier remarks. 'So?'

'I am thinking about it.'

'I will come with you.'

'Will you, indeed?'

'And I promise not to kick the chairs.'

'I'm not sure I want to make another outing to London with you, Olivia.'

There was silence for a moment.

'I'll be on my best behaviour. I promise.'

Violet waited.

'What else do you want me to say?'

Violet took a breath in. 'Your behaviour the other day was beyond the pale, Olivia. You not only upset several of the ladies around you, you also upset me. I had gone to some trouble to take you all the way to Caxton Hall, and introduce you to the suffragists. You turned what should have been an interesting and pleasurable experience into a nightmare.'

'Nightmare? That's a bit strong, isn't it?'

'No, actually. Had you told me you found the whole experience upsetting I would have understood. Completely. But instead you walk along gazing at the ground, not saying a word, not looking at me, making no effort to communicate in any way. Yes, it was a nightmare.'

Olivia's lower lip was jutting again.

'Do you remember what I said before about manners? You may hate the word, as do I as a matter of fact, but it's another way of saying . . .'

'Treat people with respect, I know.'

'Then why don't you do just that?'

Violet didn't really like what she was saying. She hated telling anyone off, least of all Olivia, who was not her responsibility and whom she really had no right to criticise. But in a world of give and take Violet felt she had given and given and received very little in return.

So what happened next astounded her. Olivia pushed herself to her feet, went to her and gave her a huge, clumsy hug.

'Dear dear Olivia,' said Violet, as she hugged her back.

'I can't help being me,' said Olivia, as she drew back.

'That is a ridiculous thing to say,' said Violet. And to her relief, Olivia laughed.

'So, will you go to the play?'

'I'll think about it.'

'And if you do decide to go, and I'm as good as gold, can I come with you?' Olivia stood with her hands clasped in front of her, swaying from side to side, like a ten-year-old.

'I'll think about it,' Violet repeated.

39: The prodigal son

She was still thinking about it a week later, when her mind was unexpectedly made up for her by the arrival of a telegram. It was addressed to 'HOUSEKEEPER' and it read:

'ARRIVING TONIGHT 5 OCLOCK TRAIN
WITH 3 CHUMS NEED BEDS MADE UP
AND DINNER FOR 4 FRIDAY SATURDAY
RUPERT'

'Housekeeper'. He didn't even bother to address it to her personally. Violet felt firmly put in her place. At least the daughter of the house called her by her name. 'Housekeeper' indeed.

No doubt the son and heir was making the most of the absence of his parents. There was no mention of a please or thank you, let alone apologies for the short notice. But it was already midday Friday and it meant Violet would have to send one or more of the kitchen maids on a shopping errand, or more likely go herself, make sure the extra bedrooms were cleaned and aired and beds made. Dinner for four on Friday and again on Saturday, so no day's excursion to the theatre for her or for Olivia. Never mind. It was probably just as well.

Olivia was spitting blood. 'Poo! How dare he?' Poo, Violet had already learned, was Olivia's nickname for her brother, full name Poopot. 'Who does he think he is?' She dangled the telegram from her fingers as if it were contaminated.

Coming from Olivia this was a bit rich, thought Violet. Nonetheless: 'So that puts paid to our outing I'm afraid, Olivia.'

'I don't see why. So we are having an outing, are we?'

'I hadn't quite decided,' said Violet, retrieving the offending missive and pocketing it. 'But this has made up my mind for me. So be it.'

'So be it NOT!' declared Olivia. 'I'll give that Poopot a piece of my mind, he has no right.'

'He has every right. It would have helped to have had a bit more notice, but there we are.'

'We shall see.'

Olivia began to march up and down the room, swearing quietly to herself. It appeared she had quite set her mind on the outing to the theatre, whether or not Violet had done the same.

'You go,' said Violet. 'There's nothing to stop you. And you can report back to me.'

Olivia hesitated for a moment.

'No,' she said, with finality. 'Not without you. I'd feel an idiot. Besides,' she thought hard for a moment. 'It is no way to treat people. Everyone should be treated with respect. Even housekeepers.' She would not catch Violet's eye so there was no way of knowing whether there was irony there or not. 'I will have a word with him,' she announced, and she flounced off.

Rupert was in his second year at Cambridge. He was three years older than Olivia, and while there were similarities – Rupert treated the servants as serfs much as Olivia did – at least Olivia talked to them. Rupert barely acknowledged their presence. Mr Gross, who had been with the household for upwards of ten years, had never shared more than few words with him. Mrs Gross pronounced, with a broad smile, that all he needed was a good spanking. He didn't even have a Trudie to keep him on the straight and narrow, so what could one expect?

Violet held her tongue. It was one of the rare occasions when she felt demeaned, and helpless. He was the son of the house and that was that.

The company arrived with a rattle in a hackney cab from the station, hollering and whooping before the vehicle had even come to a halt outside the front door. Rupert clapped a hand around the shoulders of his friends and strode into the house without the barest glance at Ned, the footman.

'Anyone at home?' he yelled.

Mr Gross appeared from the shadows. 'Good afternoon Mr Rupert.'

'Oh, you, yes. Which rooms are we in?'

'I will show you. Follow me.' Gross proceeded with dignity up the staircase. The four young men followed.

'Dinner at eight, you – what's your name?'

'Gross, Mr Rupert.'

'Oh yes. Then we're going out somewhere.'

'Very well.'

'And tomorrow night as well. Same time, same arrangement. Oh, and Gross?' Rupert halted at the head of the stairs.

'Yes?'

'It's sir. Not Mr Rupert. Don't you think?'

'Of course, sir.'

It was at dinner that night that Olivia confronted her brother, in the presence of his friends. He was not pleased to see her at the dinner table in the first place, but once she was there there was little he could do about it.

'What made you suddenly decide to come home?' she demanded.

'It's Perry's birthday tomorrow.' Rupert gestured at the

boy on his right – tall, fair-haired, freckles, smiling shyly. 'And with the ma and the pa away it seemed a good opportunity to painta da towna reda.'

'What?'

'Paint the town red,' Rupert repeated, as if to an idiot. 'Insofar as there is a town, let alone anything to paint it with.' He laughed, and so did his friends.

'At this short notice? Have you any idea how much work it involves, to feed you all, and make your beds and prepare your rooms? Who do you think you are?' She glared at her brother.

'Ooh,' said he. 'Crosspatch. Where did *that* come from?'

'You don't give a fig about anyone else, do you?'

'It's good to see you too, Olly.' Rupert lifted his glass and winked at his sister.

'You'll have to make your own arrangements tomorrow, anyway.' she pronounced.

'In what sense, sis?'

'Don't call me sis.'

'Very well, sis.'

'In the eating sense. We're going to be away all day. That's to say Violet and I. So you'll have to eat out.'

Rupert downed his knife and fork and fixed his gaze on his little sister. 'Who says?'

'I say. You gave us no warning, and we had already made arrangements to spend the day in London. We will not be back in time to prepare your lunch. Or your dinner.'

'I am not expecting you to prepare my dinner, dear girl.'

'But Vi would need to be here to supervise.'

'And who, pray, is Vi?'

'She is the housekeeper. Mrs Violet Humphreys. As you well know. So you can eat out, all of you.' She gazed at each of the young men in turn. One looked embarrassed, one looked amused, and the one called Perry carried on eating as if nothing was happening.

'Since when has the housekeeper decided when she takes days off?'

'Since she came here. Which you would know if you took the slightest notice of the servants.'

'It is not my business to take notice of servants, as far as I can see. It's their job to take notice of me, *n'est-ce pas*?'

'So there it is. It's done. There isn't any food in the house. There was barely enough for dinner tonight. So you'll have to look after yourselves. Lunchtime too. *Compris?*'

That was the gist of the conversation as related by Olivia to Violet later that same night. 'So you see the coast is clear, there's nothing to stop us going to London tomorrow,' she said.

Violet felt outfoxed. She had in no way made up her mind to go. She had even been secretly relieved to have been let off the hook.

'I had not yet decided whether it was a good idea,' she said.

'We'll have to go now,' said Olivia. 'Otherwise Poo will assume I've been making it all up. To get at him.'

'You do realise' – there was one remaining possible get-out – 'we haven't booked tickets, so we will have to queue. And we may not get in.'

'We'll get in,' said Olivia.

~

It was another day, another train journey to London, but a very different Olivia. She was all chatter.

'Are you looking forward to seeing your friends?' she asked Violet.

'Yes and no.'

'How so?'

Violet looked out of the window. 'I have a certain amount of explaining to do. I left rather suddenly, you see.

I didn't tell anyone where I was going.'

'And they will want to know why you lowered yourself to become a housekeeper.'

Violet laughed, and said nothing.

'Were you running away from a lover?'

'Dear Olivia, not everything a woman does has to do with a man.'

'Doesn't it?'

'I'd have thought you'd have learned that by now. Especially after our last trip to London.'

'Oh that, yes.' It was as if she'd forgotten all about it. Violet sighed.

'I think I'd like to be an actress,' said Olivia.

I bet you would, thought Violet. Out loud she said, 'It's a hard life, I wouldn't recommend it. Unless of course your mama and papa are happy to continue to keep you throughout your adult life.'

'All those actors,' said Olivia, dreamily. 'What are they like? Are they all fearfully handsome and romantic?'

'On stage, maybe. Offstage – they come in all sorts and sizes. I don't think your parents would approve of you fraternising with them.'

'Why not? You do. You did.'

'I am not the daughter of Lord and Lady Armstrong.' Violet smiled indulgently at her young charge.

'Phooo,' said Olivia.

'Have you ever actually been to the theatre?' Violet asked.

'Once or twice. Trudie took me to see some Shakespeare. *King Lear* or something. *So* boring.'

'Yes of course. Henry Irving?'

'Who?'

'He's one of our leading actors. He's Sir Henry now. He and Herbert Tree are great rivals. Very different, couldn't be more so. Tree stays on the outside of a character, Irving immerses himself inside it. I think Irving looks down on Tree.'

'"Looks down on Tree!"' Olivia hooted.

'Tree never looks down on anyone, even though he is very tall.'

They laughed. It was a silly conversation, but it did something to take Violet's mind off the events to come.

Queueing for tickets was a new experience for Violet. She had always booked her seat in advance or, more likely, had it booked for her. But she had seen them, queues stretching around the block for a performance at Her (now His) Majesty's Theatre: a cheerful crowd, prepared to stand there for hours, or even overnight, so they brought food to sustain them and chatted happily with their neighbours. And while they waited they were diverted by a raggle-taggle bunch of street entertainers. There were two young lads who sang songs from the music hall in makeshift two-part harmony, their attention partly on the queue and partly on the law, and who at any given moment would shout, 'Copper!' and disappear around the corner, only to reappear moments later when the coast was clear; the elderly lady dressed in furs and pearls, who danced a creaky yet oddly elegant version of the gavotte; the gentlemen in torn overcoats who claimed they 'once worked with Irving', who delivered extracts from Shakespeare and Dickens in quavering voices. They were all regulars and their repertoire rarely changed, but the crowd gave generously no matter the quality of the entertainment.

On this occasion there wasn't much of a queue. A single matinee performance of a new play by an unknown writer featuring an unknown actress was not likely to attract a large crowd. So it was less than half an hour before the box office opened, and in they all trooped.

Violet purchased two seats in the pit. Then she saw

Kapps.

He was almost unrecognisable in a morning jacket and top hat. He was greeting the punters as they arrived and directing them to the correct entrance to the auditorium, like some kind of House Manager. He caught sight of Violet and for a moment it looked as if he didn't recognise her. Then he broke into a broad smile, walked up to her and shook her warmly by the hand.

'Violet! My dear!'

'My word, Zunker, you look magnificent!'

Kapps shifted uncomfortably. 'Do I look as stupid as I feel?'

'You do not look stupid at all. Zunker, Mr Kapps, this is my friend, Miss Olivia Armstrong.'

Kapps gave Olivia a little bow.

'It is a great joy to see you,' he said. 'Where are you sitting?'

'In the pit.'

'The pit? Well, I'm sure we can do something about that. Come with me.'

'Thank you Zunker, but we prefer the pit.'

'You do?' Kapps wrinkled his brow in puzzlement.

'It's where the real people sit,' Violet smiled. 'I always preferred the pit. Or the gallery.'

'I have a lot to learn,' said Kapps, as he led the two ladies into the auditorium and to the front row of the pit. Then he gave a little bow and said, 'I shall see you later, shall I?'

'Of course.' And off he went.

The pit consisted of rows of wooden benches behind the stalls. These were unreserved seats and normally there was a good deal of pushing and shoving to get the best view. On this occasion however the theatre was not filling up, there was plenty of space to spread out.

Olivia looked aghast. 'What did you say that for?' she

said.

'Come and make yourself comfortable,' said Violet, patting the bench beside her. 'If you like you can find yourself a seat in the stalls after the interval.'

Olivia sat, with a certain amount of bad grace. Violet meanwhile looked around for a familiar face. She spotted one, seated slap bang in the middle of the stalls, the best seat in the house, and she only recognised him when he turned to glance behind him.

'That's GBS,' Vi whispered to Olivia.

'Who's GBS?'

'I'll explain later. Very famous. George Bernard Shaw.'

Of Algernon Lightly, or of Robbie Robinson, there was no sign.

Violet opened the programme and perused it. There, beneath the cast and the stage management and to her utter delight, she saw: 'Costumes by Miss Winifred Walters'.

God bless you Algie Lightly, she said silently.

She shifted from side to side on her wooden seat and prepared herself for the ordeal to come.

40: The old crowd

Mrs Morphett's Macaroons told the story of a kitchen maid called Annie Addeley (played by Lolly Mulligan with a Scottish accent), who is asked to deliver a plate of macaroons to the drawing room of a grand house, where a group of ladies has gathered to discuss the topic of women's suffrage. The event has been organised by the lady of the house, Mrs Phillocent Morphett. Rather than returning to her quarters, as she was supposed to, Annie becomes so absorbed by the discussion she hangs around until the end of the meeting and all the ladies have gone. At which point she proceeds to lecture her mistress on how to get her message to the 'person in the street, you know madam, real people'. Bemused and delighted, Mrs Morphett (clearly Mrs Millicent Fawcett, to the initiated) gives Annie some leaflets to distribute to her fellow servants downstairs, and beyond. Her fellow servants laugh at Annie, but, undeterred, she becomes more and more embroiled in the movement, and in time she evolves into a kind of right-hand woman to Mrs Morphett. Despite not being able to read or write – a fact she tries to keep hidden but which is the source of many amusing misunderstandings – her fearlessness and determination begin to win her followers. Annie pounds the streets of London carrying a stool and a bucket, and wherever she comes upon an appropriate crowd she stops, stands on the stool, bangs the bucket for attention and proceeds to harangue the passers-by about votes for women for as long as she can before the law arrives. She inveigles herself into the house of a leading (and married), Conservative MP, whom she seduces and then blackmails into forcing a vote in Parliament on women's suffrage. A counter-movement among the Conservative MPs sets out to discredit Annie by various means, foul and fouler. One of them poses as a lover in an attempt to coerce her into marriage; another tries to blacken her name in the press; yet another accosts her in the street and endeavours to frighten the life out of her, and so on. However Annie outwits them all. The play ends in the near future, where women have the vote, Annie Adderley has become the first female MP and is in the process of introducing a Bill banning men from voting and turning Parliament into an all-female institution, with the rallying cry: 'You did it to us! Now it's your turn to find out how it feels to have it done to you!'

It was a comedy satire, with a serious message. It lampooned everyone, from the suffragists to the members of parliament, including the Prime Minister and his cronies. It was a tour de force for Lolly Mulligan and gave her ample opportunity to show off her astonishing versatility and her ability to slip in and out of accents: from the Scottish maid warrior to the brazen seducer from Bethnal Green. The message? Anything a man can do a woman can do, and more so. The audience, such as it was, loved it. They laughed in the right places and were silent in the right places and there was very little coughing.

Violet was transfixed, as was Olivia. It wasn't a perfect play. It could have done with some pruning. The satire would have been sharper, thought Vi, if the jokes and caricatures were not quite so relentless. But it had drama and tension, and pathos. It made her laugh and it made her cry and it made her think, which for Violet was everything theatre was about.

As the audience began to disperse she sought out GBS and asked him what he thought of the play. He declared rather gruffly that he never drew conclusions directly after a performance. However: 'But I will say this. He gives us plenty of food for thought. He learned that from me. Not bad, for a beginner.'

From GBS that was something approaching praise.

Then it was time to think about getting back, said Violet. There was dinner to be prepared, and . . .

'Are you mad?' Olivia cried. 'I've fixed all that! I want to meet your friends!'

So they made their way back through the foyer, where they found Kapps, looking a lot more relaxed now. Beside him stood a stately-looking woman with a large nose, whom Violet assumed, rightly, was Constance. She was not a beauty – there was too much nose for that – but she was very obviously in love with Kapps, and he with her, and their arms were linked together tightly as though they could not bear to be separated.

'There's a reception at the Hungry Craw,' said Kapps, 'upstairs round the corner in Whitcomb Street. You will come, won't you?' He looked from Violet to Olivia. 'See your old friends?'

Even as Violet hesitated Olivia grabbed hold of her arm and dragged her out of the theatre and – 'Which way?' 'Right' – into the Hungry Craw and upstairs to a large room that was already half full of people.

Violet recognised some of them. Actors mostly, who greeted her warmly, with hugs and kisses and 'Darlings' and all things theatrical. They showered her with questions, which she did her best to laugh off. Then she spotted Winnie Walters, alone in a corner, beaming at the room, standing as straight as an arrow and looking like a new woman.

'Winnie Walters!'

'Mrs Graham, I do declare!'

'You look twenty years younger.' It was true.

Violet pecked the older woman on the cheek and introduced her to Olivia, and Winnie, to Olivia's delight, curtseyed.

'I have been wondering about you, Miss Walters,' said Violet. 'I was so worried.'

'It's a long story. I have been wondering about you too, Mrs Graham. Nobody knew where you'd gone.'

It turned out that, predictably, Mr Dunkett reneged on all the promises Violet had made to Winnie and effectively sacked her. And then not a month after Violet left, Dunkett himself was sent packing, and by none other than the Chief himself, and as a result of protest on the part of the company: first at the man himself, and secondly because word had got around that it was Dunkett who was responsible for the sudden resignation of Violet.

'Really?'

'Oh Mrs Graham, you have no idea how much you were missed.' Winnie's eyes were swimming with tears. 'And it is wonderful to see you again. Are you coming back to work with us?'

'No Winnie, I don't think so. My life has moved on.'

Winnie opened her mouth to say something but whatever it was was drowned out by a deafening cheer from behind them. Violet turned to see Lolly, standing in the centre of the room, acknowledging the cheers and the applause, smiling and bowing graciously.

Then she spotted Violet and squealed: 'Violet Graham!'

'Lolly Mulligan,' said Violet. She took both of Lolly's hands in hers and gazed at her. 'What a marvel. What an absolute marvel.'

'Did you really think so? Honestly? You would tell me,

wouldn't you?' Lolly's eyes narrowed, and then widened. 'And where the hell have you been all this time?'

The first question was easier to answer than the second, so she answered it, fulsomely, and then she introduced Olivia to Lolly and Olivia was so utterly star-struck she could not utter a word for several minutes. When she finally found her voice she gushed and gushed and could not stop gushing, so Lolly grabbed hold of her hand and pulled her away into the crowd, and Violet was left momentarily alone.

The atmosphere was so gay, and heightened, as it always is in those glorious few hours between the fall of the curtain and tomorrow's reviews; when everything and everyone is puffed up to twice their size with success and happiness and nothing can possibly go wrong in this magnificent, perfect world.

It was some time before she spotted Algie. He was talking to a group of people the far side of the room and he appeared not to have seen her. She looked away and as she did so, so he glanced across and saw her. When she turned to look at him again he was apparently still deep in conversation. This went on for some time before at last their glances synchronised, and there was one of those frozen moments when neither of them appeared to know what to do. Violet found herself looking around for an obvious Mrs Lightly, but it could be anyone in the room, and the room was full. And while she was still conjecturing, there he was, right next to her.

'The famous Disappearing Woman, I do believe,' he said.

'The famous Playwright, I do believe,' she said.

He bowed.

'Congratulations,' she said.

'Thank you. Did you enjoy it?'

'I did, very much. It made me laugh and it made me

cry.'

'Excellent,' said Algie.

'Although . . .'

'There is always an "although".' He twitched an eyebrow and waited.

'It could do with a little pruning, I thought.'

'A little pruning.'

'Fewer words. And perhaps a little more subtlety.'

'Fewer words.'

'To sharpen up the satire, you know. And I'm not sure about the ending.'

'Should I be taking notes?'

She laughed. 'You did ask. But I did enjoy it. It was very, very funny. And thoughtful. Was it all your own work?'

Algie took a step back. 'Of course. What are you implying?'

'I didn't know you felt so strongly about women's issues,' said Violet.

'You underestimate me. You always did.' He looked at her without blinking, and she flushed.

'So,' said Algie, 'should Algernon Lightly give it a good review?'

'He should, without question. GBS liked it too.'

'GBS? Was he there?'

'Yes. He didn't want to be drawn, he said he doesn't like to make instant conclusions. But he enjoyed it. It gave him food for thought, he said. He took some of the credit for that.'

'That sounds like GBS.' Algie was still staring at her with some intensity.

What happens now? Violet felt a terrible urge to run, and yet not to. She looked around for Olivia, or for Lolly, or for Kapps and Constance, but they were all heavily engaged in conversation. She felt suddenly like an outsider.

'It is very strange being here,' she said eventually. 'Very strange indeed.'

'Of course. You are no longer part of the crowd.'

That felt distinctly like a put-down. Violet opened her mouth to object but at that very point there sailed into view an imposing *embonpoint* attached to a large woman. She placed a proprietorial arm around Algie and, with barely a glance at Violet, said, 'Robbie darling, there is someone who wants to meet you.'

'Who?'

'William Shilversome, or some such. He says he's a politician.'

'In that case he can wait. Elizabeth, this is Mrs Graham, Violet. An old friend. Violet, Miss Elizabeth Chester-Bolt.'

Miss Chester-Bolt nodded peremptorily at Violet and sailed away again.

There was a brief hiatus, during which further explanations concerning Miss Chester-Bolt did not appear to be forthcoming, and so: 'This is quite an achievement,' said Violet, gesturing at the room and the people in it.

'It was your idea in the first place,' said Algie.

'It was both of ours, as I remember. But I never thought it would actually happen. How did you manage it?'

'Hard work, like everything.'

'But where did you find the money?'

'Elizabeth put up most of it. The rest came from Lolly's current *beau*, Mr Poll-Perkins.' Algie nodded across the room, where Lolly stood flanked on one side by an adoring Olivia and the other by an equally if not more adoring young man with floppy hair. 'Who is a Big Cheese in Shipping, so they say.'

'Well, well. And what does his wife have to say about it?'

'As a matter of fact,' Algie leaned towards Violet to

whisper in her ear, 'he is not married.'

'Oh my word! What *does* Lolly think she's doing?' Violet laughed and flapped her hand as if to fan her face.

'My word indeed. A few things have changed since you departed the scene.'

'Such as?'

'Such as . . . ' He broke off. 'How many years has it been?'

'I have to remind you that you took leave of absence before I did. And with as much explanation.'

'Ah yes.' He told Violet the story of how he'd gone to the country to sort out the family business after the death of his mother and try to make sense of the debts his gambling father had left.

'Debts?' said Violet.

'Oh yes. I did write to you, but . . .' He went on to describe how the whole family had lived alternately in deep poverty or immense wealth, and how his mother took it in her stride and therefore he was not as surprised as he might have been to discover, at the last minute, a small fortune strapped to the furniture. The furniture, of all things. He used part of it to pay off his debts.

'That was lucky,' she said.

'It was.' The rest of the 'treasure', as he called it, he had intended to put towards getting married.

'Oh? To whom? Elizabeth?' Violet glanced around the room expectantly.

'Elizabeth?' Algie laughed heartily. 'Dear me no. I can't tell you to whom. I can only tell you she disappeared before I had a chance to propose.'

'Oh,' said Violet. She felt her face flushing.

'So I decided to put the money towards other things, such as the production of my new play.'

'I see. And this person who disappeared . . .' Violet hesitated. 'Did you try to find her?'

'As I said I wrote to her, more than once, but she did not reply,' said Algie.

'Maybe she didn't get the letters.'

'I wonder why not?'

'Or maybe she did, just one. Maybe she didn't much like what was in it. Maybe he chided her for being selfish and vanishing without explanation.'

An unholy racket was taking place in the room behind them, but in the corner they occupied together it was strangely quiet.

'Is that why you suppose she didn't reply?' Algie asked.

'Partly, yes. And partly because she needed to get away from everything.'

He waited.

She told him about the man who was following her, and how she learned later it was her estranged husband who was responsible because he wanted to get married again and he was trying to catch her out with adultery. She laughed, briefly.

'And did he get his divorce?'

'Not yet. There has to be adultery on one side or the other, hers in particular.'

'Robbie!' There came a cry from behind Violet's back.

'Not now, Philip,' said Algie, and the rejected Philip retreated.

'So that is why she ran away? Because she was being followed?' He had not taken his eyes off Violet for a moment.

'That and other reasons. She'd left her job, she was desperate, she didn't know what else to do.'

'And did she regret running away?'

There was a long pause before Violet replied.

'Not at the time.'

'And what are her plans now?'

'Why, she has none. She will continue as she is. She is working as a housekeeper, you know.'

'A housekeeper?' He raised his eyebrows.

'For the time being.' Violet hesitated. 'And, she – she enjoys the work, up to a point,' she stuttered. 'She doesn't suppose she'll stay there for ever, but she will always want to work.'

'What about marrying again?'

Violet frowned. 'She's not divorced yet, I just told you.'

'No adultery.'

'No adultery. Besides, she likes to work, she has to work. And no man would put up with that.'

Algie looked away from her for a brief moment.

'What kind of work would she prefer, do you suppose?'

'Something perhaps a little more taxing than housekeeping. Taxing for the brain, that is.'

'What if she became a producer? And she produced the very play she's just seen? A regular run, in a West End theatre.'

Violet looked at Algie for a long moment. 'She might be very interested in that,' she said.

'If she said yes to that, might she say yes to marriage as well?'

'I told you . . .'

'No adultery, I heard you. But that's easily fixed.'

There followed one of those silences in which two people, for whom the world may just have suddenly slotted into place, gazed at one another with a mixture of wonder and delight and terror.

Author biography

Patsy Trench lives in London. She has written three non fiction books about Australia inspired by her own family history, and five novels about 20th century women breaking the mould. In a previous life she was an actress, scriptwriter, playscout, founder of *The Children's Musical Theatre of London* and lyricist. When not writing books she teaches theatre and organises theatre trips for overseas students. She is the grateful mother of two and grandmother of one, and her hobbies are crocheting, rag rugging and mudlarking on the Thames foreshore.

Social media

Website: www.patsytrench.com
Substack: https://substack.com/@patsytrenchauthor
Facebook: PatsyTrenchWriting
X/Twitter: @PatsyTrench
Instagram: patsytrenchauthor

www.ingramcontent.com/pod-product-compliance
Lightning Source LLC
Chambersburg PA
CBHW021812110726
47902CB00006B/1757